whose song?

Praise for *Whose Song?*

"These stories are never about anything but the most serious matters of existence — the mysteries of violence and desire; the 'plain old hurting sorrow' of why human beings have such trouble loving one another. . . . Glave is a gifted stylist . . . blessed with ambition, his own voice, and an impressive willingness to dissect how individuals actually think and behave."
— *New York Times Book Review*

"Glave's literary temperament has been described as "Faulknerian," and the comparison speaks volumes. Like Faulkner, Glave can make heavy demands on a reader. If [his]expressionistic flights are not always easy to follow, the rewards of persevering can be great. He achieves astonishing tonal effects . . . [and] has a poet's way with words." — *Washington Post*

"Thomas Glave likes to plunge us right into the middle of his stories — a crowd, a conversation, a consciousness — and smack in the center of a milieu — American or Caribbean, urban or rural, usually black, often queer. The prose in this first collection is dense, dreamy . . . as rich as a novel and a book of poems combined." — *Out Magazine*

"This book is a gem." — *Lambda Book Report*

"Glave, like so many before him at City Lights, probes the soft underbelly of love's body, ennobles it, and gives it light, all the more to make us weep when it is violently slit open. . . . The rape in the title story, and all the other transgressions, propose that the sensual song of humanity belongs to those who sing it and condemns as evil those who would silence it. Thomas Glave sings most eloquently, poignantly, and heroically, and those who should hear his song are everywhere." — *Bloomsbury Review*

"Each of the stories reveals a sensitive storyteller with the skill and fearlessness to pursue chilling, vivid scenarios, sensually charged with racial and sexual difference and the unceasing threat of their punishment, to the peak of horror. . . . Glave's compassion, insight, and writerly craft stamp every page of *Whose Song? . . .*"
— *San Francisco Bay Guardian*

"[Glave is] an extraordinary stylist, whose rare insight, boundless courage, and fierce imagination make these stories resound long after you turn the last page. . . . [His] intense prose recalls the rhythmic narrative thrust of early Toni Morrison."
— *Village Voice*

"Thomas Glave has the strong talent and courage to take up the right to enter the inner selves of both black and white characters in his stories. This is a creative claim beyond 'authenticity' determined by skin color. He also has that essential writer's ear for the way different people speak within their cultures, and what their idiom gives away of their inhibitions and affirmations."
— Nadine Gordimer

"What a writer! What a book! Glave is a brilliant writer of startlingly fresh prose, a writer who keeps you in a constant presence of experience, as if you were moving around in a clear dream. His stories are intricate tapestries of life rendered through a triumphant act of the imagination." — Clarence Major

"In this collection of short stories Thomas Glave walks the path of such greats in American literature as Richard Wright and James Baldwin while forging new ground of his own. His voice is strong and his technique dazzling as he cuts to the bone of what it means to be black in America, white in America, gay in America, and human in the world at large. These stories span the globe of the human experience and the human heart. They are brutal in some places, tender in others, but always honestly told. A true talent of the 21st century." — Gloria Naylor

"Remarkable stories by a gifted writer who explores, in prose and rhythms of imaginative moment, the stresses, the split-minds, the implicit grandeurs, the subtleties, and the terrors of emotional desire and obsession: one is drawn compulsively into character and event." — Wilson Harris

"A fiercely imagined debut — intensely lyric, driven by the desire, in the face of everything, for truth, justice, beauty."
— Carole Maso

"This collection of short stories is heartstopping, reminiscent of Richard Wright's *Eight Men*. The title story "Whose Song?" will bring tears to your eyes. It may be as important to this century's body of literature as Kafka's *Metamorphosis* was to the last." — Harry Belafonte

"I read through hundreds of manuscripts each year by many of the most talented writers in America. Thomas Glave's work immediately struck me with its linguistic vision as well as the uniqueness of its subject matter. Glave has a Faulknerian temperament that expresses itself both in style, subject matter, and method. He is one of the most exciting writers it has been my privilege to read."
—David Bergman, editor of *Men on Men: Best New Gay Fiction*

"Thomas Glave is, in my opinion, one of the finest and most important new voices on the American literary scene. His stories are marked by an energy, an ambition, a fearlessness which are all too rare. Beyond the power and originality of these stories, what is most striking is how different each is from the others. Glave has vast control for such a young writer, able to switch modes, tenors, vehicles like a much more experienced practitioner of the craft. The appearance of *Whose Song?* will, I have no doubt, signal the next stage in the development of his reputation — one of truly national significance."
— David Lynn, editor of *Kenyon Review*

whose song?
and other stories
by thomas glave

city lights
san francisco

Cover design by Rex Ray
Book design by Elaine Katzenberger
Typography by Harvest Graphics

Grateful acknowledgment is extended to the editors of the following
publications in which some of the stories in this book, several in
slightly different form, previously appeared:

*Ancestral House: The Black Short Story in the Americas and Europe, Best
American Gay Fiction 3, Blacklight Online, Callaloo, Children of the Night:
The Best Short Stories by Black Writers 1967–Present, The Evergreen
Chronicles, Gay Fiction at the Millennium, His 2: Brilliant New Fiction by
Gay Writers, The James White Review, The Kenyon Review, Men on Men 6:
Best New Gay Fiction, Prize Stories 1997: The O. Henry Awards,* and
Soulfires: Young Black Men on Love and Violence.

Library of Congress Cataloging-in-Publication Data

Glave, Thomas.
    Whose song? and other stories / by Thomas Glave.
        p. cm.
    ISBN 0-87286-375-1 (pbk.)
        1. United States—Social life and customs—20th century—
Fiction.   2. Caribbean Area—Social life and customs—Fiction.
3. Afro-Americans—Fiction.   4. Race relations—Fiction.
5. Gay men—Fiction.   I. Title.

PS3557.L354 W48 2000
813'.6—dc21   00-034641

CITY LIGHTS BOOKS are edited by Lawrence Ferlinghetti and
Nancy J. Peters and published at the City Lights Bookstore, 261
Columbus Avenue, San Francisco, CA 94133 Visit our web site:
www.citylights.com

To
Joyce Magdalene Glave
and
to the spirit and memory of
Thomas Edward Glave, Sr.
everything
and everything
and more

CONTENTS

ACCIDENTS

B Y THE TIME WE MANAGE TO PUSH AND SHOVE OUR WAY UP to the front, the cops decide to get ugly and brandish their nightsticks, looking, for all the spit and polish of their uniforms, like drunk, dangerous modern-day pirates. But we want to *see,* like everybody else, even though we're not smiling the way everybody else is — that transfixed, gruesome smile you'd expect to see on the face of a real vampire just after he licked his lips — the serial killer's smile. Melvin's with me, although since he's taller and wider across the shoulders than I am he has less trouble than I do fighting his way up there through the crowd. So, just what I thought would happen, happens: he gets so excited that he lets go of my arm. Normally when that happens in a situation like this I panic and race after him, all cold and sweaty like back in that time I hate to remember. But that time isn't tonight or coming anywhere near, and right now I'm feeling pretty safe even with this crazy slobbering crowd, because I can see his back and those two long shoulder blades sticking out like ridges beneath his plaid shirt. He can see, but the way these people are shoving — . . . just trying to hold myself up I step on a young girl's foot. I can tell from her features that she's probably Dominican, probably no more than fourteen.

"Why don't you watch out!" As she screams this at me, adding a furious *que pendejo maricón*, her face, otherwise pretty in a dark Caribbean way (like mine, some people tell me; definitely like Melvin's), contorts into ugly twisted rage. It's a little much, and before I can even begin to stammer out an apology she's already slipped away into the crowd, yelling — it sounds like her voice amidst all these other screamers — for someone named Noellia.

"They're bringing her out!" Melvin shouts. As I wave to him (a little more frantic now, I'll admit), he of course turns his head and misses me. He's not even looking for me; I can see him focusing in different directions like all these other people, with that same look on his face.

Get back here, would you . . . but I've got to say this out loud so that —

"Mel! Yo, get back here, would you? Mel!"

— he can hear me. All around you can feel a kind of rising hysteria: it's time to leave. But there's that voice I haven't heard in so long, a nasty taunting voice right inside my ear canal that always comes back to me when something bad's about to happen: *If you leave now he'll never find you.* . . . With a few good pushes it's just fifteen seconds until I'm behind him, then beside him, missing by only a few inches banging my knees on one of the blue police car fenders.

"They're bringing her out," he says, all out of breath. "She's young, too. Looks pretty bad."

I'm amazed all at once by how many colors there are, and their ferocity in the evening light: the cold red angry swirls of the ambulance light, the helpless pink and white hands of the paramedics, the snarling vicious-red faces of the police and the dark blue sweat patches under their arms, the dull refrigerator white of the ambulance and the awful brownish-red blobs and blots on the white sheets covering the thing they're putting into the ambulance — whatever it is now, it can't be alive anymore, so lumpy and still. And that car — ruined and smoking with a fragmented windshield . . . the driver's seat so crushed in that you knew anything removed from there would have to be something maybe once pretty, now hideous — *mangled* is the word; once a human, now — what? A pile of something or ash? I can tell you right now that I've never been a soldier; neither has Mel, nor has anyone of our age or generation that we know. But here we are, looking. We see. It's all colored like what we imagine war to be. Here, in this place. There'll be screams somewhere tonight . . . — all of it upended over three or four dark pools, a glutinous mess seeping over the asphalt, shallow dark-purple lakes that make sticking-sucking noises on the bottoms of the paramedics' clean white shoes.

Just for a second I look down toward my hands to make sure they're still the same color. I can't find them. At the same time somebody else's hand brushes my side, only to pull away as if burned in the same instant. What feels like a large crotch presses an intrusive, creepy tumescence against my right buttock. Now the police are furious and move closer to us, nightsticks swinging like parade girls' batons, but less gracefully, more insistent.

"Mel."

He turns after a minute to look at me; his eyes saying, not with the light of drunken good-natured foolishness, that he's about to be sick.

"Come on. Let's go." He doesn't need to get sick here. I'd probably laugh to see everybody scream and push back to give us space, but it wouldn't really be funny.

"What?" Grunting, swallowing the mess rising in his throat.

"I *said,* let's go. Come on, now." I've got a hold on his arm, pulling him back through the crowd, but now it's as if they're glad we're leaving, making space for us as we walk, although we can barely feel our feet touch the ground — at least I can't. And there's our parking space with our little blue Hyundai, still there (and why *shouldn't* it be?); I throw a glance his way as he opens the door on his side.

"Are you sure you want to drive?" Now, this is brave of me and probably even at this point a crazy thing to offer, but I have to say it. It's Mel.

"Yeah. I'm better." He looks over at me. "Get in." And that familiar smile lets me know he means it, just as clearly as I can see the glow in his face — that faint shine of sadness and weird pleasure at the uncommon fact that I am leading him away from danger, for once.

His voice was different on the way back:

"Pretty gruesome, huh?" This as he lit up a cigarette, checking the rear-view mirror in almost the same moment. The ashtray's there — I found it after a minute (and it did take me nearly a minute, you'd think that by now my hands would know *ashtray, lower left center*) and pulled it out for him. We were almost at the bridge.

"Well, wasn't it?" he insisted.

"The — yes, *yes*. What do you want me to say? I didn't know her." And I don't think I would have wanted to, either, I thought. Hell, no.

"Lucky."

"Who?"

"Some people. I don't know."

This didn't make any sense to me: a sign that he was going off into some unreachable thoughts of his own on the subject. Then he took a deep drag on the cigarette, turning to blow a long stream of smoke sideways, twisting his mouth as he did it, a mannerism of his I've always hated. It's always reminded me of a woman to whom I was introduced some years ago, at lunch with some friends in an Upper West Side Columbus Avenue cafe — a place called Café Recherché, or something just as pretend-French-silly; the kind of place that got you wondering just what the French must think when they visit here: was this some sort of unqualified, hysterical Francophilia that had dreamt its way into one hundred silly, overdone restaurants? — I remembered that woman, not so much because of the way she'd dressed, actually very becomingly in pink and lavender, but because of the way she'd blown cigarette smoke sideways out of the window adjacent to our table while rambling on about the benefits of natural foods and the company she'd soon be starting in SoHo, which would sell only *the* best balsamic vinegar and goat's-milk cheeses, and pure, fresh yogurt with absolutely no preservatives or canned fruit added. "I'm calling it *Pains aux Naturels*," she'd trilled, very much like one of those mechanical songbirds you see sometimes on the tops of expensive music boxes. "Names are important. I *love* this one. A good name adds that certain *some*thing, a little panache." She'd invited a few of us to work for her as stock- and salespeople, but I was still in school then and couldn't spare the time. I still am and still can't — now mostly because of the trouble of that time that put me out of school for a while. It all came down at once until the quiet time that helped. But at the table I'd been thinking that a better name for her company might have been *Des Crudités*. Of course I hadn't had the guts to say this. And then dessert had come.

"It's like some people," Mel was saying, speeding up to pass a small jeep dawdling in the right lane, "some people that kind of thing doesn't bother at all. It's like they live on it, like something out of — gimme an example of a sick scary movie."

"A *sick* scary movie? Dag, now, Melvin. I don't know." (Talk about liars! I could think of a bunch of them.)

"But anyway it did bother me. So I *know* it bothered *you*."

I turned the radio on. They were playing a song with slow, mournful lyrics, one we'd both heard before and liked. Somehow this song seemed right for the moment — quiet and soft, like what you'd hear pouring out of a roadside stand in the country somewhere, a hazy summer night's song for a place without any people around — until the deejay spoiled it by breaking in and announcing a new contest coming up, just keep it right there, on the power. I changed to something jazzy and cool and wild, music for the autumn season and these autumn moons.

"What do you mean, it bothered me? Why?"

He looked over at me, frowned, looked to his left and squeezed in behind a fat yellow taxi, cutting off an expensive-looking car behind us. The driver sped up and passed us on the right after making an obscene gesture at me; then wove in and out of the cars ahead, his brake lights flashing on, flashing off: quick, clipped warnings. Some of the lights were off on the bridge; Mel drove a little slower. A subway train was rumbling past on his side, grumbling over the tracks; you could see a big patch of graffiti: ROSA LOVES BILLY 4-EVER. Big white letters on the steel sides, moving over the tracks.

He was still frowning. "You *know* what I mean." He paused and gave me that look that made his eyes relax. He almost smiled. "Gimme another cigarette."

I didn't have to look at him, but I did, for a moment. The span lights overhead were forming bars, then small triangles, then crosses across his cheekbones and high, strong, dark forehead. In that light he was earth-colored; you could see in him the richest loam tones that matched his eyes and complemented the colors in both our skins. What a beauty, I thought. His beauty excited me. You know when you're lucky. I could say I had it like that. I thought about how strange it still seemed to me, sometimes, yet almost royal, a gift — one man loving another, doing things for him and to him that no one else would — or had better, I used to tease him. Loving another man wasn't strange; people can't hate the idea enough to change it, for us or anybody. The whole thing itself held the joy. And does. And having such things done to and for yourself — that simple reciprocal whatever or shadowed look; the funny feeling of knowing all the secret, intimate things our parents probably knew but had never wished to discuss, and which withholding had inevitably led to those bitter arguments that would almost always end in the icy, intractable silences of untranslatable years. It seemed so just then as, pressing one of his cigarettes into the round fiery-hot lighter, I inhaled gently on it before passing it to him; that's when I knew his fingers would brush across mine the way they always did, our way. I looked down at his long, slim fingers, where they rested on the gear shift, and thought about all the rest of him that I liked. They were brown and delicate, bony at the knuckles for such a tall man (six-one). My glance was like a flirt, one he knew well, and shy. As well I knew his smell (bay rum and books), and which joints in his body would always creak at some times and snap at others to support him, and the faint whistle-and-grunt of his snore, and the dark-brown glow of his skin when the moon managed to slip itself over our roof and through our bedroom window . . . things that were nice to know about somebody. I'd only ever wanted to know them about him.

I do have a thing about car accidents, what he was hinting at before, wanting to know if tonight bothered me. I don't talk about it much. My mother died a couple of years ago, just before I started freshman year. She had been missing for two days, on the way back from my grandmother's in Jersey, when we heard, first from the police, then on the radio news five hours later, that she'd driven her gray Sentra right off the road and into the Johnsons' lake. The lake adjoined the Johnsons' property, and they still hadn't returned from Algeria, where Mrs. Johnson had been writing a book on the effects of intermarriage in some populations.

I've since forgotten which ones. All I really remember from that time is my mother, because soon after that was when everything to do with cars started to happen. My mother had been in that lake for two days. She'd just sat there at the bottom, seatbelted and progressively becoming a mass of wrinkles. When the divers did get to her, she, the thing she'd become, *it,* had become heavy with washed-over mud. The water had soaked into her wool plaid coat. And the eels. They'd had to tell us about the eels.

That was a bad time for some of us. Sometimes I can still see it, when Melvin's not with me and everything's far away and the city darkens and all you hear are the screeches of cars, and gunshots, and screams; everybody dying everywhere, the way they do now. I can hear the songs they sang to keep each other company then, back in that place where I spent time. I sang them too, through how many hours I can't remember. I can hear them in every breath of the wind our apartment gets, and the voices and the sighs, old as the oldest spirits I still sometimes see; and the fire of that time they tried to shock out of me. I just remember, past those white-lit rooms and the strangers and the huge black spiders of that room I lived in, for a few years, it seemed. It was quiet with voices and water. Sometimes, now, I can just close my eyes and leave all this, leave Melvin and all of it, and see those leaves in that water and feel myself down there in the leaves, in the leaves. That peace.

The really bad part of it is over now. It's been over for a while. I look pretty much the way I used to, hair, weight, and all, and I don't have this thing anymore about going off piers or locking myself in with some good exhaust. It's not as if you could do it that many times, but you get better at it. And now it's like she's close sometimes, when I'm talking, and Mel's not in on it. He'd never understand how it feels when it's about to happen — the time when everybody finally shuts up.

After all that, you just want to get away from it for a while. You feel like there's nothing really good left in you anymore. It had all seemed a good place to get away from, that place of lakes with eels in them, and winding roads and skid marks and stupid, slow-witted cops, and neighbors who had been away when they should have been there at home, ready to help and guide you on which way to walk if you couldn't see, even if your eyes had been open. My mother's eyes, when they'd found her, had been open and staring and just vacant, the rusty color of the leaves on the lake's surface. The brown of her skin had paled. My father's eyes have always been deep brown and since that time they have remained open and staring — staring at nothing except the black doorknob of that room they put him in, that silent room that speaks to him with the same blue electricity the events of my time there still speak to me.

Melvin's eyes were closed.

"Melvin — Mel, wake up!" — and it was true, as he told me later, that I'd actually screamed at him — but that was the time when you felt like you weren't in a car at all; instead, you were on your way someplace else, high above everyone in the world, although you could still see them before it was all over. And also: that for one horrible minute I'd seen how Melvin would look when he was dead.

All at once he was jamming the car into first gear, then realized his mistake and pulled it back. It took me a short while, as we groaned and jerked and then swerved right up on the steel grid wall on my side, to realize that I was sitting bolt upright in the seat with the car door handle gripped in my right hand and my left knee in my left. That was the feeling you got when you were about to jump out, I remembered. From a car, from a car. This one.

Then we were off the bridge. A voice on the radio was singing a slow song now; the lyrics were incomprehensible and the singer sounded as though she were in tears.

"Christ." It was Melvin.

"What?"

"I'm sorry."

" — "

"D'you hear me? I'm telling you — "

"It's O.K." (It *wasn't*.)

" — I'm sorry. Are you all — "

"*Yes*."

"You know I never do that. It must be later than I thought."

I remained silent: someone had once told me that it wasn't good for a man to talk too much, and anyway there was nothing to say except:

"Are *you* O.K.?" — and when he nodded I shut up again. But you can imagine it. It's everything you remember: those minutes when you smell the electric shock in the air, just like when they say *Hold still please, this won't hurt*; the shock in the shudderings of the car itself, as if for one moment we had been balanced like two eggs on the sloping bridge spans and could see every cold orange light over that water without end; — then the deep blackness of the river below, knowing that we (with just a breath or a sigh) could have fallen into that blackness, unaware of any pain or trauma or sensation of falling; just that awful blackness and the power it would have to swallow us down into itself far away from any lights, lights which just then for us would have had the beauty of men on camels in the desert, bearing water and loaves of thick, crusty brown bread, rescue wreathed in smiles. I didn't release my grip on the car door handle or my knee as we drove the rest of the way home with the radio off, as we listened to all those ancient faraway sounds, like voices, echoing. Old voices, echoing.

It's our neighborhood: in this part of Brooklyn, one of those still-quaint, tree-lined brownstone-ish areas unctuously described by real-estate agents (who probably live on Park Avenue; ours did) as "charming," "up-and-coming," "the new *perfect* place to raise a family." A place a lot of white people have been known to call "delightfully ethnic." Many families do live here, most of them poor, middle-aged Puerto Ricans. There are many beautiful, clear-eyed children, almost all of whom attend the Catholic elementary school a few blocks west of the park. I moved in here with Mel soon after we met just over a year ago, after I'd gotten good and cleaned up and away from everybody. Now that I'm back in school it's a long trip every day by subway. I don't really mind. I'd never think of asking him to drive me in, since he has to commute out to Nassau County every day, to the South Shore hospital he works in. Once I surprised him out there and we had lunch on the grass; it was pretty nice even for a hospital. Most of the time that I see him he's tired. That's what gets me scared, when he drives back late from out there. What almost happened tonight could almost happen out there. Or happen. It would happen, the way things are now. The thing is, you have to be ready for it when it happens. It would be *what was left of him under that white sheet with red and brown spots all over it when he was brought back with all those people smiling and wanting to see; people we had never known. And if you looked into my eyes you would see how they would stay open for years, especially at night, because there would be those demons, those demons behind the door and the things that still live there. Because what—*

(—what everybody always tells you, what they always rush to tell you, is never true, about how those things aren't there and can't get you. They do get you. Even if you're dreaming that they got you you never really wake up. Not ever. Never and can't.)

"*Hey.*" Mel's voice. "Are you coming to bed or what?" He was giving me this very annoyed look.

"What's up with you?" he said. We'd gotten all the way up the stairs and into the apartment and through to the bedroom, and I was just standing there in front of the mirror with my shirt off, holding it in my right hand. He was smiling, weary and just at the edge of fatigued impatience, showing the smooth shoulders and pretty dark nipples that, from their place beneath his T-shirt, pressing perfect points up beneath the cotton, didn't tempt me tonight.

"Come *on*."

I finished undressing and got into bed. I was trembling. His arms and shoulders felt warm and safe. I moved closer to him.

He turned out the light, butted my arm with his face, put a hand in its favored place on my ass and grunted good night.

"Mel?"

"*Oh* . . . yeah?"

" . . . nothing — " I couldn't sleep. It was close to a full moon. There weren't any noises. Only the sound of his breathing.

Four nights later, five nights, six. . . . I still couldn't sleep. Mel was working the four to twelve shift at the hospital and then had called to say that he'd had a fight with some loudmouthed do-it-*this*-way type nurse and had told them all to go fuck themselves good, and that with luck and clear traffic he'd be home a little before midnight, but first he'd be stopping off to eat at an express-way restaurant in Massapequa with one of the guys from X-ray — Johnny Mercado, did I remember him? *No.* The rest of it was fine with me. At least for a little while yet there wouldn't be any-one else around.

 — That's what I was thinking after I hung up. I just didn't feel like speaking to anybody. In fact, I didn't feel like doing much of anything. There were a few papers I could have worked on, and some books I should have read a week ago already and discussed in the classes I missed yesterday and the day before, but instead I'd turned off the light early in the evening and had just sat there in the comfortable dark, thinking. It seemed like there was a lot to think about all of a sudden . . . like the ocean at Quogue last sum-mer . . . that place where we'd spent a week with some friends of

Mel's: a husband and wife neurology team at the hospital out there. They hadn't been all that bad for older people, in their forties, and they hadn't tried to make us feel stupid, either, the way some doctors do to people, all condescending in white. That had been their summer-weekend house, right on the beach, and we'd spent every evening but one, the rainy one, sitting and talking and drinking fancy drinks on the redwood porch facing the beach. You could feel the ocean everywhere — eating its way along the edge of the beach and licking at the legs of the neighbor's little boy who had played at the water's edge every day. Sometimes he would waddle on chubby kid legs over to us to show us something he'd found — a pretty shell or a rock — and I'd always wanted to grab him to tell him to stay away from the water because couldn't he see it was dangerous? The ocean *had* been everywhere: in the air, in the house, on our skin, even inside us; you couldn't get away from it. Every now and then a town police jeep had bumped past on the beach, leaving huge tire marks and flashing its red light like an awful, swollen, bloody red eye. Even the sun had been red. The sun had been red and the ocean had been everywhere and you couldn't get away from them.

Except in the dark. When I'm in the dark and I can't see, I can tell everything's going to be all right. It's something you know. Even if any monsters or flashing lights or greedy oceans or black rivers are here, I won't see them and they won't get to me because I can't see them.

I can't see them!

That was me, in a loud, clear voice. Before the door moved with —

"Who are you talking to? I said 'Hi,' for the second time," Mel's voice came from behind the kitchen door. He made it even sooner than he'd said he would (*but just leave me the fuck alone would you? Always breaking in like a goddamn* —).

"Hi. What's this miracle? — what time is it?"

"I don't know . . . late. We didn't bother to stop. You know that place is *not* the real deal for any kind of dinner after eight o'clock."

"Um-hmm." It sounded clumsy. Had he come home early to see what I was up to? Why the *fuck* —

"So what're you sitting in the dark for?"

"Cause I feel like it. It was quiet."

"Yeah? Since when?" He was fumbling in the refrigerator for something; pushing aside things wrapped in tin foil, rolling around what sounded like cucumbers.

"What're you looking for?"

"A beer."

"I think we're out. See if there's any Coke."

"I don't *want* a Coke. What d'you mean, we're out? How could we be out?"

"*I* want a Coke. Oh, wait." A few days ago he'd bought two six-packs of some new Japanese beer that had sounded good and I'd promised to put them away. I'd forgotten. "Mel."

"What? You're right, we are out. Jesus Christ."

"No, there're two six-packs on the floor. By the garbage can. I forgot to put them in. On the floor, the Sapporuchi something."

"Warm beer? Unh-*unh*, baby. That ain't gettin it. So," he came into the living room where I could almost see him, tall and familiar in the dark, "since when're you into sitting in the dark? You going all loco on me, hombre?"

"*Don't* turn it on." With, quickly: "It's an ugly lamp. It makes the room look pink."

"It's . . . "

"It's nice like this, when you can't see anything. Check out the street lights, honey!"

"Who can see . . . it's dark as *hell*." He was tired, affection-ate, just worn out, really. Not only had it been a long day for him, ending with that stupid nurse, but then he'd had to come home and find warm beer when it should have been fresh-cold from Japan, and me sitting in the dark, not even playing the stereo the way I used to do, sometimes for hours, until he'd come home. It was all so different so fast. And now it was like I wasn't even alone with him. I could feel it.

"Just leave it off. Did you bring my Coke?"

"Come and get it." I got up and went to him. It was all dark as I crossed the room and took the Coke as he gave me his hand and pulled me in a little. That was when I saw her. The leaves were covering her.

No sleep. Tonight there are a few noises, noises of cars and cats and the late street-sweepers. The living room faces the street, across the hall from our bedroom, and usually the few street noises there are don't reach us in here; tonight I'm listening for them carefully, watchfully. The sounds never seem to be enough; there are never enough of them. It gets so quiet you can hear your own heart, thumping like some soft clumsy thing inside you. I hear it: it's beating louder and louder, ocean-sounds. Well, the ocean's here. I see it, all white and gray and angry. This has to be Quogue or some other place, a nameless, faceless beach with only the ocean and me staring at each other. It's whispering, and the whispers sound like one big, ugly hiss.

What do you want? — quietly, so Mel won't hear.

It's not answering me. Just staring and whispering.

When this happens, you have to *make* it answer.

What do you want? Louder now. I don't think Mel can hear me here. I'm on the beach and he's asleep. Sleeping like the dead.

You, it says, shifting and rolling itself.

Why? Rolling itself over and over, back and out to the edge of the sky and back again, until it says: *Because.*

Because what? Mel's so far away — all these shadows here and him so far away with no answer from the ocean and these noises hurting in my head. Like *Hold still please, this won't hurt.* The scumbags lie, you remember it.

I nod. I'm nodding. I'm walking into the ocean and from some point far off in the distance I hear a voice calling me, *Stop,* calling my name, *Stop!* Mel or somebody. — I'm walking in with my eyes open as the ocean keeps staring *and oh dear God I will not stop walking in deeper and deeper, deeper and deeper. Marry me.*

The radio was on. Brash as a buzzsaw and loud — what time was it, what time? — and then that voice, announcing . . . a DC-10 crashed in Boston last night, killing all two hundred and seventy-three aboard. This was a dream, it had to be.

There was Mel, sitting on the edge of the bed, smoking and watching me. He looked more tired than ever.

"Morning."

"Umh." — "What time?"

"Seven-eighteen."

"Hup." It hurt to clear my throat.

"Listen."

" — "

"Are you — are you — "

He wanted to finish with *all right?* I knew it. I hated him. I looked at him and didn't say anything. He should have been dressed already and on his way out. He was still in the T-shirt and undershorts he'd slept in, sitting there calmly looking at me; only he wasn't calm. I hated him. (Since when?) I hated him.

"I'm fine." I could hear my voice, so far away, as he looked down at his hands, then back up at me. "*You* look tired. You look like hell." He wouldn't stop *looking* at me. "You don't smell that great, either," I added.

"Thanks."

"Did *you* sleep well? You didn't!" I couldn't take it when he looked like that. I felt like burning him with something, or tearing him to screaming bloody shreds. Bastard, sitting there staring at me. A born bastard. And now my head was hurting again.

"No. But take a look at yourself."

"Why?"

"Just do." (A surprise?) I jumped out of bed and went to the mirror.

So, I looked as though I hadn't slept for days. I hadn't. The only difference was that now there were black rings under my eyes, small black lines. But I still felt as though I could get into a high-speed car in two seconds and race off for miles, never touching the earth.

He was still looking at me — his head off to one side, legs crossed, drumming his fingers on his bare thigh as he blew smoke out of the side of his mouth. That habit I hated all over again, as he put the cigarette out in the ashtray on top of the blanket and came over to put his hot, horrible hands on my head. Next it would be his mouth, and then he might even have tried to hold me down, looking at me the whole time, saying *What's wrong?* — when there was nothing wrong at all. I just had to get away from him. It was him, today, now.

(To where?)

— the leaves, the lake, the lights flashing dream-red, dream-white, so pretty . . . I'd been there before, in those places, sometime. It had been so very quiet with no one.

I was already in the bathroom, trying to find something to hold on to — the toothbrush, the toothpaste tube, soft, plastic, cold — right there.

"What's wrong?" — if I'd had a gun right then I would have shot him. *Gotten rid of him.* There were noises of him opening a drawer, the drawer that always stuck and made splinters, as he searched for a shirt to wear. Those little noises made my head hurt more.

"Nothing. I'll be late," I said. The newscaster was still snapping out details of the crash and quoting the statements of airline officials. There were so many victims: *a tragic event,* one official said. But this was peace for some of us. Just to stand there, and listen.

Another night and still no sleep. Now, at last, it was nice. Finally, just some time when you could stay awake for hours, staring at the walls, watching them move and shift in the dark. With the moon's passing it was darker tonight. No noises anywhere. I couldn't even hear Melvin breathing, or snoring. It was like I didn't have to pretend anymore that maybe he was dead after all and wouldn't ever wake up, just like I'd never go to sleep. The day after tomorrow and the day after that and on and on for years, he'll be lying there next to me as I keep sitting up listening to the ocean sucking out and back and the jets that crash and burn people to ash. And that small, sneaky sound of books that have to turn their own pages because I — *I* — can't read them.

Yes; today I pretended that I was getting ready to go to classes and then came right back after Mel was gone. *Que estúpido!* the Puerto Rican neighborhood ladies would say, anyone could fool him. I was here to pull down the shades. I sat in the dark to listen. Because you never know when there'll be an accident that you'll hear that you'll want to see, and you'll know that it's an accident with all those sirens and fire trucks and people screaming as they see the runway come up closer from way down there with those huge, beautiful engines as they burn up and you know that you will soon burn with them. I sat in the dark all day to listen; I heard the voices of cats. Also the floor creakings and the shadows. I could hear them breathing as I sat there thinking. They were here for hours until the woman came. And she's back now.

It *is* her. That bloody woman from the accident that was when? A month or three weeks ago? Standing by the door next to the mirror over the cabinet, looking at me. (How can she see me?) Seeping . . . that neck is so shredded. I see the blood glinting on the walls behind her. I see that white sheet on her.

Mel, *I'm whispering,* you better get up. She's here. I can see her. Why don't you look?

The bastard's asleep. I have to wake him up, for *this. Get up, Mel!* Still asleep. *That woman is standing over there.*

(And you should know why, says a voice that is Melvin's voice but different. He's rising to sit. And I can see you better now than I've ever seen you before, Mel. I can see the demon that I always knew was in you the same demon I have been feeling these last weeks, this last year, however long the whole world has been hurting my head like this. Your face is gone except for those red eyes and red teeth red like the sun on the beach and the blood. Now you know because everyone knows as she bleeds and starts to cry that she is doing this, that you are doing this and that we will have to leave this room now, get out of here to live, because no one is crazy here, we are not crazy in any way or shape.)

A few seconds later you hear someone screaming, screaming like a monster or the way she screamed as the car smashing into the lamppost cut off her legs and pulled out her hair and ripped her neck from end to veined end; — no, the way she screamed as the muddy water swept down her throat and made bubbles in her blood until it was all darkness and the leaves in protest swirled up like bat wings around her and covered her for the living to haul up because by then she was anyway sewage, dead with the weight of sewage; no, the way he screamed when smiling white cops told him she was gone and his screams echoed through the screams and laughter and tears until the final silence of that room they put him in: screaming like the dead who will never rise to inherit the earth or whatever kingdom is promised any number of kingdoms from one daynight to the next; screaming like him now with his mouth open and dry as something under his chin tries to push his mouth shut; earwitnesses will say It must be someone out on the street dying under the cold city skeleton lights in the alleyways where cats maul and screw . . . somebody on the runway, stifling under all the foam they sprayed there, screaming for the ambulance. Trying now to remove those many arms about you; feeling the killing grip

*that will strap you into that place and drown you. What is that thing
under your chin. A hand. A smell once familiar. The hand of the lake
choking you choking all . . . the last thing now in the world of fire; that
other's burning face, Melvin's face screaming Let me help you: words spoken through red teeth until all dims to the black water color. And now
—no noises. The girl gone. How many creatures swim through the
water. And how he swims. He and he. And the silent screams and
the sirens of that time. The red revolving lights like bright hungry fish.
And the fire. Watching him.*

I can't tell you what day it is. Maybe the next day but I can't be
sure anymore when all I hear are lies, whispers, and lies. And now
*the days pass by so quickly, yellow, green, red, until the nights come, the
black nights: there must be three or four of them at a time sometimes, they
last so long. They just go on and on, like space, empty like space, and the
moon's not full anymore so you can't see anything. You can't see the stars
or the walls of your room or even the earth, although you know it's out
there. Blue. You know it's out there and you look for it but you can't see
it. It's dangerous, because if you can't see it you'll crash and wind up on
the radio after the song hour. The sad songs they play at night, the songs
of dreams.*

They're playing a song on the radio now. The words to it
are coming through clearly in this dream. We're in the Hyundai,
heading for the bridge, some bridge I don't remember, to get to
this hospital, a white hospital . . . Mel's driving. He looks so tired,
and now he looks different, like a shadow. He doesn't look real.
He's a dream-person. He looks like the shadows the sun makes on
bridges. I'm dreaming this, I have to be dreaming this. And the
dream-pictures, like photo snaps all muddled, blurry-faced, come
rushing up, stay for a second, then race off. To the bridge.

And he's driving too fast. *This trip wasn't my idea.* He planned
everything as always. He thinks there's something wrong with me
and wants me to go to the E.R. of this hospital so they can poke

me around until I come out sounding stupid. He's not saying anything. I know him. After all this time I can read his mind. He thinks they'll be able to fix me because there's something wrong with me even though I feel fine. I just don't want to go to sleep anymore. In fact I'm never going to sleep again.

"Mel, you're driving too fast." *I hate the way he drives and sits on the bed and stands up blowing smoke out of the side of his mouth—like* that. *He's doing it. I'm just glad he's a shadow. He shouldn't be real. People should blow smoke sideways when they're dreaming not when they're driving and sitting down and standing up. That woman used to do it.*

"Mel, you're driving too fast." We're at the bridge now. What if he drives too fast and we drive off the earth? They'll tell it on the radio. People I care about will go out and have an accident. There are always so many trucks. The trucks that bring supplies, the trucks that block everyone's vision, the trucks of dreams.

This truck is in front of us and somebody on the radio is screaming. *Watch out, we're going to go off the earth*

"Mel, watch out! — it's too *fast!*" And now I

— reach over and hit him and see the bright red on my hand. I must have hit him in his teeth. *They're so red. Always red, more and more like his eyes. This is the steering wheel. We can't, we can't go off the earth.*

In front of us, the noise of a crash: a plane must have crashed on the bridge, killing everybody aboard. There's a crash behind us and we are flying forward, hard, flying. I was belted in so I would never leave the bottom of the lake, but Mel's not belted so he can escape, flying, big black brown pretty jet right through the glass. I see him, there he goes. *Too much noise....* Cracked glass, red, the smell of fire . . . he's gone. He escaped and left me under this red sky. I would never ever have left him, never . . . the radio's screaming about accidents; there are accidents everywhere.

But I'm out of the car, running. I know I should be *waking up* but I'm here running on the bridge, feeling the thin, dreamy-delicious air parting itself, carrying me up. Mel must be some-where close by. What happened — ... *but you have to be okay, Mel, somewhere I can't see you.* I'm running ... my eyes are open but I can't see and I'm still running. The sun is melting over everything like hot angry orange taffy, and even the bridge is running and melting under the sky that just keeps hanging there, a world of red burning dreams, burning gold ... the neighbors who could help me see and take me home are in Africa, writing a book. I have to cross the water to get to them. Maybe even the ocean. It's there, under the bridge.

I keep hearing the horns of cars, angry honks. Only they aren't cars, they're trumpeting elephants. I'm out in the open run-ning with the elephants, and the plane that crashed is burning nearby under a red sky and a red sun as the ocean roars in anger, in terror, far away. *Africa.* I'm close. I can't find Mel anywhere. He must have melted into the bridge.

I have to cross the water. *It's the dream.* And there's the water: I can see it, black, old, deep, swirling to Africa, telling me *not to be afraid, to walk on its back, to follow it to*

Red lights ...

Dreams. Voices calling. Calling—

The sounds of elephants ...

The bridge is burning.

Dear God—

And now listen. Just listen. This is the long dream beginning. *The long dream.* You can't see anything but fire all around here. *Hot.* And now all you can hear for miles — for miles and miles — are screams.

COMMITMENT

—**B**UT LOU — , HE SAYS —
—No.
—But can't you just say it — or —
—I said, No.
—But even if I —
—Stop begging, Ricky. What did I tell you? See, now —
—Don't you want it?
—That ain't the point, now. Get dressed!
—Why don't you . . .
—What?
—make me . . .
—Boy . . . see, now —
—Uh, huh?
—You better quit playing games and get dressed! What you *do*ing?
—Proposing.
—Yeah, to the wrong one, says that other. Who is Lou Jay. Easing himself up on the bed. Thinking, mama just changed these damn sheets yesterday and now in the late-morning heat they

were already sticking to the sweat on his back. Thinking, the bedroom was all right enough — was home. Thinking, the postcards and pictures of Miami and New York and whatnot made it more . . . the way they liked it. Had liked it. Him and Ricky. Thinking: uh huh, cause the boy had been in there often enough (only one who had been) — thinking, uh huh, best friend, searching for the word to describe him, my, my — my *what?* And now that the mama and daddy were out for a while Miss Ricky was actually going to *try it:* going to try to go on and be his hardheaded self as usual and show out like a fool even with everything getting set to happen on schedule tomorrow. But, see —

—I wish Renee would catch your ass in here like this.— Looking straight over at Ricky kneeling on the floor beside the bed.

—That stupid — don't talk about that now. Don't even get me started.

—Yeah, uh-hmm. That stupid — listen to me, talking just as nasty as you! Well, she gone be your wife in a day. Less than a day.

—So? We could still —

—What did I say, fool? No.

—Why not?

—Cause I said so, that's why not. You need to listen for once, stead of being so damn —

—Hardheaded. I know.

—Well, then.

—You sound like Daddy.

—He got some sense.

—He ain't got nothing. You know he's forcing me!

—He needs to. Somebody needs to.

—I'm seventeen, Lou Jay!

—You *eigh*teen.

—I *will* be. What he got to go on and try to force me to get married for?

—Cause he want him some grand-kids.

—He got eleven already. I got brothers, Lou Jay!

—Six.

—And no sisters, neither.

—But you his baby. His baa-by Ricky.

—Shit, Ricky said. One long syllable the color of the snarl that formed it.

—Tell that to the preacher, he said.

—Well, baby, you better go on out and get you a nice sweet fancy ring.

—I'ma smack you down in a second, bitch. I swear.

—You be acting too grown sometimes any old way. Get up off your knees, Ricky.

—What you talking about grown for, trying to act like you so grown, giving out orders? You ain't but two months older than me, baby. I could stay on my knees if I want to. You want to know what Daddy said?

—About what? The wedding? Everybody far way as Decatur already knows. That's all folks do round here is talk, okay? But ain't nobody saying nothing to your daddy's face, that's all. They could shame you *and* me if they wanted to.

—I ain't studying all that. And you —

—You need to.

—You want to know what Daddy said?

—Told you I already knew.

—Don't be acting all grand, Miss Girl, cause you don't know all this. He got his gun!

—What? For what?

—You know what. Fittin to shoot off my ass if I don't marry little Renee. And you know he could shoot good. He learned me. And I learned you, Lou Jay. My baby.— Reaching over to squeeze the other man's naked thigh, then moving his hand slightly above and to the center of it. Their skins, together, all of a glow in the thickening heat.

—You'll always be my baby, Lou Jay. You know that.

—Ricky —

—Since we was thirteen we been playing *on*. I got you now, Lou. You got me. I don't never want nobody but you. We got us something! You think I could let you go for some little piece of —

—All right, now. We ain't got no time for all that sweet-talk — stop, boy, that tickles! — with some man, your daddy no less, putting a gun all up in your face. No, uh-*uh*. I ain't having it. Didn't I ask you to stop?

—Aw, girl, you love what my hands do. Anyway, Daddy ain't only got his gun up in my face. He got it aimed all up in my behind, too.

—*Um*-hmm. Cause he know what's been all up *in* there.

Laughter, until they choke. But already he is looking. Ricky, having laughed, stilled, now looking. Thinking how hard, how very very hard it is not to focus, fixate, his eyes on Lou Jay. How hard not to see, looking, just how *pretty*. How fine and all that, he thinks. How hard not to carry to dreams and private thrusts the big old shoulders and pretty lips and nipples, after his very own lips have traversed the skin . . . the shoulders and nipples all hard now hard-hard yet soft, like the eyes, beneath the shirt . . . when he wore a shirt. Hard not to think, Yeah, cause I could just take him right now, couldn't I, and do *all* a that and more. I could (uh huh, do all of it, that and *that*) get him all relaxed (the calm-down part) and whisper back behind his neck about the house they'd buy someday (or, no: *I* will buy. *I* will. For him. Ricky-for-Lou Jay. Uh huh) in Decatur or maybe . . . that one. The one they'd fix up nice with a front yard just like everybody else's and some back land too just like everybody else's so they could live someplace far away from all those others, those others with guns and bullet-eyes, those others like his own daddy. Far away from the eyes, from the Now-what-y'all-got-into-some-nasty-shit-no-doubt pressed lips and hands on hips. Far from the sucked teeth and curling sneers. Someplace where the two of them him-and-Lou Jay could just settle and say, All right, now. Because this here is Lou Jay's and Ricky's house and we been up in it together going on how long now? so don't y'all ignorant moth-erfuckers even *try* no fierce shit up in here. Uh huh. The ones with the guns (Daddy) who could never know how it felt when that part of him that was on Lou Jay, right there, slow and silky out in the fields at night sometimes or right here in Lou Jay's room like when after his mama and daddy are asleep and it's just him and me and is that your hand, Lou? I can't hardly tell no more. It all feels like soft sand, smooth reeds, watergrass. Hot silk. All water. *My face in the sand, in the soft soft reeds.* Enough to know for now. Better not to know yet about (though he knows already) the curling snakes on the shore, the blue things that, in murky rivers, curl about ankles, drag them down to drown. Enough to know, for now, what their hotsilkiest dreams tell them: that they are here, alive, and that, right here, on this hot morning beneath the pecans and the sizzling live oaks, all snakes are in their holes, all blue things uneasily at rest. Here, where, whatever else might be known or feared, each can be certain, remembering warm sand and siltyslim reeds, that the other will always be his and his. Lucky, he thinks, or something. And I'ma make sure we stay lucky. But says:

—I swear, Lou, it's like we was living in —

—You need to tell me what Daddy Malcolm said. You ain't tell me everything.— Reaching over to the bedside table for a cigarette.

—Well —

—Go on.

—All right. He *said* — get this, now, this's Daddy — he said, 'Boy, if you don't marry Renee I'll blow your head off myself. You *will* marry her,' he said. Sounding all white. Daddy!

—Lord Jesus. He got to know about me. — Blowing out a thick smoke stream.

—He do. What you think? He *been* knowing. Why the hell else you think he been pushing me all up in Renee's face?—

Looking out into the June sunlight. Turning his face to the day and noticing how the air is free, humid; how bugs are chattering between birdsong.

—I don't want to marry that girl, Lou.

—Why you so sure she want to marry *you?* She must have something to say. It ain't like you the only one out here seen her. And no matter what folks say I don't think she stupid. We know Renee.

—Well, she don't know nothing about us.

—She don't know nothing about us cause we ain't never done nothing in her face and we watched that anyway. Daddy Malcolm, now, that's a different story. He always did look at me funny. I ain't messing with that.

—Evil, you mean. You got that right. He thinks you switch. Plus you ain't never had no girlfriend.

—Ain't never wanted none.

—You should've, Lou Jay. You coulda saved us a whole lotta trouble that way. Maybe Daddy wouldn't be breathing all down my neck now if you did.

Lou Jay smoked for a while in silence, then turned his face to the freedom of the day and the birds singing and the trees looking so peaceful, quiet, beneath the bright wheeling sun.

—Can't nobody make me do nothing I don't want to, Ricky. Not even Daddy Malcolm.— Not quite believing his own words, but they sounded brave. —Anyway, answer my question. Why you so sure she want to marry —

—She do. Lou Jay, she *do*. You know Renee always liked me! Anyway her mama said she better and Renee ain't gone hardly go against her mama.

—She can't — she can't do nothing to get rid —

—Hell, no, Lou Jay! What you saying? If she even opened up her mouth to say something like that Miss Gaines would kill her with the switch before she could even say jump up. And Daddy — I don't even want think about what Daddy would do.

Besides, we ain't got all that kinda money. I don't even know where we could get one. We ain't never known nobody who did that.

—Far as we know.

—Far enough.

—Goddamn! Her mama, your daddy . . .— Falling silent once more. Turning his eyes down to Ricky's hands at rest between them on the sheet.

—I just don't see that y'all got much choice now. You know Daddy Malcolm ain't playing. I think he *would* rather see you dead. He don't want him no sissy son no matter what. And Renee gone have you a kid. You gone be a daddy.— Pausing. Those eyes raised again to Ricky's face.

—How could y'all do that? Practically right in my face.

—Lou Jay —

—You wasn't even thinking about us when you did that, Ricky. You wasn't thinking about Renee, neither. No you wasn't. And all this time you and me been making plans and whatnot. Talking shit. And now you gone come back *in* my face telling me you *love* me and how we gone do so *much*.

—Baby —

—I shoulda — I . . . that was just stupid, that's all. Don't look at me all innocent! Y'all was wrong. *You* was wrong — I can't really say too much against Renee. And I know you know y'all was wrong.— Pausing once more. Taking in the tender curve of the neck, eyelashes.

—I know you know, Rick.

—But I told you —

—You just wanted to see what it felt like? It ain't all that different. I coulda told you that.

—No, you couldn't.

—Well, maybe not.— Sucking on the cigarette. —But that don't change nothing. And now you gone have you a wife *and* a kid. I'll be damned. Ain't that something!

—Don't take the Lord's name —

—I didn't.— Smoking some more. Frowning.

—Lou Jay.

—What?

—You don't understand . . .

—What . . . what don't I under*stand?* Tell me! Since you got all the answers.

—Just . . . damn, Lou Jay! She don't mean nothing to me. She ain't — she ain't shit.

—I told you to get your hands off me. Oh, so now she ain't shit, huh? That's nice. Real nice, baby. You the one, I tell you.

—What you mean?

—She our friend, you dumb mother — Jesus! We all growed up together, you and me and Miss Girl, fool! That oughta mean something. Like more than just she ain't shit. I got to say I feel kinda sorry for her, laying up in bed with somebody she don't even know don't want her ass cept for what she got tween her legs.— Still watching Ricky, of course still watching him. Feeling the sadness rising up in him again, in that place, like the peepers' dying sundown calls: there, right at the edge of the shore, where most of the time he feels, deep inside, only Ricky. Then gathering all of it, the dusk and the shore, as they rise out of him, hover between them, joined by that lonely something else of lowered eyes, as Ricky moves closer to him on the bed. Putting first one hand, then another, on those big old shoulders. As Lou Jay rests his cheek on one of the hands. Closes his eyes.

—You know what the worse part is, Lou?

—What?

—It's like now — now I feel like —

—Yeah?

—Like I hate her. Renee.— Whispered.

—Like — like I ain't never hate nobody in my life — not no girl, and —

The eyes, opened.

—I know, I know. Don't look at me like that, Lou Jay! You know what —

—What you saying?

—I — I don't know. I don't know why cept I know I been laying up in bed at night thinking about how much I —

Lou Jay looking at him.

—. . . how I hate that girl now, Lou. Can't even stand to look in her face no more. That —

Lou Jay looking at him.

—Don't look at me like that, Lou Jay! I can't —

—I guess you want me to say something.

—I can't —

—What you going on hating her for? *She* ain't done nothing to you. Last time I heard takes two to make a baby. And she settin up in that house knowing she gone have you a kid and her mama looking at her all cross-eyed and you settin up here talking about some you hate her. What you doing hating folks?

—You don't like her neither.

—I don't like what y'all did but I don't hate nobody. I hope.

—She so proud, walking around telling everybody, 'Yup, we getting married!' Just yesterday she was up the road telling folks, 'He so fine, wait til y'all see him in his wedding suit.'

—Well, you are.— Very quietly. But I swear to God I won't never tell you that too many times, he thinks, cause you just too hardheaded for words.

—Uh huh. But just watch me wear some tennis shoes to the church.

The other silent.

—Why can't we go away, Lou? Up to New York — even Atlanta! What I'ma do, married to some —

—What you did the night you got you a baby.

—Lou Jay —

—You do what you got to do. Like I'm going on to college. U.A.'s waiting.

—You really gone do that, Lou? Go on and leave me here with her and Daddy?

—You left me.

—I didn't! Listen, Lou. Listen to me. Whyn't you leave Alabama for school so we could go away? I could work.

—And get Daddy Malcolm up on my ass to come on and shoot me dead. Uh-*uh*. No, thank you.

—Coward.

—No. See, now, listen. Try I don't want your mess all up in my business, fucking with my shit again. Try that.

—Oh, bitch —

—No, baby, no. We ain't gone have that, now. Didn't I tell you how long ago now to go on and get dressed? You gone stick around here all day, when you getting married in — what is it now — twenty-two hours? Besides, Mama and Daddy'll be back in a few.

—Where they went to?

—Probably out with your daddy, looking for your ass. You need to go on home.

—They know what we was doing last night?

—When did we ever tell em? Do they *know*. Do they *know*.— The disgust in his face and voice cruel enough to slash cane. Hiding from the slash or seeking to conjure the face of the water and the reeds, Ricky put his own face in his hands.

—So I'm just gone ruin my life, and you ain't gone do shit to help.— From between fingers.

—Help you ruin your life? You don't need no help. Gimme one a your cigarettes.

—I ain't got but two left. You don't even care, do you? Bitch?

—Excuse me? Ain't nobody your bitch up in here. I got to buy me some.

—I said, you don't even *care*, do you?

—I heard you. What you expect? You want me to drop dead?

—Whyn't you try? Ricky said, but the laughter returned. Later, Lou Jay would remember that just then he had noticed neither the glimmer in Ricky's eye nor its presaging the speed that followed as, with the barest shifting of a thigh, Ricky leaped onto Lou Jay's chest and farted loudly and squarely on the most sacred spot, just below the neck. A way of possessing it, the victor knows; the surest way of leaving behind his most private smell where before only the mouth and skin had been. Then feeling the strong hands attempting to push him off, but the feeling of those fingers about his hips once more, even in protest, nothing compared to the victim's grimace and the victor's delight.

—Now see if I give a fuck about some Renee, Ricky said, purring — for, like many, the foul gifts of his own innards entranced him.

—Well, thank you, you nasty —

—Aw, you love it, honey.

—Take your hand off me.

—Lou —

—Come *on*.

Ricky moving lower over him, then closer.

—Let's just run away.— Whispered.

—Aw, shit. Here we go again. I swear —

—You could cook. Make me chicken in dressing. Pear preserves and biscuits. In our own house. You could cook, Lou Jay.

—I know I can.— The beautiful smile at last emerging in full. —Did I or did I not ask you for a cigarette?

A reach over to the table, a cigarette pulled from the pack. Lit, then placed, ever so gently, into that mouth.

—See, Lou, I could light your cigarettes for you.

—Uh huh.

—We could get married.

—Boys don't *get* married. To each other.

—You need to look at the news, girl. Boys be marrying each other up in Oregon —

—I ain't moving to no Oregon. And if it's boys marrying each other, you know it's white boys.

—Or in California where it don't matter. Where don't nobody know nobody.

—Fuck that bullshit. U.A. U.A. You got it? September, now!

—Why you acting like — damn, hold still, boy! Can't I even get me a kiss? What you scrunching up your mouth all stupid for?

—You got your kisses from Miss Renee.

—Lou Jay — goddamn! — I told you —

—Speak the truth and shame the devil. Now! Tell your Daddy *I* said that.

Ricky silent. Watching those lips move over the cigarette.

—It ain't even like that, Lou.— Very quietly. —You know I just —

—It's time for you to go. Now I ain't —

—I'm serious. You think I'm playing?

—I'ma say one more time —

—Just one kiss, baby. Please? Then I'll go on. Please? Open up.

This *is* one hardheaded fool, the other thinks, *the kind that sooner or later* —

—Don't you love me, Lou Jay?

A look at those eyes, asking; a look away. And now Lou Jay, lying on his back, feeling what's on the way, doesn't have to say anything, not a word or even a tune, because it's all there — yes, right there beneath the watcher's curling lashes that match his own, there in the neck's curve, where the veins are exposed, where the look is hot silk, *where you can't even hardly stop it cause you are*

—What you doing, Rick?— But all at once his voice is all water.

—Get up offa me, he says, but how the silt of the smooth river glides, glides across his moving sand.

—You can't say nothing now, Ricky says, sucking air where there is none.

—Get your hand out from all up under me, Lou Jay whispers, but how the waters have already parted, a circle of ripples pushing gently where the weeds are thickest.

—Ain't nobody gone be back for a while, neither, Ricky says, wetting his face where it is warm.

—See if I marry that girl.— Straining the weeds, the soft grasses, through his teeth.

You will if your daddy makes you, Lou Jay thinks, running his fingers up and down, up and down a single blade.

The bugs, still conversing. The jaybirds, over the water, darting. Everywhere blue, black to blue, blueblue.

Renee will be there soon. Lou Jay, remembering. But moving now faster against the weeds, pushing more deeply into the sand, up to his buckling knees, until the entire river, its source and moan, rises and swells, swells and flows, wetting his sand, soaking his weeds. Filling every space of that warmth in his open throat.

—A beautiful dress,— she was saying. The three of them walking out along the Stone Bridge Road that led down the long hill to the Creek Meadow valley just outside of town. And she *was* pretty, Lou Jay had to admit — the type who surprised you with that devil in her that came out when you least expected it. And when you most expected it because it didn't. The Gaines' least favorite girl, folks in town said, who from the looks of things spent half her time daydreaming and should have been quicker than she apparently was considering she was Elvira Gaines' girl, since you could see Elvira had known quick enough to get Renee off her hands and into Ricky's, whose daddy owned not only twenty acres here in town but fifty more too up around

Decatur *and* his own house and business and had those seven boys, six of whom had already come close to doing the same. Nice girl, everybody said, but looked simple sometimes too, like them Birthwright brothers up on the hill who fooled away the day playing with cats and whatnot — the kind who ought to see things she needed to and didn't, things that sure enough, please, Jesus! didn't bear mentioning. But then others said no, not simple, just innocent — who wouldn't be, by force or His holy reckoning, raised under Elvira's switch? A few to whom almost nobody listened said naw, that girl was *deep* if you just looked. And — who knows? — maybe with that fury (the source of which they'd quickly forgotten or had never known) that in ever-shifting forms still took nightly and daily aim against them even as they slept, and which now firmly in their grip propelled them to devote the meaner, smaller parts of themselves to caring too much about some things, like the image of two boys pressing hands to each other's bellies in the slow velvet dance of a kiss — maybe with that same fury that moved them to cut their eyes and storm over policemen's bullets and marauding church fires in their midst, they'd never bothered to look very deeply into the most quiet part of that girl's eyes — or not far, anyway, beyond so many guesses as to the eventual worth of that girl and her kind as sweet fast pieces. Her gaze darker, deeper than ever today. Skin shining in the heat, hair permed and tied back in just that way that made so many of the other boys in town think nothing of going right up in her face to whoo-zop a little of the Bird they hadn't known they'd owned, za-bazz out some of the 'Trane they'd not suspected still seared in their veins, and say Miss Renee, hey, hey! All right, girl. Cause, well, uh huh. So, why don't you. And. Not that she couldn't handle them, Lou Jay thought. And Daddy Malcolm too had welcomed her into the Malcolms' with wide-open arms (a little too open, some said) because he'd always loved her anyway (a little too much, some also said) — like the daughter I ain't got, he'd said more than six times, and loved her even more these days, some folks murmured, now that she was marrying his baby son. Everybody swears Miss Renee got herself a man, Lou Jay thought, but I had him first, y'all, in places y'all couldn't even *dream* of. Shocked at how much it scratched at his heart to think of them having a baby together — what was a little baby, after all? But scratched even more to think of it now because they'd all been friends and he wanted them all still to be so long as he could just have Ricky and they could get far away from here and everybody and get that house, something, someday. Away. And none of it fair to her neither, he thought. She hadn't never hurt nobody, not once. But even harder now for him to like her when he almost wanted to. When the wedding was getting closer and they all were together here talking about (but what? please, Jesus) her wedding dress. Ricky! he cried out silently, what we gone do, Rick? Distant field noises coming drowsily across to them in the mid-afternoon heat. Lou Jay's parents having returned from visiting somebody's sick wife, and Renee come looking for Ricky (where else but at his best friend's? Boys would be just like that, getting married and couldn't care less about tomorrow). The Stone Bridge Road walk had seemed to suit all but the soon-groom. He would fidget, the other two thought, and be his sillyass self, but why looking evermore like he wanted to kill somebody?

—What's wrong with you, Ricky? What you looking at Lou Jay all evil for?

—Nothing.— Skipping stones in front of his shoes on the road.

—I ain't paying him no mind.

—Go on ahead of us, Lou Jay. Me and Ricky got to talk about something for a minute. In *private*.— Raising her eyebrows at Lou Jay and jerking her head toward the road ahead of them. The two young men exchanged startled looks.

—Anything you got to say to me Lou Jay could hear, Renee. I don't know what you got to say that could be so —

—Let me go on, y'all, Lou Jay said quickly. Moving ahead. —I'll wait for y'all on up some.— He was already gone by the time Ricky opened his mouth to protest, then turned back to face Renee standing in the road; her face grave, upturned to the source of light. The light in her eyes not golden, the face not smiling.

—Well, what?

Her eyes, looking at him.

—Well?

—What you taking that tone with me for, Ricky? You acting like somebody did something evil to you. What's wrong with you?

—Just tell me what you got to say, Renee. It's hot out here.

And there's so much he don't even know, she thinks. That he won't ever know.

—Well . . . — A pause.

—Yes?

—I just . . . I just wanted to say I hope everything's gone go all right tomorrow —

—What you mean, go right?

—Just what I said.— Pausing once more. Continuing:

—I mean I hope you show up on time like Daddy Malcolm said you would and don't come in the church looking all evil like you looking now. Mama and Daddy gone be settin right up in front with your mama and Daddy Malcolm and we don't need to have no kinda fuss. Mama picked out my dress and Daddy Malcolm paid for it, so that's that. I guess you know all that anyway. I know you're nervous, but I'm nervous too. You acting like you the only one. But don't forget — I'm the one's having the baby!

—Girl, you don't even . . .

—Listen! This ain't no joke, Ricky. You think I ain't scared too with a baby coming? I ain't never had no baby. I ain't even so sure I want one, to tell you the truth. I don't know. But we gone have one and that's why we getting married.— Stopping then to look at him with those eyes suddenly filled with dark birds in rapid flight through a country he'd never known — or had never wanted to know.

—Renee —

—You listen to me, Ricky. I got a lot to say and I don't know if I'm gone be able to say it straight out like this again.— Her feet planted squarely on the road's dry, hard, sun-baked earth. Looking almost as if she will rise into that other country from which her own voice seems to be coming, thinking, But this can't be me talking like this, not to him, not to nobody, who ever gave me the — ? *Or did I always* — ? But maybe too scary, right now, even to think. Rising into the sky might be easier than continuing to speak, continuing to look at him burning at her that way as the birds race through her eyes, their wings' beating her own secret desire to soar with them, so secret even she is unaware of it, *how could such a soaring ever take place?* she does not quite think but senses. Senses that the question itself is rarely, if ever, permitted, at least (but why?) to her; that the freedom to dream in a language of wings, if that is what freedom is, to fly, the sort of freedom her almost-but-not-quite dreams intone — such freedom truly must be a journey, must lead to grace. Petite, pretty girl on a country road. Hair tied back, lips parted to speak or to fly and so much, so much now and always, an entire world and beyond in her eyes. Now speaking from that place where she continues to stand, knowing that it is in fact her own voice she hears, her own words and the wings between them, as the words' weight and her feet so planted continue to pull her down into another vital yet hidden part of herself — a small, reaching figure outlined and illumined in the merciless sun.

—It's like I been thinking . . .— Her voice almost gentle.

—You said one time — only one time, Ricky, that you loved me.

But I know just like I got two eyes in my head that you ain't been showing me that side much lately. Daddy Malcolm's been real nice to me like always. Why can't you act right? You got the same face like your daddy but you don't act nothing like him.

—Renee . . .

—I ain't finished. Just listen. You got to understand something, Ricky. I don't want nobody in this town talking about you and me and our business. One thing I can't stand is a bunch of *nosy* — . . . The vehemence in her voice halting him.

—Renee —

—No. No. Let me tell you. Already somebody come up to Mama saying something about how it must be hard to have a fast girl in the house and how still waters run deep and all a that. Mama picked up the switch so fast I ain't even know what hit me. She said she ain't raised no fast girl for folks to laugh at and I know I don't want nobody laughing at me or you neither. So I'm just saying we gone have this baby and live right and since you gone be a daddy I hope you know we ain't gone have time for you to be running all over town with Lou Jay like y'all ain't got nothing better to do.

—Renee, lemme tell you something . . .

—Hold on, Ricky. Whyn't you listen for a minute? I'm just saying we could all still be friends and whatnot but he *is* going off to college and you and me gone have to get jobs and work, you hear? Cause I ain't about to put this baby off on Mama so she could take up the switch on me again and tell me something about how it's time I acted grown. We can all still have fun and get together but we — we gone have to be *responsible*. That's what Mama been telling me all along and I think she right.

The birds fluttering, settling. A new fear creeping into the spaces between their wings.

—I ain't gone feel that switch no more, Ricky.— A small, quiet voice.

—Renee—

—I ain't, Ricky. And, see, I'm not my mama, neither. I'm me. You know? I mean, *me*. And *me*, I mean me and you, *we* ain't gone use no switch on this baby. No, we not.

Opening his mouth to speak but the sweep of those birds stopping him.

—Don't say nothing to me while you still looking all evil, Ricky. Just come on.— As she turns and walks up the road, shoulders a little lower than before, he doesn't see the falling birds beginning to die in her eyes. As he follows with that slow dull heat that begins in his ears and continues on creeping down into what still feels like his neck. When they catch up, Lou Jay will look back at him, see that new (but what is it?) searing out of his eyes, and turn quickly to her. Will put his almost-burly arm through her fine-boned one and say:

—What about that dress, girl?— Pulling her forward. —What was you saying?

—Y'all got to see it. It's got satin — wait'll y'all see it! — satin ruffles. And —

—It's bad luck to see it til I marry you.— Gazing off toward some white houses on one of the surrounding hills.

—Well, excuse me, you ain't gone see me *in* it til tomorrow. Didn't I already say —

—Don't pay him no mind, Renee.— Shooting Ricky a Don't you start no mess out here! look. Behind Renee's back, Ricky grabbing his own crotch. Flicking Lou Jay the finger.

—You gone act right today or what, Ricky?— Over her shoulder, walking on.

—I got a headache.— Renee missing the kick he aimed just then at Lou Jay's behind.

—Well, don't talk then.

—Go on, Renee.— Smiling so that only Ricky can see. Smiling, the other thinks. But not smiling that day when I asked you why, Daddy. Why, and you saying Cause that's what you gone do, boy. Nothing else. I know you know why so don't be asking. You man enough to put a baby in her, you gone be man enough to marry her. You *will* marry her.

But I don't want to, Daddy. I — I can't. I don't —

Why *can't* you? Why don't you *want* to? Boy, don't be telling me nothing that's gone make me kill you up in here.

Would y'all quit that fussing and come on.

Mama. Mama, talk to Daddy.

What you want me to say, baby?

Quit crying, now! Quit crying! — you little asslicking sis-syass. I wouldn't even call you my own. You think I don't know? You my own and you done shamed me. Shamed me!

Daddy, don't hit me! Don't —

I'll kill you.

But didn't say all that. Even though he did hit me we ain't said all that. But we should've. We should've so I coulda known sooner he did hate me. You. You hate me and him. But I just want him. And I don't give a fuck cause we gone get the hell outa here anyway no matter what and buy us a piece of something some-place no matter what cause it don't matter what you say you ain't never gone make me marry no girl, Daddy. You could kill me if you want to. You could try. You could just try.

And she told her mama but ain't told her daddy she got a baby in her. Didn't mind telling my daddy but she ain't told her own. Maybe I could blackmail her. I got less than a day.

But now he sees the car coming down the road toward them. Raising dust clouds, an air-wake in the bright distance. The enveloping heat, disturbed, breaking into shimmers. The dust after a moment circling back on itself, settling on the thick grass, on the leaves of the heavy dark pecan trees along the road.

—That's Daddy Malcolm's car, Rick.— Lou Jay, seeming prepared to run.

—Not his daddy — my father-in-law, Renee corrected him.

—Not yet.— Ricky threw a stone over her head.

—Since when y'all got a station wagon?— Lou Jay looking from Ricky to her.

—Since you know when.

—Maybe he could buy us one.— The snort from behind her that followed her words not reaching her ears.

The car pulling up to them. Ricky's father, sticking his head out.

—Well, what we got here? Three pretty rats.

—Sir. — Lou Jay, not looking.

—Daddy Malcolm.— Renee, moving closer.

—You— to Ricky —you ain't got nothing to say to your daddy, boy?

Something just beneath the surface of his father's face swiftly urged the bloodsnarl trembling in Ricky's throat to a mumble that, in the wavering heat, passed well enough for respect.

—*Sir.*

—Uh huh. And so now where you all walking to?

—No place.— Her voice low as she cast a brief glance at Ricky. —You know we got rehearsal in a little bit. You coming, Daddy Malcolm?

—Church be too hot for rehearsal now.

—We know. Later on this afternoon, we going.

The gray or heavy thing beneath Mr. Malcolm's face softened into a smile before he glanced back at Lou Jay. —That sounds better. Just call me when. I got to bring the preacher.— Sharpening his gaze on Lou Jay. —And you, boy —

—Sir?

—Guess you must be fittin to go off to U.A.— Moving something on his lap.

—Yes, sir.

—You won't be coming back too much, then — this summer's the last we gone see of you. You'll be so *busy*.

—Maybe.

—Ain't no maybe about it.— Pulling up into view a long, shiny rifle he'd been holding out of their sight on his lap.

—Ain't she good-looking?— A smile. —I'm fittin to get me some hunting. — Patting the rifle fondly, looking from Lou Jay to his son, smiling at their unsmiles.

—I could knock off something *big* with this.

—You could shoot us something.— Moving closer to the smiling face until Ricky's hand reached out for, tightened around, hers.

—Honey, I'd shoot anything for you, looking so pretty. We know why, boys, don't we?

Dust, heavy things, silence. A memory of birds, rivers, blue things. The two young men unsmiling, wordless.

—Got to say, Lou boy, nice to see you talking so sweet with a girl — even my son's fiancee. Ricky!

—What?— Slow steps forward from where he'd been pulling leaves off a few bushes on the other side of the road. Lou Jay and Renee walking farther down the road to stand in the shade.

—Don't you *what* me.

His son silent.

—Come closer, boy.

His father's eyes, burning into him.

The older man looking straight into his son's eyes to say:

—I know you member what we talked about.

—Daddy —

—Seven sons,— his father continues, a sudden bitterness hardening that deep voice, —seven sons and my baby son gone leave us tomorrow to take him a wife. Thank you, Jesus! he shouts, shattering the stillness beneath the trees. Looking about as if expecting Christ to come down off the cross, then driving that hot gaze toward his son. Only then does Ricky see the face that had stormed, kissed, wept over, sang to and cajoled him through the years in that house they lived in up on the hill change in that very second into something utterly destroyed, like the face of a person in flames — a face all at once of hideous suffering. Melting, shifting, a face of pure rage and something else, unspeakable: what in that moment the witness knows has been familiar to him all his life, throughout every cold space back of communal keening, visions of dark birds in someone else's eyes, beneath blue things lurking in rivers and deep within his own frightened silences — a face offering no escape for itself or anyone. In that collapsed minute he sees in the face too much like his own every twisted face that once torched barns and left fiery crosses in their place, faces that have stalked his dreams; then the face of every corn-whiskey peckerwood coon hunter; then all the faces before his time and of it, that above jeers and fire had strung up heavy women and ripped out their insides, to crush beneath the heel the dreaded commingled issue so desired and despised. *Daddy.* Backing away in horror from the face as he feels himself drawn with a greater fearful yearning than ever before for who and what he is sure, this time, are behind it — the strange human power or just the pain, in the body of a man or a lurching, broke-spirited god. And then in that other very old language which possesses no words but only the power of harsh vision and the brute killing force of pain — a kick to the stomach, a sharp knife to the groin — he knows that the terrible something inside himself that burns what he feels for her, for *her* — maybe just something like hate itself, looking for an easy place to settle and spit — forms part of this face, corners its edges; as he knows too where sensation blows cold and fierce enough to slay everything that all faces of this face were devised long ago, in three (or two, or four, or eight hundred) closed moments of the most deadly cunning, silence. Sensing all at once a weakening in his knees that feels as though — yes, as though it's accusing him of something. Backing away still further from the face. But it continues to speak.

—You mind you tell Satan to get behind you, boy,— it hisses, —for the rest of your days on earth. You hear?

The faces staring at each other in the heat.

Then the older face is gone. Become Daddy Malcolm again, same as before.

—Lou Jay! Renee!— Mr. Malcolm, shouting. —Y'all come on over here now.

The two of them running over, sweat-faced. Lou Jay not looking at Ricky.

—I know y'all gone get to the church on time. Mind, now.

With one sharp movement, Ricky turned away to face Renee. And she ain't even nowhere near ugly, he thought, I wish I could say I did like girl-pussy.

—I got to tell you something.— Looking her straight in the face.

His father raising the gun. Lou Jay's eyes opening wide.

—What, Ricky?— The birds gone from her eyes, now reflecting back only the stone certainties of the future.

Daddy Malcolm's gun pointed directly at his son's back. A click from the trigger.

Ricky turning. Gazing at his father.

—You really would, wouldn't you.

The face emerges once more, but by the time the skin has finished its shifting and melting the scream strangled in Ricky's throat has risen up into his head, to remain there.

—He would what?— Only Ricky's body preventing her from seeing where the gun is aimed.

—I would love to see my son get married tomorrow. Y'all know Ricky's my baby son. Seven boys, six married, tomorrow the last one. And it's gone happen, too. So nice to see young people loving each other, living a normal life. Lou Jay!

—Sir?— Lou Jay's voice thick through the clustered reeds in his chest. In that moment looking exactly like what he had never been known to be in that town: completely stupid.

—We will miss you, boy.— The gun lowered. The look on Ricky's face unchanged. Renee looking off into the distance with what none of them can yet know — a memory of dark birds from another country dying at her feet. Nice-looking girl, the older man reflects, and a shame, only seventeen in two months, she coulda saved it for a real man.

—Yes, sir. Thank you.— Backing away as the car slowly begins to move off. As it runs right over where he'd been standing.

—I'll be with your mama and daddy for a while, Renee. Y'all don't forget — later at the church.

—We won't! she screams, but the car has gone. —What's wrong, Ricky?

No answer. Trembling in spite of the intense heat, he turns to Lou Jay, says:

—You coming?

Lou Jay also shaking. Hands stuck in pockets. The shoulders stiff.

—Nope. I need to get back. I got things to —

—Wait a minute. Am I gone see you after the wedding?

—You gone see him later, Ricky! What you —

—Don't say nothing, Renee, fore we get into a fuss. Am I gone see you after?

—Ricky, your daddy — you saw —

—I asked you something.

—Well, sure, you gone see me. I live here, don't I?

—That's right.— Her voice still low. —And Lou Jay, if you —

—Renee, shut up.— I'll knock you down in a second, he thinks, but only Lou Jay can see how she is staring now at the face none of them had ever glimpsed in the man who must soon be her husband.

    —I asked you, am I gone see you? I mean *see* you.— Hands folded into tight purple fists.

    —Ricky —

    —I got to see you, Lou Jay! You don't know —

    —Ricky, now —

    —Tell me!

    —I got to go, y'all. I'll see y'all in the church.

    —Lou Jay!

    —Bye.

    —Lou!

    —Bye, Ricky.— Walking off quickly up the road in the direction from which they'd all walked earlier. The air becoming cooler as he mounted the hill — and strange, he would think later, because there wasn't hardly no shade up there, after all.

Feeling Ricky's stare burning into him all the way up the hill, until he rounded the curve near the higher meadow that bordered the farm-fields where there should have been a gentle breeze and wasn't. Recalling the horrible burn, like the feeling, he'd received only once in his young life, when he'd put the wrong finger at the wrong time into a beaker of hydrochloric acid in high school biology lab. The finger hadn't ever been the same, not really. One of the fingers he would need to write postcards from Birmingham, like those pasted on his bedroom wall, if he could find them on that campus seen only once. But Birmingham was far enough away. . . .

When, just as he finished rounding the curve, he heard the screams far below and behind him, he ran all the way back to the part of the road where there was a view right down the steep slope into the Meadow valley. He saw Renee. Down in the dirt on the side of the road. And saw Ricky, pulling her hair and kicking her all around, especially in her stomach. Saw her bleeding, spitting up blood. Saw how she tried to get up, and how Ricky punched her hard, right in the mouth, then kicked her in the side of her head. Again. And again. Even from that distance, perhaps because of the day's still heat, the sounds seemed audible for miles. Soft, wet noises. Thinking, before his mind began to scream along with Renee, that to some people there was no better proof of love than that.

—Ricky! he screamed, running as fast as he could down the hill, —Ricky, stop! You want your daddy to kill me? You fittin to get you and me killed! I got to go to college! You gone kill your own child, Ricky! You gone be a daddy! That's Renee you beating on! We all friends! Ricky! You hear me? You can't go beating up on no girl like that! Stop that now fore you kill Renee!— Then feeling his heart chugging up inside him in the way of the heart attack that had been predicted for him before he reached forty, just like his daddy. But still he couldn't stop, not even when one dark bird and then another and then still another flew out of nowhere right into his face and he fell flat on his behind in the road, tumbling over and over on those sharp little stones until he raised himself in the dust to see the blood and dirt on his hands and forearms as he tasted it in his mouth and felt it warm and sticky and dirt-smeared all over his face. Thinking that it was, yes, Mama, like he couldn't even taste or feel Ricky in that private place inside him anymore, *Then take me now, Lord,* or the water and the reeds, *and wash me, Jesus,* or the sand and the soft soft grasses, *and O shall come on a cloud descending,* but could only sense that big new bitter taste, *that* one, inside every part of him that he knew he shared with the one who knew it all and had been all up inside it and back around, cause *thou art the light,* cause *I ain't never wanted nobody else not nobody but you,* cause *I feel a fire in me, Lord, when I see you riding up this way, but O your daddy learned you good and you ain't know til now how good did you,* he thought, flying: knowing that it was that terror and all before it back to the

time of the holy rider and his blazing flight unto the fiery angels
and their swords and light that were lifting him now, exploding in
sharp fragments inside him as he ran and felt the sun and the
sweat on his back and the familiar blood on his face, as just then
and for the rest of his descent a million dark birds released from
dreams charged blindly up into the sky turned a deeper red with
the heat of the day, as each eye of that face came out to look at
them and score into them the curling marks once recognized in
blistered skin — right there, where the prophets spoke in flaming
tongues, the flier knew, and where the first words of their lasting
flame were always, before anything anyone could call truth or
love, just plain old hurting sorrow.

FLYING

THE WORDS —

and in preparation for our final approach into Boston's Logan Airport we'd now like to request that all passengers make sure that seat belts are securely fastened and all trays returned to their upright and locked positions/flight attendants will be through the cabin shortly to make sure (yes, yes): *— hope you enjoy your stay in the Boston area and we thank you for flying with us*

— and now he will take them in, slowly, with that slow comfort tempered by the casual boredom so common to the frequent traveler, yet with that hint of mild surprise, his own still-boyish expectation. Looking down at his hands. Placed in his lap, moving slightly every now and then through no effort on his part along the folds and creases of his dark, expensive business suit. And where did I ever learn serenity like this, he thinks, where'd I ever come across this kind of peace when yes now we're about to touch the earth again and look here we are falling falling through the air coming home to I don't know what, not anything anymore except that she'll be there to meet me. To meet me. — Nice hands. A hint of his athletic youth in their trim and intricate vascularity; lean but not too lean; long, clean, clipped. Neat, and capable of love, perhaps. He had always liked his hands.

He is Craig. This afternoon, on this flight so like so many others, amidst the drone of the engines and the paper-rattlings of so many other business travelers (and how serious they are, he thinks, their faces so lined with money and routine), between the noises of a few squalling infants and mother-clucks and shy, we're-not-well acquainted conversations, he allows a small slow and (unbeknownst to him) cautious smile to play over his face. His face is smooth, the sculptured yet soft face of a black man whom you wouldn't know was black if you didn't know it, although you wouldn't take him for white either. It betrays none of his forty-two years. His green eyes light up for a moment with the catches of the smile, although he himself doesn't know that, any more than he is now or ever has been aware of the many admiring glances he receives from those who take in his lean sensuality and think *the marrying kind* — slow and easy, they see, with a simple sort of goodness about him born not out of simplicity but sheer lack of deep thought; in full possession of the mild insouciance that now and then is permitted the handsome.

And not thinking deep thoughts now. Nor of Mercedes, who will be there to meet him with her nervous hands and her mouth stinking of liquor. Enjoying instead that almost-easy and welcome comfort in thinking just for now only of flying. Of soaring. Far above the earth and leaving behind the dirt and crowds and street horrors of New York, where this flight has come from, as he thinks of neither business nor home but the blessed restful interstice of this hour in the air when he can be everyone except who he is, or nobody, and must answer to and be called upon to cajole or court or reprimand nobody. The other passengers might be so much human floss to him as he drifts into that world of not-quite dreams and jealously cherished images associated with the flying he so loves. This afternoon's flight feeling like his nine hundred and ninety-sixth. It very well could be. All of it so much of a standard *formula* he thinks, bringing along now its own comfort in those established patterns: the flight attendants' pre-flight demonstrations of the use of life jackets; the ticketing crews' brisk unsmiles with each passenger *(Any bags to check in sir? Thank you, next—)* that never change he thinks, because remember last year Mercedes we saw that play in New York three times and every evening was different from another so different, remember that? and we were different too I guess we knew who we were then. Spontaneity! Nothing like it, he thinks, nothing at all.

The other passengers are a study, when he permits them entry into that rarefied quiet realm of his dreams. Noticing how most of them pay scant attention to the landing announcements unless it's been a rough flight and they're all nervous (stupid idiots, why didn't they listen before? — his bit of meanness, he indulges it); observing how they'll lackadaisically leave their seat belts free until a flight attendant's patience-in-steel admonishment galvanizes them into appropriate pre-descent procedures; watching, with that dreadful ironic scrutiny Mercedes loathes and fears in him, how even then most of them will only worry and fuss about the quickest way to retrieve their assorted hand luggage once the aircraft has come to a full stop at the terminal. Then that long walk out into the letdown of being home again. Home. . . .

But couldn't think of home now. Couldn't: wouldn't he thought because home used to be Willemstad, then New York, now Lexington, Massachusetts, and maybe someday (who knows?) would be someplace else, free, warm, where they could be, Mercedes, just be: home. There. Wherever. Remembering even now (but why?) those days she recalled too: heat, sun; heatsun in that place they had first called home, that had been (uh huh, it had been) filled with their own, their own theirness. Remembering again now the sea, its power to calm the soul; the water so aquamarine feeding the soul, as the youthful walkers he and she had wet their feet there yes. Where, together, they had waded again, yet again, through the tides and the shores beneath that rainbow soaring up to the spirit higher and higher and: recalling how full he had been yes there with her. When he had laughed with her she had laughed and he had not thought of— . She just arrived from her own city across the water. That city of labyrinthine streets high up in the mountains. Her eyes utterly open. Her mouth. . . . Speaking that Spanish (and seeing her there again, touching her skin copperdark and:— holding her again, that hair falling black over her face his face and). Where everything had been clear: shirt, shorts, saddle shoes; seasun drowsing on the skin; faces and hands between, beneath; pressing into the parted folds. The Dutchbuilt houses by the harbor. Home. And flying from Willemstad to Miami and saying America and taking the train up to New York and seeing now again all that land sea highway and ending up now where Mercedes? where?

But some of the things which he loves most about flying are those things which seem never to change: the pungent smell of gasoline at the airport and the flaps folding and unfolding themselves into and out of the smooth silver surfaces of the wings; the very odd sensation of standing on end during the steep climb of take-off and then those peculiar unsettling rolling bumps of the wheels on the runway upon landing . . . that contact and brushing like nothing else in the world for him at all thinking and praying *please don't change it* and *just leave me something I can hold on to and don't have to answer to:* reflecting. Reflecting how so much of it now was determined by *they*, the bastard they of the ruling circles and exclusive clubs which he (more out of a type of sociological curiosity than true sycophancy) so desperately sought to join: where his very light skin did not affront them nor immediately summon images of the desired rapist. They who would try, had tried, to transfer him out of Boston yet again as he with every muscleinch of his junior vice president stature and slightly halting eloquence had fought and would go on fighting them to allow him to remain. He all the while happily (they thought foolishly) flying back and forth between New York and Boston and Hartford so many times per month, running up his travel account; the running-flying, of course, just what he needed, what they could never quite sense — the hidden raven's quiet upswing and the starling's plunge, the guarded crestings of sustained flight and need so well-cloaked beneath the green mendacious good humor always just there, behind his veiled eyes, when he walked into their midst.

But useless to avoid her.

(But he could try—)

— but useless. He saw that now, uncomfortably strapped into his seat, accustomed to but not welcoming completely the capricious visitations of memory, wistfulness, hapless rage as, slowly, implacably, her fragrance encircled him and, for just that second so unbearable because of the image pressing itself through the hollow space of his lonely hands, her soft body loomed astride him. Even in those few interludes when she came to him now, always with the stink of liquor and her hair fallen in that way over her face that produced in her the appearance of some terribly tragic, impossibly vulnerable heroine, he knew that it happened if it happened only because she was still so dimly aware of that cat- alyst side to herself that he had never fully (or bravely, he thought; yes, ruthlessly, *recklessly*) managed once to meet head-on, head thrown back and throat utterly exposed, in all their years together: the fury of that strength unpredictable that, summoned up and out from her eyes, could still call him to her side to lower his body over hers as he restrained the gag which would inevitably come from her stink of liquor, as not quite together they moved their not bodies but *shapes* in those writhings in darkness which revealed nothing new or old to them but verified only that they had both finally succumbed to every gray force of that other larger (and now inescapable) habit. Those silent hours most diffi- cult, unnavigable, when, naked to the flesh, stripped of the moun-

tains of paper and trivia that protected him from her, far from the
constant roaring planes that whisked him off to distant or nearby
cities away from her, anywhere, just far from her and the shadows
in those eyes that he preferred to remember alive with a light long
gone, he would be most lost, in fact very much like that long-ago
child he remembered with that face he remembered (his own or
another's) showing that child's terror of horrors not easily brought
to rest by Mommy and Daddy because in this case Mommy and
Daddy had caused them. And then, lying beneath him, occasionally hating him as neither he nor she could know she in fact did
(but — surely? — didn't want to and even now couldn't admit),
she would become aware of that lately-useless tigress in her that
(long ago, aided by so many silent years) had retired whatever
tawniness it had stretched out beneath the sun of their earlier
years to the coldness through which he reviled her (had he
known the full extent of that reviling, he would have blamed his
upper-class island upbringing for the nothing-wrong-here dishonesty it had permanently instilled in his eyes; then blamed his
eyes; he who had never been one easily given to admitting that
he too could be dishonest, which was or yet would be his most
fatal dishonesty). They both had become increasingly helpless
before the silences. With the help of so many pretty little brown
bottles she had descended even further into a soundlessness where
he could hardly ever reach her; where the tigress, though limp,
had still been known occasionally to spring open-jawed for the
easy kill of the futilely protected heart. But they had loved each
other! — so he would tell himself now. But then lately too there
had been shimmying through him that greater duplicity of which
he had been aware for some time but no, wouldn't, couldn't think
about that now, no, not yet, please God, not yet, no; plus the fer-
vent desire to believe that they *could have* been, *would have* been,
could still be very happy together if only she would not drink in
front of him. There was, or at least he saw, in her drinking in front

of him a challenge lately as intimidating to him as the desires skiplancing through his genitals. For they had wanted children, they did want children . . . a child was the dream of the world, they'd thought. As long as she didn't drink in front of him . . . that, coupled with that secret mental duplicity which assured him in his most truthful private frightening moments that the so-called integrity he had struggled for years to build was slowly being eaten away. A question finally of stamina, he thought. The stamina that makes a man. And a woman. But love . . . — the person next to him —

Saying something about Puerto Rico? Children? They were at it again: *breaking in.* He might be a million miles away from all of them, safe, clean, at peace, and they would insist on *breaking in.* Tearing apart that silent orchard where he walked with no one, envying nothing . . . in that place for once not fearing the endless silences of trees and fragrances. Lifting his face only there to that always rare and forever longed-for gentler beating of wings. *Breaking in.* Talking of children or what the hell —

"I'm sorry, what?"

"I said, you got any kids? You look like you do."

I look like I do? What the hell does that mean? Turning sharply to look at the speaker; seeing a young eager-faced Latino-looking man with radiant eyes that say *travel.* Who looks so happy to be flying, the accustomed traveler thinks, as if he could just throw up in joy right here from the experience. To those green eyes, a something-or-other just enough of Mercedes in that other golden-dark face to make him worth looking at and maybe even listening to a little longer. Her beauty, though younger, softer; a suggestion even of her rarest light, though lacking the terrible grieving glance, the depth of those currents and the riptides. Why you'd think he'd never even flown before, Craig thinks, and he's not all that young. But says:

"Oh?" — lifting his eyebrows a touch.

"Yeah," says the young man. "Do you?" Such eagerness in his voice as he reaches for his seat belt to fasten it, all the while watching him, if I were that age in the world today I wouldn't be so damn eager, Craig thinks, turning his face to look out the window and then locating the pocket watch in his vest and beginning to rub it furiously and now looking down beyond his hands moving on his thighs and thinking all right, there's the harbor; now we're turning, left over Boston Harbor; good good (the plane's shadow on the water); the sea so gray today (but it always is). Only in the goddamned young is there such simple excitement. Only in the goddamned beautiful young.

"No," he says, more to the window than to his neighbor. "No. I don't."

"Oh."

"Yes."

"Well . . ." the young man begins, will try again — "I bet you'd have some real pretty-looking kids if you wanted. I mean" — what else can he say? — "where you from?"

Those green eyes shining with that calculated yet diplomatic cold ferocity so pleasing to clients and strangers turn back to the young man — sweep over him, in fact, in a single furious glance.

"Curaçao. Do you know where that is? Willemstad. Do you know it?"

"Naw. That's South America, right?"

"*No.*"

The golden face already fallen. The mouth (soft, the traveler sees; full, the lips moistened, generous and parted for the syllabic glide, the slow easy sliding of shape and sound in and out) saying, "I just swore you was Spanish" — now revealing that accent Craig knows from so many city streets as urbanized Caribbean Latino, and which he hates. Thinking how Mercedes would hate it too, goddamnit, she can't stand the way those people speak. But realizing now that it's more than just this young man's accent that he hates.

"What kinda people they got in Curaçao? You all speak Spanish down there?"

"My *wife* speaks Spanish. I —" — and, suddenly furious with himself for revealing that much, snaps out (but why so angry? why so — ?) — "How old are you?"

"Me? Twenty-four." Smiling a smile that brings a greater glow to his skin, the fresh beauty of a late adolescent, the over-much gleam of the almost ingenuously indifferent. Youth. Teeth clean and white. A kid, half his age.

"What time you got?" the young man asks now. "We gonna get into Beantown on time?"

"I hope so" — and yes, he ought to cease that distracted rubbing of his watch before the design wears; the one thing there will always be, finally, is time. Just then, as he settles back into his seat with what feels to him like an odd and sudden personal lassitude (or age?) the wheels release with a bump that shakes the entire plane. "Someone's meeting me," he says, slowly. Staring out now at that approaching land he loves; at those trees beneath which, somewhere, lies his home. It's the young man's face, however, with that something of Mercedes' face in it, and her face, that now more than ever will be intertwined, in confusion, in his mind.

And they will look at her but never know. And look at her and *look* at her but never see. Never see never know that that dark tall somehow wild-looking elegant woman, so well-dressed, clasping and unclasping her hands as she moves them with that fretful nervous intensity now to her face, then over the fretted hair, then back down to her face and to the lips that part slowly, almost shyly, as if seeking something they've long been denied (another pair of lips, a caress, a drop of heaven) is thinking *Who are you? Nobody. Me too. Not anybody? Nobody? No. Not whore? Not*

slut? No. Not filthy little stinking drinking little housewife whoreslut?
No, goddamn you. Why? Because. Because I am. Because I am . . .
drunk. Drunk? Yes: Mercedes Sint-Jago, drunk. I want a drink now.
Just one. Just one. Who are you? — They'll never know, looking
at that face that is still the face of a beauty but fading, fading
unknown to them and to her, that she hates waiting in this terminal for the simple reason that it is in fact so ugly. They'll never
know (eyes now on her expensive nervous hands, on that shining
lizardskin purse) that in reality she hates them too. All these people. I'm not coming to get him anymore. He's lucky I do. I could
have gotten into an accident. *(But you shouldn't drink and drive.* Oh,
hell! Drop dead. I only had a little one at three and it's almost five
now. *Liar.* One *at* three. *Liar. Liar.)* These fucking Boston drivers.
South Boston trash. Scum. I've never liked coming out here. I
hate this city. Hate it. Hate.

    (want just onemore I want onemore just only be three
today a little bit of ice give me nice clearandcold let me one-
just one please one)

    Liar. When he looks at you with that look that says you
stink of liquor you'll be a whore. Fucking whoreslut. Stinking of
liquor. Dirty stinking puta. Borracha. Well fuck! I can look at him
as if I hate him too.

    But I don't. I don't hate him!

    They will look at her and admire. In envy. Curiosity. Lust.
Imagining sliding themselves along that smooth skin, tasting her
darkest pleasures. Imagining taking her down a few notches, the
cunt, with a few good thrusts. (Imagining her screams for mercy:
the crying and the bleeding, they think, hearing it, O Jesus *feeling*
it.) Envying her expensive tallness and designer dress but not
knowing. Awed by the bold perfection of her cat-features, not
coming close enough to see the small dark lines under her eyes;
in which they will instead see, erringly, the day-weariness (of
plans, they'll think; travel; parties; adventure, though they are

wrong) they for reasons of their own so desire to believe a woman like her must own; or the world-fatigue (she's seen so much, has traveled so much, *now just spends her days counting money probably, the rich bitch. Dark spic rich bitch from the looks of it*) that must be her inheritance as easily as her beauty is. They won't know

But O God now what if I forgot his flight number or the airline or even what city he's coming from (but they're always the same): what if I forgot them. He would hate me. Hate. The one thing he hates is a mess. Would hate for anyone to know. But no one knows. What is there to know? (I don't think you know, darling, how much I worry about you every time you fly. Do you.) Nothing to know because nothing except that I hate this airport and these tall ceilings and all these people and you Craig might have to drive home this time because I think I'm going to get sick over the wheel.

(And sometimes — sometimes I'd just like to die. Go where it's veryvery quiet. I know there's a place for me there. So soft!—look, everyone is smiling. Everything is white. Falling . . . — oh my God now but why am I falling   again and now they're giving me fresh blood to drink   and now smiling like that and sticking their fingers down my throat to choke me and   )

They'll never know. They won't even come close with guesses, or care or dare to. They will leave her there, alone, utterly defenseless in that statuesque isolation begun long ago in the casual, awesome accidents of nature and physiognomical illusion. And, leaving her that way, they will never learn of the needing and the fearing — yes, and the wanting (what? *what?* — but wanting); nor will they know of the hushed or sometimes ranting imprecations and the daily, bitterly enforced preclusions. They'll never know, and she will stand alone, not knowing either but feeling.

Feeling. Because in New York at least she had been happy for a while. *They* had been — hadn't they? — when they'd lived in that town on Long Island (like here yet different) where the people had at least pretended to like them until somebody very honest had burned that cross on the lawn that was *theirs* and had sloped down to the water and all around where for once (for the first time since they'd left everything important behind) they had come to a quiet place softgreen and blue beneath the sky, except that people like them couldn't live in a quiet place softgreen beneath the sky like that one for very long (if at all) because there always would be a somebody to burn a cross or scrawl NIGGERS over their garage or throw the first rock with SPICS GO HOME written on the paper tied around it through their pretty window. Then the second rock. The third. And Boston? Rocks hurled at schoolchildren, epithets screamed at schoolbuses. Worse. Lexington? Worse. Marblehead. Beverly. Everyplace worse because everyplace the same and colder.

(But my country so warm, my love. Remember? Sunwarm. A view of the sea from the mountains. O but so full of the poor and never with that government or this one nadie tiene ni una mierda, not anything at all . . . not like it was in Miami or New York or even Curaçao . . . not like the pretty pretty white of here —)

But yes so happy they had been on the rich North Shore. And what would he have done if when they burned the cross she had been pregnant too? But hadn't been. Because now like then she didn't get — (pregnant). *She* didn't get. *They* didn't get. Had they ever forgiven themselves for that? Had she ever forgiven him for wanting it . . . but she still wanted it too! Because he did. He —

(Liar. Whoreslut.)

And now, like them, in that great game of revolving glances and unseeing stares, she will look at them and will not know: their thoughts, curiosity; their speculations about the tall dark woman who seems in her imperious distance to be remembering or inwardly moving in an elegant pattern of unknowable steps to the songs of black South American mountain-nights; yet in reality is trembling in confused hungry impatience for a drink — right here or anywhere. She will pass through this spiritless, vague dance of the inconsequential with them, all thinking about the people they'll meet or what they will do that evening. She will pace and yearn for vodka, chablis, cabernet sauvignon; Chambord or Kahlua, Frangelico or Courvoisier. In that dulled yearning, before which all other things must blur and muddle, she will misinterpret the look of sadness on Craig's face as he walks out into the terminal toward her. Seeing but not seeing the heaviness in his body as one more encroachment of the business side of his life she loathes upon their personal sphere; not seeing (or not rightly understanding if she does) his eyes' quick sweep over her face: his taking notice of yet almost immediately disregarding the alcohol-dimness in her eyes — she's so tired these days, he'll think (from *what?* he won't dare think), she needs so much rest to get back her spirit. In his weariness, in his laziness, in his increasing and uninventoried despair, he will think that, and she won't know. She will take his briefcase from his sweating hand as she does now, and, with her old customary humorous gallantry, carry it for him to baggage claim, her matchless legs moving with only the slightest unsteadiness before him. Neither of them knowing that, once again, she will mistake everything in his face for something else, as she has for years, as he'll again not know how clearly his face registers his own inner sadness and quiet, growing terror — as he will not know either of the rage building behind her drunken smile as she recalls his yearning eyes and wonders, What the fuck have I done to displease him now?

Quietly, very quietly, their voices coming out from themselves to each other in the darkened bedroom. Sitting up, two dim shapes aware of each other. Untouching. As quietly, very quietly, her hands wrap around the bottle to pour its contents into a glass that he can hear but not see. And still won't see, and will hate to hear. Quietly, as she says:

"So you . . . "

"Yes. All of next week. In New York. Yes."

"A whole week?"

"Yes. It's happened before. It's our scheduling time again. Yes."

"A whole week gone. And I — "

"It's not a problem for you, is it?" (And even now the words *darling* or *my beloved,* they will not come, although he wants them to, he tells himself: wants them to come rocketing up out of his throat on a charger of their own and move him, yes, *require* and *compel* him to take her there, to hold her, that way, the way he once did, I, someone, *goddamnit:* but no rocketing registers, no forward thrusts engage. Such imperatives must always be imagined, she must always be imagined, and now again he can imagine she and he as only the smallest parts of that lonely space in his arms pressing so hard back against his chest, leaving him reaching out for still another irretrievable what-had-it-been from the past. Because you hate me so much, don't you? he thought — or you wouldn't sit there in your slip like that, watching: drinking in front of me and thinking I can't see you and hating me and liking it. You wouldn't.)

"Is it?"

Mocking me. You wouldn't. "Is it? That's what I'm asking you. If . . . "

"When is it ever? When did you ever ask before?"

"I'm asking you now, Mercedes. Now. Only — "

"No."

"No what?"

"It's not a problem."

" — "

"Yes? What?"

"I'm only trying to . . . I mean — if you — " (*Look* at her) " — if there's anything — if you need . . . "

"*Need?*" That laugh, so full of the riptide. "I don't. I won't!" The current in her voice sharp and clear yet quiet still in the darkness, distant as that still longed-for fluttering of wings. "I might do some reading again." (But — what? How? Books, like the world and her nights and days, had become more stupid than ever.) "Maybe I'll go into Cambridge and get some new books. Everybody's reading Latin Americans now. Gringos love reading about the exotics."

"*Gringos?* Why do you — "

"It *fits*."

"It — "

"I need something from home. Like Mistral or . . . Vallejo or . . . I just want to — "

"*This* is home. You can — "

"It re*minds* me of home. *They* remind me of home. I miss them. Is that so hard to understand? Can't you ever just — "

"Vallejo and Mistral . . . "

" — are close enough. What else do I have? Nothing." Nothing but some ice to suck on, she finished silently, but the melting in her mouth of that hardness always left only a coldness from which no promise of new life had ever flowed, nor left any explosive fire-circles or sweetwatered rivers to course up those smooth neglected paths of her thighs, endless, endless: no pulling apart of the infinite universe, only down down down to the drowning and the ice. Down.

She rattled the remaining ice in the glass. A dangerous heat was beginning somewhere at the back of her neck. One is always fire, she thought, and one always water. But which is which?

"I'd like to see you go back to school. This might be a good time. Now, for the spring."

"And study what?" Fire and water.

"You always liked — art history, wasn't it? We couldn't ever pull you out of a museum when you wanted to . . . — you could pick up where you left off on your master's. And that book of essays you wanted to do on the Aymara women. Remember that?

And the Guajira. Why — " he stopped, shocked at the hot grip of her hand on his shoulder in the dark.

"I *can't*" (fire had won out, a whisper very close to his ear that brought with it the heavy brutal smell of rum) "go through all that again. How could you even think I'd want to? I *won't!*" The taste of steel shavings in her own mouth kept her from feeling his almost-cry out from the cruel renewal of her grip.

"*Things have changed*. You can't see. . . . Listen. I'm telling you. I'm saying: I'm too *old* for that. I *feel* old."

"Merced — you're *not* — don't — "

"Wake *up.*" The heat and coldness right in his ear, hissing with that old horrible tone of command he knew. "You keep on dreaming," came the fire-hiss and the rumsweet smell. "You always have. You can't see how different everything is now. The *world*. What do you think I'm talking about? Look at you! Look at me!"

"Keep your voice down, goddamnit! Get your hand *off* — " (but couldn't push away that fire he had made, he thought; couldn't and wouldn't dare put his face in that revealing flame and *walk with it* nor *pick it up and carry it* to the fierce illumined center and the source, the matrix of all that glowing anger and ash. Couldn't, turning to avoid the glare and the flash. Not ever).

"You're thirty-seven years old, 'Cedes," he said quietly. "You can do anything you want to do. You always could. I've never stopped you." (So he would trade one fire for another and lie. Otherwise she would scare him, terrify him; the wounded tigress would leap, the blood would rush and O yes he thought tell the truth damnit tell it.) "So just tell me," he went on, hearing that new surprising bitterness in his voice, "just how in the hell the world is so different with that!"

She was silent. In the darkness he could feel the heat and ponderous weight of her eyes once again on him, watching him but not seeing him as they could see nothing of each other; feeling himself moving on the bed and realizing with a sudden yet welcome shock that he was actually moving to embrace her — the rocketing, the charger — when her voice rang coldly out across that immeasurable distance that had opened up again:

"It *has* changed. Everything has changed," she said, getting up with the hard musical sound of ice-in-glassware clutched close. "You just don't see it."

"Mercedes — "

"You don't have any insight. You never have," she said, and was gone, fire chilled to ice, eating ice, a moving thin shadow beyond the bedroom door and down the stairs.

He lay back and stared at the ceiling for a very long time; certain that if he closed his eyes he would see only an advancing, harshly outlined world of strangers. When he did close them, the young man from the plane came to him. He opened them at once and looked about the room; felt his scalp prickling slightly beneath the fingers that had just moved there. But no, it's all right. She'll soon be back. *You're still at home.* And closed his eyes again. But then saw the young man again, just there, behind the lids. The vision this time completely undressed. Those muscles, *those,* before him, as the young man smiled at him, beckoned, then leaned forward and whispered something into his ear; then the long lean approach, the crouch's curve; the knees bent in the crouch, the starling's swift descent, the heavy smell of pregnant ripe things ready to burst and O my God he thought with eyes closed still what is that coming down now over my face or is it — (but whatever it was found his face, settled, and so there above the fleshmask and skull was at last content not to reveal to him anything of distance, time, or the fury of the pounding inner source at the end of that long interior pathway — the sensate journey); then the full smell of ripeness again. A softness and a warmth . . .

His eyes opened again. He would not close them until Mercedes returned what seemed like hours later and dropped into bed beside him, a full half-quart of white rum running through her veins. Her breathing told him that. He pulled her to him as he had never done before, unmindful for once of what wafted up into his face from her sleep-smile. He whispered her name and even shook her once, twice, to no response. Then the heat-heaviness exploded out from his face, stinging his eyes as it burned as if in escape from something deep within him that he couldn't name. As he buried his face in Mercedes' sleeping breast, which wasn't her breast for him just then, he gave himself over at last to that which had returned yet again, which would stay with him, astride him, within him, in place of the living breathing woman next to him, until the second visitation exploded into that last cyclonic current of exhilaration and fearful rage. He raised his eyes up to the darkness of night and sky through which he was now coursing, listening. A soft beating of wings presently came to him, but not the pair he was looking for.

Feeling the light and now descending through it hazedrawn into the day of the silent and vast hours with the churning of the clock and the carpet's creeping beneath her feet and now again the buzzing of that greedy angry thirsty fly in her ear obscene and worrymaking and *because of the silences* she will think or *because he's gone off to New York to be a big shot again* or *because of the emptiness of this fucking house so big*. What do we need a house this big for? My father never had one this big and he was practically a *patrón*. Then the dull, casual little day-pleasantries: the arrival at ten o'clock of the cleaning woman with whom she could speak in Spanish briefly before that good woman (but tacky, poor, not *gente bella* but from some Caribbean stock) went off to break her back mopping and sweeping and brushing the floors and walls and unused rooms of that rambling house, cleaning today and always that empty room they had planned to use for a nursery, cleaning and wondering why they had no children, giving her *señora* that pitying mother-look that would make her want to kill the old bitch puta de la mierda porque para su información señora nosotros no queremos niños, entiende? No queremos.

(Liar. Whoreslut.)

(No! No queremos!)

— as the old bitch de la mierda went off in apparent happiness (but couldn't be that happy) breaking her back cleaning houses all over Lexington. Wellesley. Newton. On and on to the *Buenos días, Señora Mercedes. Buen día, señora, cómo le va?—Bien, gracias, sí, señora* — that would tap at the brittle enclosure of her solitude and make her Mercedes sola see that what she needed above all else was people: with their hateful but so needed kindnesses to show her that, yes, she *did have* a purpose on this earth, in this house, in the state of Massachusetts, distinct and aside from her steady inflexible aim of courting a coward's death (but vengeful, vengeful, she thought, because then he'd realize what he'd lost, he whose green look of repulsion had never been completely lost on her through the merciful hazes of rum and regret) through the many brown bottles that clanked through her consciousness, in the kitchen, in the backseat of the car on the days he wasn't there, clanking like so many spirit-chains dragging her down to that sea of vomit and bitter dreams in which she had found herself choking on too many mornings after he had gone, leaving her so cold from his not-touch to her aching body, so cold and alone from his repulsion. People. But then imagining them (would they love her? Would their touch dress her in babyskin the way his once had?) and thinking North Americans are so cold, so inhospitable compared to us. He's so cold, compared to what I could've had except that having it would have meant I would have had to stay — there. People. If only to smile in unknowing stupidity and gather around

when I feel like I'd like to die.

Why do you want to die, señora?

I don't know why. I don't. Except that

— *She could have written a book of essays on the Aymara women. Could have written articles on the fishermen of the desert of Sechura. Could have finished a thesis on the people of La Guajira. Could have finished a masterpiece on the weavers of Tarabuco. Could have — could have —*

She could have had a child. With someone else.

The coldness of the thought chilled her shoulders and spine as it tightened her throat into that knot now pulling closed. Hairy fibers filling the throat to choke.

No air.

— looking around herself in confusion. Finding herself fully dressed, standing up and swaying slightly in the living room. Standing on the Persian rug still creeping thick and elegant as it always had been in those intricate designs beneath her feet. The bookshelves clean, dustless, packed with the fat books neither of them had read in years. The banker's lamp on her desk off in the corner, shining with a brilliance savage to her eyes. It was then that she realized that, though feeling the burn of that still-smoldering inner fire, momentarily caught up in the maudlin posture of the lonely drunk reaching out to gather in the little mean agonies of dead coals and sorry comforts, in those instants she was also clearly alive, listening to the beatings of her heart in mid-morning, bird-chirping Lexington; the quotidian noise of a dog's bark coming in from somewhere off in the distance. The Javiers' dog, probably, that annoying car-chaser. Alive, standing stock-still in the middle of her living room on the ground floor of a house too creakingly large for two people to live in, two people like themselves, a house of day-ghosts where she was suddenly caught up in listening to the beats of her heart that all at once *there* and *there* were slowing down to mean nothing less than that she was going to die, yes, she knew it: I'm losing every bit of my mind, it's going to happen right now, here, before I can stop it or move, and, why, I didn't even notice, I'm holding a glass of white rum. It needs ice.

"I have to get out of here," she said to the desk. "I can't breathe. I can't breathe. I'm going to die. I can't breathe!"

"Señora?"

Bitch! she thought, *how'd you get in here?* The cleaning woman's grandmotherly face and sad, kind eyes she could see now through the descending haze had, with those hard-life imprints and unbearable kindness, always spoken to her of that other world's forgotten poverty and the useless, eternal hope begged for by the pious faces of the saints, and had incited in her a wicked impotent rage that no solitude or escape could ever comfort: a Latin-lined face that brought back too many memories of the isolation and dreadful patience of tortured villages. But since when did you have keys? Do you *have* keys? Did *he* give you keys? Typical of your kind, nosy sneaking — but this is *my* house. And I can say —

"Sí?"

"Dijo algo?"

"Sí . . . the keys? Tiene llaves de la casa?"

"Sí, señora. The señor gave them to me" — the small, wrinkled woman held out three shining keys in a withered hand — "ayer por la mañana."

"I'll take them."

"Pero . . . el señor — "

"*Give* them to me."

The woman handed them over.

"A ver . . . sí, hay tres. Gracias."

"A usted, señora."

"Where's the telephone? I have to call the airport. Did you take it out of here?"

"No, señora. Allá está en la mesa, como siempre . . . se va?"

"Sí." But where am I going? Why? "To New York. I'm

going to New York." *(Why? Are you out of your mind? For what the hell?)* "Mr. Sint-Jago has a very important meeting tonight and I have to be there, to — " (to *what?*) " — to help him."

"Ah."

"Sí. Pobrecito, alone in New York sin su señora. Imagínese!"

"Sí, señora. Terrible." The lowered eyes took in, but wisely did not acknowledge, the brimming glass in Mercedes' hand.

The telephone felt hot. "Yes," rasped the voice into the mouthpiece. Is that my voice? *My God I can hardly talk I've got to get out of here. I've got to*

" — about flights to New York . . .

"I don't care what airline. Any airline . . . "

Clouds had begun to gather in the sky, looking very rain-like as the air in the room thickened and the breeze which earlier had rustled the trees and now smelled of cut grass began to blow. I hope there won't be any turbulence, she thought, I'll get sick.

"And — is this directory assistance?" — gasping in the no-air quickly closing in around her head. Finish that drink, señora. Have another one, señora. "Because — because I'm going to need a taxi." I'm having a heart attack. Raising that voice, her voice, still sounding as though both it and she were scraping through a wall of mud — "because I can't drive. Do you understand? What kind of people are you? Don't you understand that I need a fucking taxi to get to the airport!"

The cleaning woman. Standing very small off by the book-case. Watching the tall swaying figure with the now-empty glass in her hand shouting words not completely understood into the telephone. From that cowering, awed stance picking up in one hand the vacuum cleaner she had left on the floor. A wrinkled, trembling hand rising up to cross herself as she turned away and shuffled out in bent-over smallness to the kitchen.

II

A hand and nothing more. A hand he knows is attached to his body although even now he can't quite believe it. In that hotel suite high above New York City, with that view he loves of the park and rushing lights on Fifth Avenue, in that safe sphere the world cannot easily enter, with a thick carpet beneath his feet and soft lamps which light what he does not wish to see: himself, no more. No, not in the sparklingly clean bathroom mirror, nor in the shapely glass vase holding chrysanthemums, statice and calla lilies on that shining wooden table in the corner. Not in the gleaming doors of the elevator he rode up in that afternoon with that smiling, obsequious bellhop, nor in the shining closet doors behind which hang his shining clothes. For the moment, just that hand. Reaching down out of his expensive business suit to pull down his expensive pants. To feel the soft cotton underwear and the hardness beneath it. To put a finger to the wet spot caused by that hardness, then return it to his mouth to taste and smell the raw smell and taste of himself, no more. To think not of the glowering hard faces ringed around a conference table that morning, talking endlessly of mergers and acquisitions and letters of credit, but of the newer, graver, infinitely attracting tantalizations. This, destiny. Vaguely pleasant. To appear in the heat-daydreams now flooding his brain and body. A mouth upon his chest. (But *not of her.*) Then a hand to his thigh, that imagined hand oh so wanted. But not of her. Yes, of her. Has always been her. No one else but her. But now in the safety and danger of this solitude as he collapses upon the bed it is not of her in the sudden race firing his loins recalling oh recalling the past

— but all at once all of them. The beautiful boys he remembered from Willemstad as he'd laughed with her in those years before and hadn't thought of them. The insolent suntanned shoulders of Venezuela. The dark muscled thighs-in-shorts of Jamaica. The hairless exposed nipples of St.

Kitts and Nevis. The dreadlock-framed long eyelashes of San Andrés and Providencia. The young man on the plane. The concave depressions of his corduroyed buttocks. Places for hands. Places for thighs. Mouths. Thinking now if you'd told me ten years ago or twenty years ago that I'd be doing this now and feeling it and seeing it   thinking but it wasn't this way when they had walked and laughed and later when his face had eased beneath and they had struggled tried and held on crying even to make that baby they couldn't make and   feeling her and being her holding so tight and   then what was happening now who and with I God that water still walking because even now flying but falling down I Mercedes even now loving you and conjuring you here conjuring like you've never conjured me   to feel you inside   to feel   even now   love and wanting you wanting moving   filling   there

A hand now wet, still clenched around him, trembling satisfaction. That now goes to his ass, to rub the wet heat of his dreams there, to feel what it would feel like to have another man's heat jetting between there, to conjure as only he can conjure a mouth to fill there, a face to lower itself into that wet heat and whisper his name. . . .

— A hand that will not surrender. That fears itself in the act. Inured to old habits, motivated by his brain. Now and then thinking of her within the dream, maybe, but acting on him.

The flight had not been rough. Through the haze that had thickened on the plane and was now limitless and blue with the sweet fire-heat of Amaretto, she smiled to think of the surprising ease with which she had obtained a taxi at the airport. The plane had landed late, right at the beginning of rush hour. Look at the people rushing. But people in New York are so polite. So much nicer than in Boston. To me. That's because I'm a person of quality. Soy una persona de calidad. Cal-i-dad.

That was what she was thinking when the urge to vomit came upon her right there in the taxi in the middle of a city that was all at once as suffocating as the living room had been that morning. What she was thinking as she gripped the door handle on her right side and told herself that she was not going to choke *or* splatter the nothing she had eaten and the plenty she had drunk all over the front seat of the dark little taxi that stank of cigars and plastic leather and cheap cologne. Fifty-second Street, Fifty-third, Fifty-fourth. . . . The spasm passed as quickly as it had come upon her. The great furry rodent that occasionally crept through her darkest dreams had raced up out of her belly and paused and scratched a moment in her throat; then returned to her stomach to beat its whiskered head against her heart. The fearsome pounding had started again. I'm going to die, she thought, right here in New York.

The hands that were not used to kindness and showed it were in her coat pockets that fast, searching for the tissues that years of what had started out as jealously guarded class habit later altered to paranoia had placed there: tissues for nosebleeds, vomiturges, afterwipes. In the soft, dark, warm space of her pocket, so like a mouth for her hand, something cold and jangling struck out, sliding against her wedding ring. The keys. The keys he'd given to the cleaning woman without telling her. To let her into the house to spy on her. Now remembering that she couldn't have a moment of peace without that old bitch looking at her with that look she hated (but when did I ever notice it before?), that infuriating look of Lexington, of Boston, of every shrieking place in the world that offered no rest. *Ay Dios mío, pobrecita señora . . .* now another thing they would take away from her before she'd even possessed it. Before she'd even had a minute to hold it in her hands and say *This is mine.* Whatever. *Mine.* And then the fury which didn't quite make sense even from that twilit place where the rodent turned itself to sickening sleep in her belly as it fed upon the pulp of her pounding heart began to build, fanned by the heat waves of a moment's clarity when she realized that whatever it was she now again wanted to possess, like hope (if hope could be possessed and not merely borrowed), had long ago been forgotten, was past reclaiming, had never been clearly defined nor understood. But that was why she had come. In search of . . . but she couldn't name it, and her tongue thickened with that namelessness as the rodent stirred within her.

But the keys would do. Anything would do, in this city she suddenly hated like the rest of them. And so in that heat which was a comfort as it stepped up to a new bitterness in her mouth icing over the Amaretto-linger, she didn't notice the two credit cards and cash she dropped on the seat when the taxi pulled up in front of Craig's hotel; didn't notice the looks of recognition, then of surprise and confusion, she received from the reception-area hotel staff as she stumbled, though still elegantly, through the revolving door past the gold-epauleted doorman into the lobby to inquire with consummate aloofness-through-haze as to the room of Mr. Sint-Jago, whose name and face they knew well as belonging to that gloomy colored or whatever he was businessman who, though colored or whatever, always stayed in an executive suite, carried the right type of briefcase, sported a fine pocket watch and natty cordovans, charmed them all with his sad-dreamy-distant green eyes, dismissive smile that could turn chilly in an instant, strange accent they had never identified as Antillean, and who — the most important — tipped well; nor did she notice the elevator operator's watching after her as she stumbled down that very tastefully carpeted hallway to knock on the door of he whom she knew would open it, who did after a few too many minutes she did not notice, and who now stood speechlessly before her in his bathrobe with a sheaf of papers in his hand and the most dreadful look of weariness and something else in his face, new, that she couldn't place, mixed in with the unfamiliar oldness she decided right then and there she didn't like, it made him a stranger to her, it brought unease, he looked

— *awful,* yes, that was it, *awful, why do you look so old all of a sud-den, Craig, work never did* that *to you before,* yet still an odd light shone out from somewhere within him, a luminescence very much like the after-sex glow that she had not seen in him for years and for that reason fortunately did not now recognize, as she reached into her pocket and held out between them the jan-gling evidence of his betrayal before she threw them hard into his face and the jangling hardened into that voice of rage she heard but could not place or at the last minute shrank from placing as her own: "Why did you give her the keys, you son of a bitch! Why — " — as he managed to pull her into the suite and slam shut the door, but not before " — did you give her the mother-fucking keys!" flew out into the hallway to the glee of that under-paid elevator operator who would give himself over that night in unrepentant fury to a sometime-or-other half-woman he would fuck until he wept, in unforgiving celebration of this new evi-dence that these people, yes, baby, *these* rich snotty cocksuckers had their little problems too.

Much later, in the time that would follow implacably on the heels of what had been set into motion that night, they would remem-ber, selectively, exactly what had taken place between them there, as they would summon the old requisite stamina so carefully folded within the realms of cowardice and illusion that had served them until Craig had left the following morning for his confer-ence call meeting. That is, after the anger and the confronting and the shouting, until he realized that she could not, would not, lis-ten and he could anyway neither listen nor talk, he would recall how he had wavered before the cold contempt and unexpected power that had surged up through the haze in her eyes that had accused him of everything gone wrong with the world in those moments, and the deeper, older wanderings of which in his soberness only he could know and at which she could only guess, even as they swam upriver to hold each other; guess she had, but wrongly, searching out his face, seeking explanation for the eerie luminescent fatigue there which somehow did not make sense, or if it did, or would, should not, because what was it? From where and when? Why? — surprised that the rage and haze allowed her so much interest, shocked to think *how complex is the human spirit,* that her heart and mind, though drugged, numbed, world-sickened, still pulsed and yearned for the both of them, and for him especially then with his suddenly old-looking face. The feeling had been an ounce or more of what they would call, correctly, compassion, as it hit them both. Yet she was still she, possessed that intellect and curiosity that had led her from the Andean altiplanos to the coastal deserts of Peru, owned that intellect that would not then nor ever give up, give out, nor climb to rest and shake itself out, that there, on the bed, high above that gray city bluing itself to nightfall, sought him, would go on thinking that the mystery in his face was surely connected to something ridiculous or picayune in their past, having no idea that it would tie in more immediately than she knew to her future. No, he hadn't come to New York to see another woman, what kind of a silly question is that, Mercedes, just business as usual, he'd said, although pathetically, she would remember later, but no matter; she'd accepted his feebleness by then, it bound him to her more tightly when she felt she needed that — whenever. And so, yes, amid the searches and the little reliefs, they would remember: how (rather foolishly, he would tell himself later, and to no proper end) he had buried his face in her neck and felt none of the old back-and-forth desire and repulsion but only the worst frightening sort of deadness because yes, oh yes, that afternoon's pleasure and discovery were still sending heat thrills and kisses down his spine and along the lightly haired undersides of his buttocks, beneath which he dreamt lay a featureless face tongue-grazing its way deeper into him; and how maybe, just maybe, she'd thought (for the stirrings of the rodent had frightened her, and the heart-poundings that invariably accompanied them had terrified her), she *could* begin, with the last grain of strength she knew deep in her soul was finally not an illusion, to put aside at least one of the pretty little brown bottles each day, through which perhaps — only perhaps — she *could* write those essays on the Aymara women, or on the desert of Sechura, or whatever else awaited that long-ago brilliance put to rest far away within her.

But suddenly the strangulation of it all was too much — the strangulation of years as they held each other there, trembling like two shipwrecked; the strangulation of that particular hotel suite with its gleaming lamps and bathroom faucets and pristine closet doors, high above that insomniac city shaking out its streets to hunger; the strangulation of living room mornings drenched with the stuff of shining bottles, of wind-voices that still held the smells and memories of soughing yew and deep muddywashed undercurrents. And with the strangulation came both their rodents roaring up out of their insides, hers well developed and his just awakening, to break through their skins into the protected place they'd both thought the world, with its men on planes who brashly appeared in dreams, with its mocking faces in airport terminals and those inevitable grinning faces of skeletons, the advance guard of death, could not touch. With that, all at once, to her suffering questions and his memory of that wet spot she hadn't seen that represented everything new in his desire on the soft sheet beneath them, he found himself choking out the rodent-scream that now (but it had been a long time in coming) racked his body, as he gripped her face and held her familiar heat tightly between his hands and felt the hair and skin that he told himself he still loved — to shout at her now-still, staring face the words that had to be true. That —

"I love you, Mercedes. Do you know — you know — "

" — Craig . . . "

"I'll never leave you. Never leave you. Will you ever leave me?"

" — Craig — "

"You" — shaking her shoulder — "want children, don't you?" he hissed. "That's what we want, isn't it? *Isn't* it?"

"Craig!" The shy bird of their most intimate moments, distressed at this new desperation, flew up out of her face and across to him to signal and mirror what he knew more than ever was his own madness. But he couldn't stop. Not now.

"We can *have* them."

"*Stop* it, you son of a — you're hurting me, stop it!"

"I *prom*ise we'll have them." — His voice not quite a scream now; reverberating through the room as she shook free from his grip and got up to back herself against the bathroom door, looking at him with the fear and revulsion he had never seen in his own face.

"I *prom*ise we will," he said, more quietly, getting up to move toward her.

"Stay away from me. Don't touch me. You crazy son of a — " (And then he would remember too how pathetic and unprotected she had looked just then with her hair fallen over her face in that way that had once driven him wild: — small, vulnerable, even though she wasn't and never had been small, was his height in her Italian high heels, though swaying. Would remember more than any of it for years the deepcurrents passed between them in the next moment as, backed against the bathroom door, the room's soft lights showing up the alcohol-flush in her face, she had opened her eyes wide in utter haze-penetrating realization that had signaled the end of something, and the beginning, aimed straight at him.)

"My. God." The words thick, hoarse — "You're. Crazy. Do you know that? You're — *crazy*.

"It's not *me*," she went on. "It — never. Was. Me. It's — *you*. You're — "

"Mercedes!"

" — *crazy!*"

With that he was upon her, feeling his own unsteadiness as he reached for the neck that he wanted not to tear apart but to hold on to with all his strength for the rest of whatever remained of his days. To make her listen, to make her see, he would tell himself later. Listen to me. You can't walk out on me. *Listen to me.* But he hadn't counted on the fact that even when stone-blind drunk she had never been too awkward to elude him or even hurt him, as she did now with the elegantly manicured, terrified fist that shot out and smashed hard into his jaw, slamming him into a world of bright colors he had never known. She was already out the door before his complete vision returned.

"'Cedes." (And he had never been the sort to shout, he thought, shouting.) "'Cedes!" But like so many times before, she was gone. Stumbling to the door on legs that nearly gave way beneath him, he was just in time to see one dark Italian heel disappear into the elevator as the leering face of that faithful operator peered out to greet him, then vanished within with her.

He stood there for a while taking in the hallway's subtle lights as traffic sounds floated up from the street. He put a hand up to his cheek where her wedding-ringed fist had met his jaw. Then he closed the door and went back to sit on the bed as he closed his eyes in an attempt to quell the urge to vomit. When the vomit came flying up out of him to land squarely on the rug in front of him, the burning bitterness in his throat and mouth tasted exactly like the earth he was crawling through, eating as he went, in that new country into which Mercedes' fist had knocked him — that land of dim water and mist through which he could make out only his own skull-face amidst the rattles and the silence.

And he will look out the window past the wing's flashing green light to that darkness and those blue and yellow lights far below that he recognizes as the beginnings of the Connecticut shore: they drove through there three years ago on their way back from Westport that summer, would you remember that Mercedes — too tired to put a question mark at the end of the thought. He will sip that lukewarm coffee brought by the flight attendant, and wave away the offer of a late edition or two of the New York papers as, childlike, tonight on the way to New York where he has recently made his home, he presses his face to the window and thinks of things left behind, and of things awaiting him, as he offers silent thanks that there are few passengers on this flight.

After everything, it had taken him a year and a half to tell her what had to be told. But still he hadn't told her everything. He hadn't told her about the men, and the one man in particular, whose caresses had lit up the submerged smile in his eyes and made him throw his head back to receive that touch to his throat, his hair, his eyes, although he had told her about the feeling, the marked intensity of the *it*. He hadn't told her about lying beneath another man, or about the fingers that had brought brisk shudders to the back of his neck and found their way down his spine to the further, deeper chill and heat. Wisely, he hadn't told her that her skin and smell and hair were still a part of it every time, would be a part of it for some time to come, though less, a lessening which brought a different chill with that intoxicating ecstasy and residual guilt. And no, he hadn't told her about his new increased knowledge of condoms because, well, he had never let things go that far . . . or near. And couldn't. Not when the first thing he told himself he was truly seeking was the peculiar blessed intimacy of a caress, the elusive *Hold me* in another's eyes . . . the rest could come later. To his mind, speaking of the *felt* and the *need,* he had told her everything. Most of all, and what would be most jarring for the both of them, he hadn't told her that in that way, with that man, or another, or even alone, he might have a chance to get close to happiness, to know it once more, to hold its soft fleeting features in his hand — for many reasons, but mostly because happiness, whatever happiness had been, whatever they had defined as happiness, recollected or hid from or lied about to themselves and each other, had been dropped between them long ago, in the harbor at Willemstad or later, from a thin white ship that had sailed very far away, that perhaps had never even existed, a pale phantom ship of dreams. So often what they had called happiness had seemed irretrievable. Who could tell now?

And how her face had hardened into a face of rock. A Peruvian mystery-face, a Mesoamerican face so ageless. Ageless she had become as every nexus of her had hardened out of those numbed accumulations of outrage and atrophy; frozen into that cold yet brittle beauty that had shed not one tear upon learning of his new yearning for and acting on love away from her, outside of her, beyond her reach. But she knew that he had loved her. That he *did* love her. That nothing could ever change that. (But the truth —) *Nothing* would ever change that. Yes, tell yourself that. But she too had changed, for in that crucial moment she had neither cried nor screamed but (with the grave silent dignity of those whose bloodskin and ancestral cauls still informed her dreams) simply ordered him out of the house. And he ... had left. Incomplete with just that other part not knowing, he thought, not knowing anything at all except that there had to be a way they could live, just *live* for once or maybe even twice or three times: all he wanted, he thought, before it was all over. For someday it would all be over. She had been right as always, he thought; not only were they not nearly as young anymore as he had once dared to think or childishly wish-dream them into being, but it seemed suddenly impossible, obscene and almost terrifying, even, that, having come this far with so much eye-knowledge and so little, they ever could have been; that he in particular, the becalmed yet still searching traveler, ever could have been; knowing her then and forever in all that shared pain and searching as the oldest spirit of them all, now wrapped within that approaching and more audible beating of wings; he now drifting far beneath them all back to the heatsun and the memory, letting the baptismal water of all that openness once again wash his many scattered parts in stillness and supplication, holy light, eternity. . . .

Then remembering her face. The hardening, the mask. One of those masks their people and all the people of the world had used for centuries for survival, for the celebration of death. Seeing it on her as he had felt the skin of his own. And now they never would have a baby, would they? Could they ever really have wanted one? For what? Leaving them just that, then, for the time they both had left: what they didn't, couldn't, make.

She stopped drinking that day. Didn't touch a single drop. Probably won't ever again. That coldness she developed to the level of a sacrament did it, won it, moved it, finally did what everything else couldn't do, although he'd wanted it. And now? Could they ever love each other again through all that hating the way they did? Could they—

Just then the plane took a huge bump that made everyone cry out. He continued to sit there, knees crossed, wrists relaxed, barely raising an eyebrow. He would never be afraid of anything again, he decided; just tired of it all, a weary specter, which might be worse.

And then, just that fast, he *knew*. It came to him not with the speed of blinding revelation but with a rapid beating of wings filled with all the spitting fury and amazement of a dead weight long dragged in willful silence suddenly awakened to screaming life. He knew that she had cried and stormed and screamed. He just hadn't been there to see it. As he'd never been there to see it. As he'd never wanted to see it because seeing was the most excruciating, most reckless terror of them all. Helpless so helpless now before the brusqueness of those truths and the irremediable helplessness of the past. — He knew, as he had always known, that she had been alone without anyone to comfort her, as he'd been with someone who had not known him well enough to comfort him, and knew that he would not have been able to comfort her because everything back there in that city to the north he still loved with all his heart had flown quickly out of his reach. He hadn't been there to carry her smell away in his arms for the many nights he would sleep alone while some form of her slept next to him. He had missed the last chance to crystallize in his vision the dark terror that had lived in her eyes, that he would have compared to the terror or lust or loneliness of every strange face that lately had inhabited his nights and days and even his fantasies. Those staring faces had shown him that the world was not the world anymore as he had known it. Now it was and would be forever what it had always been — that world he and his kind had sought not to know from the safety of high hotel rooms and lawns manicured to preserve the faith, that shrieking world where presidents dropped bombs on unsuspecting nations and dispatched soldiers to quell riot fires of the restless . . . *that* world. Imploding on itself in the last throes of rushing chaos, with planes that would fly through it all until the final, eternal fire.

— *But I can avoid all of you even now,* he thought, *we're still in flight we are flying* —

— Oh, but no. It'll be useless. You can see that, can't you? Use-less. Let it be, let it rest, let it fade, he thought. Like a man long denied water, walking the desert earth in search of that once-healing orchard or a benignant presence, an aspect of grace in silence or only a last merciful absolution before the weighted fall — the end of all things and the beginning, the fiercely rapid wings descending — he raised the coffee cup to his lips and drank. Some other passengers glanced his way every now and then but missed that vision of the world in his eyes. *I don't want to think about anything else, dear God, I've had enough.* Fine, then; no thoughts. For now, he will see that something or other of himself reflected in that darkened window as he grips his coffee cup and stares out at flashing lights and flaps he doesn't see, as he feels the pounding of his heart. For a little longer, a last kindness: *open your eyes, the world's nowhere near.*

And now, with the chill of sudden panic, of bygone years, let the old spirits descend to greet him. Let them tighten that aureole around his head. None of it will matter. For now he won't think of anything, nor take his eyes from the window, nor hold any long conversations with death or with the living, or with those other lost shattered voices of the past — no, dear God, please, no more, nothing, *none of it* — not until the old assurance of the captain's voice comes again over the speakers, from way up in the cockpit, announcing, Passengers, fasten your seat belts, because it'll soon be time to land.

— AND LOVE THEM?

O NLY NOW I HATE THEM.
Well, no, I shouldn't say that, I really shouldn't and anyway you have to be careful saying things like that and especially who you say them to because it's the kind of thing they're always looking out for to hold against you, the kind of something or other they think they can use. And they always use it, without ever understanding the feeling. They always use it, without ever taking responsibility for their part in it. They're always waiting to jump on you for something, catch you in something — that's the way you've got to deal with them, that's what makes it so hard every time. And after a while you learn that you can't hate all of them anyway or all of anybody. Not for long. Sooner or later it passes into something else you recognize, and I guess deep down *hate* anyway isn't the right word. I consider myself an educated woman. I'm logical, I read the papers; I observe, I think, I respond. And react. I'm still pretty good-looking for my age, people tell me — you couldn't tell I'm getting close to forty-whatever, it doesn't matter how old, it's no big deal anyway and if it is you know it shouldn't be. A woman's life begins

at forty, some people say, and I think they're right. Someone I used to know who's really honest, one of them but still really honest, told me once that I could still even pass for a teenager and I believed him because I know it's true — how you keep yourself, it's all in the mind. My mind's really sharp, that's what keeps me going. Like when I sit next to them on the train in the morning on the way to work and think about them. That's when I try to feel them, feel what they might be thinking or feeling. But most of the time it feels like you can never tell what they're thinking or feeling. One of them used to work with me at the office — a sweet, very charming girl from Guyana or one of those islands. She spoke so nicely on the phone, people said; she was so polite when she took messages and spelled out their names correctly. It was like she always had a smile in her voice. But she left two months ago — she was finally pregnant, she said, after trying so hard for so many years, and wanted to have the baby in Guyana or wherever it was. I found out later her husband was involved in some kind of trade union thing down there on one of the islands. I wish them a lot of happiness together. I certainly will miss her. She was so polite, so kind; what I call a real human being.

But that's what I mean — that way they have of holding back. I still can't understand it; it hurts me deep down and makes me really furious, to tell the absolute truth. And then after some more time of it I just get sick of it all, the same goddamned situation over and over again, and it's like I'm always thinking, what should I say? What should I do? What went wrong *this* time? But you can't let *them* know that because all they ever are is angry, very angry, and it's like they think they've got an exclusive corner on it so they can bully the rest of the world into shutting up or being afraid. And as soon as you even try to open your mouth to explain that maybe, God forbid just maybe *you* might have some feelings too they give you that disgusting sickening awful look that's no look at all and then go into that sulky silence they're so good at.

I'm pretty intuitive, I can tell moods. It's like they don't want you to know they're angry, oh no, but then, oh, believe it, they *do* want you to know. They force it on you. You've seen it: those ugly expressions. The ugliest expressions in the world. Their lips get thin then and they stare at you with that hating look. But then (if I said this to one of them, you could be sure they'd take it the wrong way) at least when they react that way you know, most of the time, that things won't get out of hand. It won't be like when they get *really* angry and go out into the street and do all the wild things they do, setting fires and turning over police cars and killing innocent people just in the name of anger. They're not human then. I've seen them, everyone's seen them — like what they did in L.A. in '92. The thing is — they could never understand this — I *agreed* with them. I didn't think they were wrong to be upset. I told two of them, friends of mine (Tracy and Angela, two girls who work with me in the legal division; they don't always seem to be looking for an argument like some of the others) — I told them, you're right, you've got every right to be angry, that was a ridiculous miscarriage of justice, I couldn't agree with you more (I told them this, oh yes, the truth, I told them), I can't believe that even with a videotape of them beating him and everything else that they still allowed those men to go free. Awful, I said; just not right, I said. And I meant it. It was all true. But then — here's where it gets so hard — I wanted to tell them that maybe they *should* have looked at it all a little more closely before they got so upset, because those men *were* police officers and they were only trying, really, finally, to do their job, can't you see? — it can't be easy going through what they have to go through every day of their lives, imagine being a policeman's wife, would *you* want to have to experience that trauma every day of your life? Well, yes, all right, you could say maybe they went a little too far. I've never seen police violence like that before in my life. It upset me for an entire week, I almost had nightmares like everyone else,

I've got feelings too; but maybe — did they ever stop to think? Did they ever try to have some compassion for the other people in the situation? That guy, the criminal, might really have been dangerous, who can ever know these things when they're happening? Because even after they hit him a few times he kept on trying to rise up from the ground toward them. Maybe *they* were afraid, after all. Wouldn't you have been? Wouldn't anybody have been? Because you can't ever tell what someone's thinking. And they showed some compassion, finally, the officers, because they didn't shoot him the way they're trained to do. It's like you just can't tell who'll try to kill you in the world these days, everything is so dangerous now with all these drug dealers and crackheads and all out in the streets, everywhere, and all these rapists and serial killers too. But no, you can't tell *them* that. I couldn't tell them that. They would just get all upset again and tell me I'm being what they always call you when they can't call you anything else — it makes them feel good when they call you that because then they can sit back and hate you and blame you all over again for everything that's wrong in the world like you made it that way. It's always you, never them. It's so hard, so sickening, because I really like Tracy and Angela, they're nice girls, so well-spoken; we even go out to lunch sometimes together and manage to talk about all kinds of things like books and music and even modern art. It shows you how much people can have going on upstairs when they want to. I really value their friendship so I never tell them these things, and that's one of the things that makes this all so hard and horrible because — if you don't already know — imagine how hard it is to be friends with someone when you can't even tell them the truth because they're so sensitive about what they think is right that they can't deal with reality or what anyone else thinks. They're very emotional. All of them are, there's nothing wrong with it, it's just a cultural thing, and it's like you know they've probably been hurt in one way or another by things that have happened to them — little, stupid things. But after a while even that begins to sound too much like another excuse. Haven't we all been hurt by something? But some of us still manage to *think*.

Besides — and this I know I can say, it would make them smile — why do the people always burn their own neighborhoods? Why do they hurt themselves? It's always like that. If I was in their shoes, and I am in a way kind of because I'm a woman, I would march right on up there to the good neighborhoods, all those places in Beverly Hills and whatnot, and break a few windows and turn over some cars *there*. That'd show those rich bastards who's got the power! I did say that, and I meant it. And Tracy and Angela laughed, but they also looked at each other really quickly and strangely afterward with that look, that look they're so fucking famous for, I've seen it before, you've seen it before, I know it like I know the back of my hand, but what they mean by it I couldn't tell you, I still can't tell you. And sometimes it's really like I just don't care anymore, I just get so sick of it. Another thing they keep to themselves, not really angry but not what I'd call friendly either. Had I said the wrong thing? And we laughed and laughed, yes, we laughed, on and on and loud, for sure, yes, but that's more of what I mean, do you see? — just that no matter how hard you try you can't please them. You can't win. You can't get through to someone on a really human level, never, not even when you have true painful compassion for them; compassion so deep it hurts, what we've all felt at one time or another. Never. And you hate them for that, you can't help it, because they won't ever let you in.

I know I'm a very compassionate person. I can feel sorry for anybody. The world is so full of suffering. When I see those homeless people on the street talking to themselves, muttering to themselves, all bent over like cripples, I just want to cry. And sometimes I do. Because you know people shouldn't have to live like that. You can't even call that living. It's wrong and it's unfair. I try to give them money when I can, to improve their lives in some little way so they'll be able to thank God again, feel alive again and know that somebody, even a stranger, cares for them, would like to help them, and really wants them to do well in the middle of all this crazy sickness. Sometimes they say thank you and sometimes they don't. I know I can't change their lives — only Christ can do that, or the government — but a quarter or a dime will make their day a little nicer. You have to have compassion for people, no matter what color they are. It doesn't matter. I was brought up to believe that color doesn't matter, just like how much money someone has doesn't matter, or what kind of house they live in, or whether or not they're educated so they can get a good job; even if they're living on welfare with a whole bunch of kids because they don't want to work, you shouldn't judge them — that woman you're judging might have been raped or maybe her husband beats her like lots of them do, or he's in jail. You don't know, so you shouldn't say anything. Only the person matters, my family always stressed to me. And the truth everybody knows is that we'd all get along better if it mattered less to them. They're the ones who always bring it up. And then they'll look at you and say you hate them when they're really the ones who hate. That's when you know you should just try to rise above it and leave hatred in their laps because they're really the ones who want it. Always.

It's like that old man in the subway. Sometimes even now I think about him and even as I feel compassion for him I still get furious. He was a cruel old man, just cruel, that's all, and he didn't have to be. He was very old, filthy dirty and very black, sitting on the subway steps in everybody's way as we were coming out one morning on our way to work. That day I remember — it was such a pretty morning, the sun was out, and people in the rush didn't seem as pushy and nasty as usual. I didn't have any change left because just that minute I'd bought a ten-pack of tokens to

last me the week. Why did he have to pick me? — maybe because
I looked at him? Or because of my clothes? (People are always
envious, even homeless people, although you could tell he was a
good type, sort of, not one of those people pretending to be blind
or the kind who would try and rob you like some of them.) I just
felt so sorry for him there, sitting there alone looking so old and
dirty as everyone stepped around him and over him, and when I
gave him a kind of sympathetic look he started screaming —
screaming — that I wasn't going to give him any money because I
was white, wasn't I, and why didn't I just go (he said something
too unbelievable to repeat) because he didn't need my money
anyway, you white bitch, he said, and kept on cursing, *you white
bitch, you white bitch,* over and over. Over and over. He actually
called me that. And I couldn't say anything. I couldn't feel anything except the hate and the real rage that came up. Because it
was humiliating. Because I didn't deserve that. No one can tell me
I deserved that. Not even the worst kind of person would deserve
treatment like that. And for no reason, that's what makes it worse.
Just because I happened to be the one he picked on, because he
was a sick crazy old bastard who didn't have anyplace to live and
needed to blame somebody for it. And I swear, and I'm not apol-
ogizing either, in that minute I wished something really horrible
would happen to him — I didn't care what, just something to
show him he should watch what he said to people, people who'd
even wanted to help him and didn't have to but wanted to
because that's what you should do for people who are suffering
so much, they're so unhappy. I don't care if I shouldn't feel that
way, I don't *care* what anyone says, I'd just like to know how one
human being could say something like that to another. Especially
when I felt so sorry for him sitting there so alone, so black and
dirty. But then you learn that some people don't deserve anyone's
compassion. You learn that they'll just take it and use it against
you. Because I didn't cause his pain. I didn't put him on those sub-

way steps. And you could look around and say that there are more of them that way than anybody else, but that's one thing they can't blame us for. I can't be held accountable for what society does to people and I shouldn't have to suffer for it. I wasn't around a hundred years ago and I've never stolen anything from one of them, never. But you can see it in their eyes: how they try to put it all on you. And when I think of that I just want to scream, or break something, or kill any son of a bitch who even looks like him. Because — just ask yourself — how can they keep on blaming everybody for things that happened a hundred years ago, two hundred years ago? I've never even been in Georgia or any of those places. And after that he could have sat there and starved to rotten death for all I cared. I know I'm a good person. I have a life I can call my own. And a *job.*

It's like what happened last week, I swear to God, the same thing almost, for nothing at all. One of them in the office got all mean over something really stupid. I'm talking about hair. Can you get that? Hair. I was like, let's get real already. It wasn't as if I was asking her about God or her boyfriend or whatever. And then it's like, you try to talk, they won't even let you get out five words before they get all hysterical and upset. It's getting so you can't even ask how's it going or what'd you do this weekend, and, God in Heaven, don't dare to take it further. Let me tell you right now — I wouldn't *care* if anyone asked me about my hair. It's brown, I comb it out in the morning and tease it and put on some hair spray and sometimes a barrette if I have the time. That's all. But this one in the office, this girl who's always wearing all these African clothes and things, she had some fancy hairstyle one day, all curls and twists, and I thought it looked great, kind of foreign, almost, like what one of those models or someone would wear, and I asked her, all I did was ask her how she got it like that and how she washed it because it was great I thought how they could do all those things with their hair that nobody else can, make it long or short one day or stiff and whatnot. And the way she looked at me — like she wanted to kill me. Cut me out before the sight of God. Hate is what you call it. Hate. Over something stupid like hair. So she went around the rest of the day saying "Miss Blue Eyes wanted to know how I did my hair" to the rest of them, laughing, and they laughed too. I don't have blue eyes and I didn't like her tone — that nasty mean sound in her voice. It's what always happens, isn't it? You can't be a real human being, except maybe with a very few — the nicer ones. And now I won't ask anything, never again. Ask and they'll laugh at you. Ask and they'll humiliate you. And then you know they'll say things — I've heard them, you've heard them — like how you don't ever want to "learn" about them and all kinds of things. What's there to learn that's so special it has to be a big deal all the time? People are people, and with all that it's just another example of how they always want to make themselves different like they're the only ones who have problems and all the rest of us are just living the high life. Am I living the high life? Do I have to pay taxes? Do I have to ride the subway every day and smell the vomit and the piss stink with everybody else, or what? And then it's like I want to say (but you can't tell them this, so it ends up burning you to death inside) that if I'd wanted to take care of children I would have had some by now, thank you. *Stupid* children. This same girl had the nerve to tell me once that if I wanted to learn anything I should go to the library. It was like she'd smacked me right in the face. Go to the library for *what?* I'd wanted to say. When I could just ask her, a real, living, breathing human being, and learn from her? That might have meant something to me. We might even have become friends if she hadn't been such a mean-spirited bitch. To tell you the truth, I don't even see why she always wears all those African clothes, either — she's not African. That's another thing now, another fad they can get angry about, every day something different, like how we're supposed to say *african-*

american not *black.* People are never happy to be just who they are, I'm learning. They dig their own graves that way, holding on to all those labels, and then try to pull you down into the sickness with them.

She doesn't even know what kind of a person I am. How I try, as God is my witness, how I try. Like that time I was walking down Lexington Avenue, alone, late at night, on a Sunday after some friends and I had gone to the movies up around Seventy-something Street and they all took cabs home because of the hour, but they knew me, I couldn't be bothered to spend that kind of money, you never know when you might need it and anyway I love to walk late at night sometimes and just feel the city quiet and sleeping around me, quiet and peaceful, so quiet. Yes, well, I know I could be raped sometime, I know what's happening in the world, but no one's ever done that and when they try it God forbid I'll be ready because I never go anywhere without my Mace and the pocketknife a friend gave me one Christmas. I could easily kill someone who'd try to rape me. I'd have no choice. What's a woman supposed to do, live locked up in a castle? You might as well be dead. Anyway, I'm walking down the avenue and it's dark, a really nice night, quiet, cool, the entire city sleeping behind windows, making love, maybe, or watching TV, maybe, or just out walking like me, thinking whatever. And after a little while I can tell there's someone walking behind me, kind of following not too fast but fast enough so I can tell he's there. I kind of look back, you know, just so that I can sort of see his outline, and I can see out of the corner of my eye this dark guy, really tall, walking back there, keeping pace with me. Did I get scared? Did I think about running? So maybe when I thought about it later I did in a small way, you know, I thought plenty of women get raped in this city, you have to be really alert for creeps if you're thinking at all. But this guy — just because he was a big one didn't mean I had to be scared, really, maybe he was just out enjoying the night like I was . . . people have all kinds of ways of enjoying life. And I'm telling myself You're not going to scream, stupid, just let him walk behind you, he's probably never even raped anybody, he's probably a really good person with a job and everything, just because you see a lot of them hanging out in front of those neighborhood stores doesn't mean anything now, right now, just relax. But then all of a sudden he starts walking faster, then faster and faster, and it's like I do start to get a little just a little scared, not much but I'm also telling myself Stupid you know people just like him in the office, Tracy and Angela sort of and all the other girls too and the guys who work in the mailroom and the messengers and that bitch who got so pissed off about her hair, remember that remember that you know all of them. But then it's like — I don't know, all at once I'm thinking about how angry they can get when all you do is ask them a simple question, oh God a simple question, that's all, and how angry they get at people who're just trying to do their jobs like the cops, you see it on the news all the time, they're ready to kill people who never did anything to them, just like that guy who shot up or no he *massacred* all those people on the railroad that time just because they were — just because they were there, just because they were — because they were *white,* he said, it's like Jesus God how could anybody be filled with so much hate for anyone, it's like he hated the whole country, how, why, for *what?* — ask yourself that, then ask yourself why can't people forget about things and get on with their lives, because for God's sake the people on the train weren't doing anything to him and he even admitted it, remember, he said it was because he was so angry and full of hate, he hated everybody, even Chinese people who never do anything to anybody, they're so quiet always and really decent and clean, they don't bother anybody, everybody loves them. I cried and cried for days after, and that time I did have bad dreams, because think about it, those people could have been anyone, they could have been you or me, and it's like you know everybody shouldn't have called him an animal but that's something only an animal would do, isn't it, only an animal, what else can you say? That's it, that's how it always happens, they're ready to kill people just for looking, just for smiling, you can't smile, no, you can't look, no, never, they'll kill you or start a fire or:— angry all the time for nothing at all, really how can anyone live like that, that's why they die young, they live to be angry, killing people and even each other sometimes and then:— wondering I'm wondering really fast is this guy angry too for some reason because Jesus fucking Christ God I didn't cause any of it his pain or whatever they're complaining about now, living in the past still *they won't let go of it:—*

(should I scream or should I)

(they won't get beyond it they won't

should I scream or)

and so suddenly so fast I start to walk faster Jesus God walk faster almost running I should run but not almost running and trying to find the Mace my knife a cop I haven't got a gun why didn't I but I am not scared the Mace the Mace but it slips out of my hands or maybe I don't know I forgot to bring it this time I am not scared:

because lots of lots of women do get raped in this city   all over the world:

everywhere   Jesus God you better run you better fly or is there somebody a cop or:—

because this anger in them that gets out of control it gets out of control and if he raped me but I can't imagine being raped but if he rapes me Jesus God Christ I'll die I won't

—survive I won't because it can happen to anyone and it's like this panic I'm not scared I'm not trying to run but running not running and is he there

running oh God   is he there

—and then I see him running out into the street and hailing a cab so I guess he must have money or something, only the cab

doesn't stop for him and the next one doesn't either and the next doesn't either and you can see he gets this kind of frustrated look, sort of angry, always angry, and now I'm sort of calming down and thinking *I wasn't really scared I wasn't* — and what's happening is they're not stopping for him and you can't blame them but not because of how he looks or anything but they probably just want to go home and eat, they've worked hard for hours and it's late, really late, and they deserve a break too. I know, because some of them wouldn't want to take me out of the city either. At this time of the night they only want to go to SoHo or Tribeca or maybe the Upper West Side or the Village. They hate going anyplace else because they want to go home and eat. It's also really hard to get one these days because now lots of them are from so many foreign places like Pakistan or Africa and you know how people are in those countries, if they see a woman out late alone they'll take you for a whore, because it's like they show on the news, in those countries you know a woman can't just be herself, she's either somebody's property or she's a whore, that's how it is. And now slowing down but still watching him, looking back, I feel this incredible warm feeling, it's like happiness or contentment, that he turned out to be a good person after all, I almost want to cry for some reason, and I look back at him and kind of wave and say (I don't know why my heart's jumping around like this, it's so stupid how darkness and dark streets can make you feel so jittery, nothing's ever happened to me after all, what would ever happen?), I say, Having a hard time there, huh? — and I smile, really smile, because it's like this really human moment when there's nobody else around and it's just us two out in the dark in the middle of the quiet quiet city when nothing matters, none of it, we're past it, we're just two people. A truly human moment, and I feel like, God, what an incredible world this is in spite of all the pain and the suffering, and you can see some homeless people carrying their beer bottles and bags and everything down the street, looking the way they always do, dirty and run-down, but at least they're alive, thank God, they'll live to beg another day and you know somewhere deep down there's some kind of mercy in that at least. And now he's still out there and he looks back at me for a second before he turns his face back to the lights of the oncoming cars (his face, it's so beautiful, really, like one of those bears with the gentle eyes of a child), but then — I swear to God — looking at me he gets this look on his face like he hates me. *Hates* me. And just that fast like before, so many times before I'm thinking I hate you too, you son of a bitch, somebody tries to reach out to you and be friendly, who the hell are *you?* I hope you never get a cab now, you bastard, and then I'm thinking something really awful and I'm sorry, I *know* I shouldn't think that, God forgive me, but it's just like before, like always . . . they drive you to it. You can't share anything, not the night, not the darkness, not any kind of human moment. And now it's like I feel a little sick, a little hot, the moment's over and it feels like somebody died, there's something dead here, ruined, and I'm sorry I went to the movies at all, something always has to spoil it, and I'm not walking alone anymore tonight I tell myself, no, I'm sick of walking and running out here and anyway you can't tell what kind of animals are out here at this time of night, you can't even walk alone without somebody coming up behind you. I put out a hand and hail a cab and one comes, thank God, everything'll be okay now, and yes, I'll pay the goddamn fare all the way home because I'm on my way back now anyway, after all, on my way home to a quiet place. Get me home fast, I'm thinking as I get in. Fast. . . . It's safer that way.

And — just once — one time —
    I don't know why. I don't. I just —
    I dated one. . . .
    One time. Just once. A long time ago. Not now. When I was a little more. . . . I know, I shouldn't talk about it. I should just let

it rest and be quiet. Just forget about it already. It's all over now and it'd be better not to go over all that again but even now I have to, something inside me's saying I should, I have to. Get it out of my system. For the last time. Let it out. I have to.

It's like I wonder sometimes how it happened at all. How it ever happened, I mean. It's not as if I don't try to be really careful. Even back then when I didn't. . . . You know you can't ever tell about people. Like if some guy comes up to me and tells me I'm gorgeous that doesn't mean I'm going to go out with him. Even though I know I'm lucky, like I said I'm in great shape and everything, you know guys use that line with women all the time when they're looking for a good time, that's how they are. And maybe I shouldn't say *they're* especially like that but it's like I said too you have to be really careful with them always. I know that even more now, because it's like nothing ever changes; you can't change things. And I guess that time I just *looked*. Everybody looks once in a while, right? And maybe you shouldn't. You know you really shouldn't, but it's like you can't always help it, they're out there more now, not just in their own neighborhoods, and then sometimes you know some of them try a little harder, sometimes, like Tracy and Angela, they really try. That doesn't mean you're going to — but we did, that one time we did, and it's like now I still can't. . . . That's what scares me the most sometimes. Just that we — that all that stuff happened. I know — I know it was one of those times when it's sort of like you just let go. You slip a little looking for something and you just let go. You don't know what it is maybe and maybe you don't even care. It's like all you know, you *feel* it, my God, like you want to really let go like you never did before. Not ever. And when you do that's when everything happens, when you end up alone wondering, like oh my God how could you. . . . That's it. It's like you jump, really scary and far, and you fall. And maybe part of it was even my fault. Or even all of it. But we never talked about any of it because I knew he was really embarrassed by what happened that time, and even though I think I'm a modern woman and everything, I mean even though I believe in equal rights and divorce and the right to do what I want to do with my own body and all that, still I know one of the worst things you can ever let a man feel is embarrassment because of something he did with you that he shouldn't have done, because you know how guys are with their egos and their pride, they can't help it. They're always like that. And guys like him have pride too, this kind of noble mysterious pride, except that — I know more than ever after him — they always get kind of stuck on themselves. They really start to think they're special or something, as soon as things get close. The way he did. And you know it's probably because of what's happened to them in the past, like they're so ashamed of it they feel like they have to take it out on you somehow. And that's when you feel the most sorry for them, because you know, you can see it in their eyes, what they're holding back; it's like they really want to reach out for once, in a way, the way they do when they do it, but they're afraid. And then you can almost forgive them for it because you know they want you — they really want you. And you can, because it was worth something to you, that time, because how often did somebody do that, how often . . . it was really worth something. It was a real human moment. You felt it. You always feel it and you know it too.

Because he really cared about me. Loved me. I know, he really wanted me, he was always telling me how much he loved me and how beautiful my hair was and everything. You're fly, he used to say, and all those other things you hear them say. And even now I can forgive him for everything except that one bad time, because I know he cared about me and I know too that I really believe in the power of people even more than the power of God sometimes. Because I've seen it.

We met just like other people meet, I guess, at lunch, in the street, in the subway, in an elevator — how do you ever meet someone? You see something you like and you start talking. And from the very first I could tell he would be good to me — really good. He spoke so well and said he'd been to college and I believed him, a college up in Massachusetts or someplace that cost twenty thousand a year or so and gave scholarships for minority excellence and whatnot. You could tell it was true because of the way he spoke, and he carried himself in a really special way, not like the guys in the mail room or the messengers. (They're nice guys, they all know I like them and everything, but you can tell they're more like the ones you see more often on the street and always in the subway too.) And so we would take walks and all that, only I could never invite him to my place because it was never clean enough, since I work all the time I never have enough time to clean, you know how that is. . . . People might've stared too, although that really wouldn't be a problem because I could always say he was a friend or something and just leave it at that. And maybe they wouldn't even stare, who knows? — but anyway we always wound up going to his place that was on the edge of a kind of awful neighborhood but not right in it so you could feel kind of safe, you know, and then we always took a cab to get there which was sort of romantic, I guess, and safe too. The people around there actually seemed friendly; they always smiled at us and laughed and talked about him being on top of the world now, calling him brother and all that the way they do and slapping his hand and so on, and you could see it was like they were really proud of him for something, like he was a real star to them or whatever. And his apartment! — it was really special. It always smelled like incense, just like him; he had it filled up with all these cultural things. And he loved to read! I never saw so many books in my life — all on interesting things. You wondered how he did it. That's why more than ever I don't like to hear anybody say anything about this country and how bad it is, because it looked like he was doing pretty well, once you got inside the apartment. You wouldn't ever see *him* out there burning things.

We did talk there, sometimes, but most of the time we did other things, and I guess that was when the bad times came. It just happened so fast, that one night, I couldn't stop it. I wasn't even sure I really wanted to stop it. It's not like I had anything against him; it could have been anybody who did it. It was just that time, that time it was feeling so good, it never felt that good with anybody, God, no, not anybody else, never, always scary and sort of sick for some reason which made it feel even better in a way. You know what I mean. Because for the first time in my life ever, I mean the first time, I felt wild, I mean just free and wild and then scared and thrilled too all at the same time, and it was all so bad in a way and dirty and sick too but in a kind of good wicked secret way, because you could just let go for once, when *no one* was watching, and *give* yourself, I mean really give yourself to it. Whatever. It was like for the first time, I swear to God, I didn't care about sin then or anything, not Jesus or my family and what they'd say or anything, and it's like I swear I'm telling you the truth when I say that for once, really for once I wasn't scared of any of them, not the loud ones on the street or that mean bitch in the office or even the crazy killer one on the railroad. Because I'm telling you it was like we were having a real human moment, him and me, right there, in the dark, private, nobody else around, sort of dirty and sick like I said but good too, God, so good, and all you could see were his eyes, looking at me. Like he was catching something. Holding me. Like that. And then it was like I could feel his skin next to mine and how it smelled and felt, kind of rough, and how it tasted too, really rough and smooth and black next to mine, God, like the way he felt on me, really wild, it was like you couldn't break or catch that thing in him at all because whatever it was, *him,* Jesus, would kill you first, and then it was like you knew you really knew you'd never see anything like that again in this life, like that, *on fire:* out of control. In me. In me. Fucking God. Just wild. I didn't care. God forgive me, it was so much, it was so. . . . But then — I didn't want to remember this, I really didn't have anything against him, it wasn't because of him — I wanted him to stop because it began to hurt, really hurt, and it was like I couldn't cry or scream or do anything, God forgive me please, because I wanted to but I didn't want to. I couldn't, I didn't want to. It was like all at once, I don't know what happened, it happened so fast, like all of a sudden he was really angry like all the rest of them, like there was something angry inside him and he wanted to kill somebody. Kill them. And I got so scared, it was like. . . . That was when I wanted to get out of there, I wanted to leave. But I couldn't. Do you know what I mean? I *couldn't*. And then, God, I started getting this really cold feeling, sort of cold and almost dead like when you know one of them's going to hurt you, you didn't do anything except maybe look at them and they want to hurt you, cold, dead, and he wasn't saying anything but you could tell he was angry and he knew, he *knew* I knew. It was like that *very real* angry that makes them burn things and kill people, always with the police, the guns, the blood, *angry,* and then so fast even though I was cold and so scared, God, I started to get angry too but in a different kind of way. *Get off me you bastard,* I thought but couldn't say, *Get off me you black bastard,* I thought but couldn't say, God forgive me, *I'd like to kill you you black bastard kill you* — I thought but couldn't say, Jesus, and it was like a nightmare or something. I was feeling blood everywhere, blood all over the place even though I wasn't bleeding, Jesus, it was like there was this blood you could feel but you couldn't see hot and sticky the way blood really is. The blood. Angry. He was burning me with it. You're killing me, you fucking animal, you black bastard, you're hurting me, this fucking hurts, stop it, can't you see I'm crying, you bastard, *stop*. . . . I *hate* you. — I couldn't say that to him. He loved me, I know he cared about me, I couldn't say all that to him. He just got out of control. He wasn't paying attention. He didn't mean to hurt me. He didn't even know. If he'd known he wouldn't have began to look old, small, mean and shrinking in, so dark and ugly and even creepy all of a sudden, really spooky, and I couldn't breathe that incense smell anymore because I was feeling sick, kind of, and falling again and still so dead, falling way down with nothing to hold on to anywhere. That's when I got my things, fast, and got up, fast, and I was beginning to get scared again even though I knew for God's sake he wouldn't hurt me, stupid, I was being so stupid, he wouldn't hurt me, all that stuff was in the past already. I knew that. But then so fast it was all beginning to be like a dream again all filled up with red and those shadows I didn't want to see anymore with those weird colors in his eyes that you always see in their eyes sometimes. . . . I was up already, walking to the door, not in a funny way or anything but just quietly kind of, but I had to look back once to where he was still sitting with his hands so tight around that mug holding the black coffee. I can remember that — the tension in his hands and his eyes kind of hard and soft too, almost innocent, looking sort of like how I was feeling, just out there and really cold. And I did look at him for a little while but he never raised his head to look up at me. Then — I don't know what, I still don't know — something came racing up in me really hot and I wanted to tell him that even though I was feeling that way kind of cold and dead like his eyes and even his hands and his mouth, like that, it wasn't that bad, I wanted to tell him, he didn't have to feel ashamed for any of it, it was over, I was forgetting it! It was history already, no more, please! It's like when you're dead you don't have to think about all those things. We could just pretend, you know, that we'd never seen each other or anything. It was like we hadn't, really, and couldn't, at all. You could tell that. And then I was really out the door, leaving him there like I could feel him still sitting with his head down, remembering things maybe, remembering. . . . The guys were still out on the street, almost invisible in the darkness, laughing and smiling again this time and asking me if I was going to hang with them, and even though I was still feeling dead and cold and hot too I didn't feel afraid of them, I'd never been afraid of any of them, I thought, afraid of what? I walked right on past them and smiled back and didn't look back. Walking not running to the subway wishing I could've found a cab but there were no cabs. Walking down into the subway, like falling again down into that dark thing and *Jesus God oh God I'd never be the same again God oh God*. Angry. Not scared not of them but just wanting to get home and take a shower, to wash it all away the blood and the heat crawling up my legs

to take a shower and

walking very fast yes very fast not looking back and

is one of them behind me in the darkness is he there and will he will he:—

— not looking back. Not ever. Not once.

None of that ever happened. I'm telling myself now. Never.

Put it all behind you, I'm telling myself. It's all in the past.

It never happened.

Only one time. That time. Just once.

Once. God. Once.

THEIR STORY

A ND THEN IN THOSE AFTERNOONS THAT WERE YET TO come after so many other events of that time and our days too had passed over into our dreams, even after all details and memory had merged into those rivers of our nights, you would see the two of them walking together, past our windows, past our front porches and our doors, through Sound Hill: Mr. Winston and Uncle McKenzie. In summer, the trees fluttering down their eyes and watching so quietly the heat-drowsed life along those streets; the smell of the Sound (the water only yards away behind the farthest of our houses) hanging heavy through the air as first one pair of hands from behind a fence, then another and still another, waved at them in greeting, and large heavy dark eyes all along that street — through the heat, through our dreams — looked out from every other memory with easy smiles of recognition.

You will not see them walking quite that way now, and our summers, too, have grown more silent. But even then, as starlings chattered overhead and our backs strained over hedges and coaxed geraniums to turn their hands to the sky, you knew that it hadn't always been that way: that the faces of those two, and later our own, hadn't always borne that sadness; that once, you remembered, there had been more of a lift to those old shoulders lately so rounded, and a spryness to the step that no winter of the heart nor mind could remove. Some of the older folks, like my grandpa, remembered that time so many years ago when Mrs. Winston also had walked through our streets: the iron-gray hair framing the heart-shaped face, the heavy body that had known many years of difficult labor, the pair of long legs ending in bright sneakers beneath a flowered dress; remembered (and carried into the dream) that voice singing away the long hot days in her garden down by the water, where, among those hydrangeas and the peonies that had done Sound Hill proud, she had worked tirelessly in a relentless quest for color. And memory of her could not be summoned without bringing to mind Uncle McKenzie's wife Icilda, and the smells of curried goat and ackee and saltfish that had always breezed out of her kitchen. In that time, when the world still allowed those of us who were young to be children, scraped knees and pop-eyes turned up without fail at Mrs. McKenzie's front porch for Jamaican bun-and-cheese that not even the best of the Jamaican bakeries in Baychester and up on Boston Road, even years later, would equal. There, between taste-swallows of an island of whose mountains we knew nothing, we always greeted Uncle McKenzie, who invariably found time to put himself all up under Mrs. McKenzie in that cluttered kitchen — "a goddamned kitchen jack!" her voice shouted as her always-crisp house dress rustled in ferocious blue; as, softer, came, "Here, pickney, take it, nuh?" — and we felt the caress of rough hands we also carried later to our dreams.

Uncle McKenzie was play uncle to all of us: What you Americans call play uncle this or that, we in Jamaica call pet name, he said, and that is mine. And so, without fear of what was to come later, reaching up to those hands and running back out into that time of protected ignorance, we called him Uncle, for the rest of his life, in fact, as we ate bun and hard dough bread and gizzarders conjured out of that distant unknown place called *Trelawny,* from where they both had come, and where, they always told us, lived creatures called *duppies* — ghosts.

Ghosts in and of themselves wouldn't have been enough to scare us in Sound Hill. In our isolation in that forgotten and far-off North Bronx part of the world, so far removed from the churnings of a city whose streets permitted their prisoners no real vision of the sky or light, we had already known them. We had learned long ago that even the vaguest rustle of a bedroom curtain on nights of the most abject loneliness only betokened — in most cases — a visitor of the gentlest and most yearning benignancy, longing from so far off (within that other darkness, emblazoned by that light we couldn't yet see) to share and comfort our solitude and theirs. We knew they came and went as surely as the summers came and went until our fire-shadowed days of autumn; there were beneficent ones and those troubled and — depending on how one had treated their personages in life — those who could bring terrible dreams and vengeance. All of them, if permitted by us the living, possessed the power to access and decipher our thoughts, appetites, memories, devotions, regrets, and even our most secret and thwarted obsessions; mostly when we walked those night rivers of painful remembrance, which was often. So that even many years later, when so many of us had moved out of our parents' homes in Sound Hill and into (smaller, lonelier, meaner) apartments in the city, leaving behind the lilac-fragrances of those ghostly night walks, we would summon again to the rushings of our own shame just what had happened with Mr. Winston and Uncle McKenzie, as we learned the truth.

When Mrs. Winston died — Miss Ardelia, we called her — all of Sound Hill turned out for the funeral. Because we had no church of our own, it was held at a church way up in the Valley.

Midway through the service, all the ladies, my mama included, bent low over their knees and raised their palms high up in the air — supplicating that light which had never been kind but which they so devoutly believed would someday fall from the unyielding sky and maybe even now, especially now, Jesus, into their reaching hands; as their men, like my daddy and grandpa, sat like stalwart sphinxes beside them — afraid more then and always of the quiet storms building within themselves than they were of the future explosions a lifetime of such storms could cause at any moment to rip open the tender flesh of their hearts. Mr. Winston was the worst. His daughter and son-in-law came all the way from San Francisco to see Miss Ardelia put to rest; they had to help him into the church because his own knees would not. That last week of spring he had turned sixty-six, and last June he and Miss Ardelia had made forty years together. "A man can't take but so much," my mama said. "Taxes, killing, young people dying, Social Security that don't feed nobody. That's all one thing you could put into a box and just say God help you try to sleep at night. You'll lay off worrying and go on to sleep when you get tired enough. But a wife sick so long and then to go off like that and leave him, sweet Jesus. A man can't take but so much. Especially a man like him."

Mama was right. That day when we were all in the church up in the Valley feeling the spirit and Miss Ardelia's spirit too with Mr. Winston bawling and then being real quiet and the light that wasn't ever kind falling over us and us listening to the preacher's words about how Miss Ardelia was now with the Lord our shepherd in the sight of all His goodness and His grace, I watched Daddy holding on real tight to Mama's hand as he looked straight ahead and held me too and I knew she was right. Everybody's mama knew and everybody's daddy — those who were there — knew too. Mr. Winston was a soft kind of man, good soft — the kind you had always seen on those later spring and summer and even winter evenings walking down past the fences and the lawns with Miss Ardelia almost-tall at his side — walking, you remembered, a little stiff; joking with Noah Harris and Hyacinth-who-danced about how that lawn sure enough looked like the ragged-torn side of some trifling nigger's head, hadn't they never heard of Bill and Acie's Lawnmower-U-Rent on Gun Hill Road?; greeting the Walker twins, Timothy and Terence, telling them apart only because of the fiercely protective look and arm-about-the-shoulder Timothy always had for his born-twenty-six-minutes-later brother; making Yvonne Constant, the quietest little girl in Sound Hill, look up for more than a second and even smile; with Miss Ardelia not humming quietly then to herself as she often did but just smiling and laughing softly once in a while; admiring O. K. Griffith's irises or Johnnyboy's front-yard eggplants; putting a hand now and then to that white straw hat she always wore on warmer days; then the two of them walking down to the Sound, when you would hear the man's soft voice telling her how someday when they had not three but four grandkids he would build them all a sailboat and take them up off over the water, past Westchester and Connecticut on one side and Long Island on the other, and wave to all the rich whitefolks who'd be watching with the same wideopen eyes they'd always imagined us to have, and say Hey, y'all, looka here! — I got my family out with me for the day. So whyn't y'all let them maids and chauffeurs free for a day so they can come on with us for a swim? — Hush up, Win, would come the woman's voice then: very like a flute, more light than sound; as you imagined her resting a thin hand on his thin shoulder still moving with the laughter he had learned to embrace as joy — a small, pithy sort of joy, but the form and shape of joy enough. The hand would remain there, moving over the joy, as the curve beneath it leaned slowly into the arm and hand, feeling it long after eyes and flesh had joined and gone home to watch the nightly news, watch the outer darkness descend, watch the inevitable. There, where eyes mattered less than touch, the feeling continued, you knew, as we felt the hint of it or the breath or the moment amongst ourselves, even long after everything had happened.

How, then, did those future events come to occur? Some would say later, after they were over, that they had begun with a sort of blindness. Uncle McKenzie's blindness, after Icilda McKenzie's death a few years before from a cancer that in her earlier years had begun gnawing away at the smooth flesh of her breasts like a tenacious but unasked-for lover, been arrested by several pairs of surgical hands, savage machines, and scalpels, and skulked in her body for twenty years until, the tenacious lover finally turned vengeful, it had silently exploded into her brain on that gray morning none of us would ever forget. After the explosion and the memory, Uncle McKenzie did become blind. From that morning on, he had been able to see nothing except that long dim pathway leading yet further down into a valley of utter silence, where all trees and even the most humble ground-dwelling creatures had long ago learned not to weep, stricken with the knowledge that all about them grew the most unimaginable sadness which no tears could redress. So that, as our restless spirits showed us, it wasn't quite a literal blindness. And then some of us thought that actual no-sight might have been almost a blessing on those nights we dreamt Icilda McKenzie's ghost came back in her grief to wander past our sleeping houses, past the house of her dead friend Ardelia Winston and so many other passed-on or sleeping friends who wept and reached out to her from the endless sorrowing rivers of their dreams, until she found that particular green house down by the water she was looking for: where the kitchen still smelled of bun and curried goat and calves' feet jelly, and pictures of Discovery Bay and Port Maria hung on those weary walls; yes, that house, whose structure was of slight wooden frame like all the rest; where the walking shadow paused for a moment to embrace those summer-night delights of ripe apricots still hanging on the front yard tree her own living hands had planted so many years ago, the man with that ease of the sea in his voice laboring not far from her. Then, like that which she had become and which the object of her eternal searching desire was fearsomely becoming, she entered the house — patting the clay-potted geraniums on the front porch to make sure they were still properly dry in that season of frequent thundershowers; drifted upward into the room whose walls had watched her die; where the mirrors had watched her watching herself making love throughout the years to him whose sleeping, trembling cheek she then, in the dark, began to stroke; caressed the grieving forehead, and kissed, with the fleeting touch of ghost-love, those lips so lately useless throughout the new appalling silence of so many sightless days; as he, mired in the mud of that dream-riverbank that continued to hold him fast, called out to her from a place she could not reach him, to save me, Icilda, help me, Icilda, I'm ready to go now, Icilda, I'm ready. Ready. She would calm him then. For while she could do little or nothing to lighten the blindness of his days, which she anyway passed on the banks of a distant shore he wouldn't know for some time, she was able at least to quiet the fury of his nights. When, in that dark solitude, he awoke sweating and fever-pitched, grasping the air wildly and crying out for her, feeling the pounding of his heart and thinking, praying, that this might be the heart attack at last, Heavenly Father, that would finally bring him closer to her and allow him that sweetness of resting his fevered head in her cool lap once again, forever, she was there — just behind him, out of his sight but close enough to lay her hands on his neck and rub him there, pulling him with that gentle, ghostly insistence back down into the twilit country of sleep and the river where, at least for the space of that time within earthly boundary, he could rest his fatigue on the shore and listen in peace to those rushing waters.

In those hours of silent, immeasurable time between two worlds — one raging, the other in the most unknowable and confident serenity — what secrets, we wondered, what wisdoms did she share with him? Our own dreams never told it all, being currents allied with the nocturnal unspoken mysteries of death. But we learned then, as everyone gradually discovered, that only those ghosts we knew among us were capable of telling the complete truth, unencumbered by twitching lips or the diurnal cutting of an eye. They alone possessed the fortitude and the power, buttressed by the breadth of eternity, to stare down the remorseless intelligence that outlined and directed our destiny. Fearing death — perhaps because we did fear it — we knew that their knowledge was infinitely greater than our own not only because they had already faced what we feared — loss of life and the awful pain-resonances of human grief — but also because they had long gone on to whatever it was our surviving hopes, wisely or in pathetic human foolishness, insisted we continue to believe in. Our spirits, like Icilda McKenzie's, had only to face the circular time of what to us for our time on earth would remain unknown, as we yet walked through our days and nights in constant fear and avoidance of the certainty and ostensible closure of death. So that when the living, fretting Uncle McKenzie stuttered out the pain that had so tightly coiled about his heart and spirit, protesting the entry of yet another presence into his dreams, wanting only her in the flesh, in his arms again, or himself with her on that farther shore, she the wiser spirit would shush him who was still her husband and lover, whispering to him that he must allow to occur what was beyond his power to alter; that soon, some night, they would again be joined in always-time, and that, for now, he would do best to listen to the sounds of all those other wandering spirits who, for all he knew, might be bringing him news of her sojourns on those quiet shores along which she had so lately walked. Oh, she was strong, our night rivers told us; she would never allow him to descend of his own miserable willingness into the deeper parts of that current from which, for him, at this moment in his destiny, there could be no return. In her patience, and from within that firm and infinite resolve deepened by the requisites of death, she soothed the bitter maledictions of his raging heart until the restorative river-melody sighed once again in the more steady sound of his breathing. It was then — only then — she knew that she could (as she must) remove her hand from the relaxed grip of his and, just that way, a vision diminishing, a force once again released, make her way once more out of that bedroom and down the stairs, out into the sleeping world so uneasy from its own day-terrors, to walk again in her own aloneness until the unrevealed hour when the longing of their separate courses would meet for all time in that other world of light.

Thus, in that way, until the end, some of us thought, Uncle McKenzie's nights gradually came to be illuminated by those private moments of transcendent vision, even as his days began to descend into that most terrible form of blindness which preys on the living bereaved. It wasn't long afterwards that we saw how he began to stumble, not walk, through our streets he knew so well. When, one evening, he fell down on the sidewalk in front of O.K. Griffith's irises, O.K.'s boy Walter R. later told his daddy that, as he'd reached out to help the old man to his feet, Uncle McKenzie had looked dead straight up at him, right through and past him, as if seeing a sunset world behind and beyond Walter R.'s nappy head, and in the most terrible earth-filled voice had whispered, "Icy. *Icy.* Got to get home to help Icy with the curry goat. She waiting pon me, you no see, pickney?" — so that later Walter R. would tell his daddy too that the look in Uncle's eyes — that vacancy which saw nothing in this world except those sunsets laying waste to desolate fields beyond a river which in daytime did not exist — had terrified him as much as the hopeless weight of those old, fragile bones held up in his arms. Later that summer, when the police brought Uncle McKenzie to Noah Harris' doorstep with the news that he had been frightening women at the Pelham Bay bus stop by asking them through his tears if they had by any chance, please, seen his wife Icilda walking through the river, several of us wept into the most private spheres of our own hearts, feeling the dreadful certainty that, from all appearances and more, Uncle McKenzie wouldn't be with us much longer. It was as if, seeing what was to come very much later in the ashes of tragedy and reborn gods whose acts would forever terrorize our survivors, and not having the good sense to run then from what would be that later horror, we sought in both Uncle McKenzie and Mr. Winston a glance of the forever-survivor, who might lead us into a possible future and more fearless re-sketchings of ourselves. In our sorrow for him, we were obviously feeling also a more prescient sorrow and fear for ourselves, sharing the knowledge that even more unnerving than the final rivers of our dreams were those inescapable deserts of our surrender to the ashes of the future.

But then — thank God and the spirits — through the workings of unseen guiding hands, it came to seem an almost natural occurrence that, neither too soon nor late, the stronger of the personalities between the two old survivors began gradually, cautiously at first, to guide that one who had fallen to his knees up to his feet and to a place where, far above that night river, two old wrinkled men could begin to weave out the intricate patterns of their common distress; as the trees in that place gazed down upon them with wise and silent knowledge of the miracles humans might still achieve after so much time of blinding loss.

And so it happened. As the hazed languor of those late-summer days crept into the cooler fires of the coming nights, we began to see them together — bent-backed, shuffling, wary of step — in the steady company of shared grief, perhaps, but also in the occasional slow surprises of that elusive light that children, and all others who find they still have much to discover in the world, know. Thank Jesus, our mamas murmured, because a man at that age needs someone he can slap thighs with and trade jokes with about the good old days that were already past most of our recalling, and about which practically no one wanted to listen anyway beyond the necessary polite smile of one minute or less. So that, even years later, well into the time of our own separate and lonely autumns, we would think back on our pleasure at the sound of their mingled voices, low music frosted by age, as Mr. Winston guided Uncle McKenzie down to the Sound they both loved; relating to him over their slow steps the joke about rescuing the maids and chauffeurs from the whitefolks. It began there — the unraveling of a tale of his grandchildren in San Francisco, who knew only what the evening winds and their parents' whispers told them of their grandfather's distress, were sent by their mother and father to "quality" schools where they were taught nothing about themselves, and — most unforgivable — had been raised by the lawyer his daughter had become and the architect his son-in-law had always been not to believe in spirits. That was why, he told Uncle McKenzie, those two children had learned all about the lives of so many important people and all the gleaming cities they had built in the snowy wastes, the anchors they had tossed on the coral reefs, the radioactivity they had brought to sun-scorched deserts high above the secret lairs of scorpions, and even the luxury housing developments they were planning to erect on all the bright planets still reflecting the moon's ageless light on the earth, yet to this day could not have midnight conversations with their departed grandmother, who, like Icilda McKenzie, also walked steadily between this world and that one. None of his living people knew how to listen to the older spirits, Mr. Winston said, nor to those tall trees in the South he remembered that still brought the tortured last words of so many skeletons that only some years ago, and even yesterday, had swung in white silence from those long branches, a length of charred bleached bones and shame drying in the sun. So what kind of way to raise children was that? he asked; and Uncle McKenzie only shook his head and said that it was no kind of way at all, Massa God, for pickney must raise up to know the spirit and true. Amen, intoned that other, thinking again of Miss Ardelia; and they would stand there for a while, looking out at the glistening waters of another vision, another dream, as the hushed waters of the Sound lapped up at their feet on shore.

The days grew chilly, the light thinner; late flowers offered up to us their resolute and noble last, falling fast before the proud marchings-in of our stately chrysanthemums. We returned to the dreaded boredom of school, weekend leaf-raking, honors projects; our grandmamas again turned to preserves, worryings about the world and scoldings; our parents once again every day rode the Sound Hill bus to the Pelham Bay station to their jobs in the city and back again. Between these dull, regulated spaces in our lives and nights of TV telling us how not to think and feel and what winter would bring, we heard: Mr. Winston, with Uncle McKenzie at his side, leaning on O.K. Griffith's fence; regaling his companion, O.K. and Walter R. with that long-ago truth he had never forgotten, about how the most persistently disapproving eye to his marriage had been not Miss Ardelia's mama and daddy but her grandmama, who had died six years before the marriage yet had insisted from that calmer world on making an appearance at the wedding of her beloved third granddaughter, and who indeed on that hot South Carolina June day had appeared at the ceremony in her cream linen suit, spanking new as forty years before, that had matched her cream high-heel shoes and the yellow-cream flowers on her hat. Settin up there big as day, Mr. Winston said, and didn't leave off bugging 'Delia about what her duty as a wife was til two weeks *after* the honeymoon. Even then they'd still been aware that she had been lingering, a presence, carrying her aroma of mint jelly and beeswax through the big new house young Mr. Winston had moved into with his bride; a presence gently ruffling lemon fragrance through the bedsheets before the newlyweds turned in for private hours of love; plaiting Ardelia's hair with gardenias throughout the night as the bride slept in her husband's protecting arms; dusting off the kitchen table, always leaving behind her beeswax scent, scolding Ardelia for walking around like a lovestruck rabbit instead of with a broom in her hand; until, on a gray humid afternoon which promised a cooling absolution of rain, the old lady felt the ponderous weight of an earlier rain in her soul and, her face wet with sudden tears, cried out, "Your grandfather's calling me! It's time to go home for good! He's calling me!" — and, bestowing one final kiss on her granddaughter's stricken face, disappeared into that seamless memory of rain, drawn back into her lonely husband's embraces awaiting her at the edge of the world. In that moment Ardelia put a hand to her own cheek and felt her grandmother's tears, which would remain there and bring to her face a glow of supreme life touched with an implacable sadness her husband would not be able to caress or kiss away until eleven days and twelve nights later, when she would sit up abruptly in bed to cry out "Nana's home! She's with him!" — and sink with a sigh of deepest relief and contentment, yet edged by a lingering melancholy which would never completely leave her, back into her husband's wait-ing arms. The earliest dreams began then. Late one night, the elderly couple returned to the newlyweds from an uncharted place on the other, broader side of the world where, nightly, the sea crawled with a maroon skin beneath a ceaseless moon, and in every tide carried back to shore the intoxicating unmistakable scents of beeswax and mating crabs. "Me and 'Delia never was much for writing letters," Mr. Winston said, "but can't nobody write letters to folks passed on no way. But with the dreams at least we could *see* em." It had remained that way always, he said, as O.K. Griffith snorted and said he didn't believe in no ghosts coming back like that and leaving tears and whatnot on people, especially on people that young. Mr. Winston just came right on in with Hush up, boy, letting O.K. know he hadn't hardly lived his life yet and probably still didn't know the difference between a real live ghost and a baby coon's fart.

A shining then. Uncle McKenzie's face. Almost wet with the memories that until his last hour on earth would call to him from the framed photograph of Icilda as a young girl, kept on his night-table, close to his heart. With those elbows easy on fences, at the side of his indomitable-spirited and trusted friend, what occa-sionally came close to the surface in him was clear. And watch-ing, as we did, you would feel that gladness for him in the something — a flicker of that other, deeper knowledge he hadn't yet either named or uncovered — that had for the immediate present transported him, too, back to those days of his youth.

So, then, should any of us really have been surprised when — quite suddenly, almost forever — all memory of the present was swept up into that slow breeze's beginning and the signaling of evening's arrival off the Sound, as that other aged voice we knew so well began recounting once again the events of that time of the relucent miracle of the dolphins who, in a sadness so griev-ous it couldn't be shared even by the spirits of countless other creatures long ago hounded to extinction, and bearing in their eyes the foreknowledge of an impossible destiny even the most self-congratulating marine biologist couldn't explain, had begun to wash up and suffer out the last days of their stricken dreams on that long thin palm-lined strip of land Uncle McKenzie's country-people at that time called the Palisadoes, which years later would be renamed for one of the nation's most illustrious and forthright heroes, whose name, even in times of willful collective amnesia, would never be forgotten by the wisest. No explanation ever emerged for the dolphins' appearance on those shores, nor for that deep lingering sadness in the eyes of so many once-sleek sea acrobats which, particularly in that part of the world, had been known to chase sharks to the farthest ends of archipelagic exile, rescue children from foreign ships in distress, scratch their own backs on the spines of silent sea eggs in that tropical midday heat, and — most astonishing — balance in perfect stillness on their fins in the undulating open sea, bottlenoses stiffly pointed toward shore in upward-facing attention, when, at events of great historical moment, the anthem of national pride and independence was sung by uniformed schoolchildren at the prime minister's residence. They had faithfully guided fishermen at dusk past hordes of camera-wielding tourists out to the deepest, bluest waters where green-dreadlocked mermaids and their seaweed-bearded lovers (the older, oceanic true brethren of the Maroons) forever sang the wistful political songs they would later bequeath to the beloved dreadlocked singer who, until his untimely death some years later would, with the peerless talent bestowed upon him by the sea and the sky, sing those sunset chants of hunger, suffering, and triumph before endless mockeries of justice, with a style which would catapult both him and that green island of blue mountains into fame throughout the world which, nonetheless, would continue to insist that what the poor everywhere really needed was charity, only charity, don't you know.

The dolphins continued to suffer. The wails of their dying young could be heard over the tin roofs of those shacks in neighborhoods on the other side of the harbor, in the southwestern part of the city, and even up in the hills, in the larger homes of those who blocked their ears with mango leaves to keep out the suffering creatures' cries, and who daily told their maids not to speak amongst themselves in those spotless kitchens of such things as dying sea-mammals on the causeway and so many terrible visions of hunger and prostration before death. Three hundred dolphins arrived on Monday, by Wednesday there were close to seven hundred, and by the week's end over a thousand;

in the midst of their agony they continued to horrify curious witnesses with their grotesque dying smiles as, shrinking further into the suffocating indignity of their last hours, they dreamt still of leaping away days on the open seas where, as everyone knew, only one man had ever walked. Why the rass were they so desperately unhappy, everyone wanted to know, and why the backside had they struggled to the land's end of these particular shores? Those questions were never completely answered, Uncle McKenzie told us, even as the victims continued to wash up in horrendous numbers, continued to die, continued to decompose beneath that trenchant sun with those gruesome grimace-smiles beneath their bottlenoses. Even if they had been edible no one dared eat them, for to do so in that region would be supreme and utter blasphemy on the spirits of those deities who, even after so many years of modern building on their sacred lands, continued to appear nightly in the surrounding waters and in the hills, and who centuries ago had taught the first inhabitants of the region exactly what the sea offered and what it withheld. So that it was finally clear to all, even to the wealthy who stuffed their ears with mango leaves and studied North American TV programs in order to expand the vacancies of their own minds and lose the precious music of their accents, that without doubt the condition of the dolphins was inextricably linked to the nation's condition, which at that time (and, it seemed, forever before and since) was gripped in the stern throes of not-enough, the wretched condition the singer crooned about. A mean little thing, not-enough. But big. Nasty. Not-enough, that had crept through every tin-roofed shack, pissed its salty waste beneath ragged clotheslines, pecked at the scabby feet of bangbellied children, cutlassed off a woman's arm for her bracelet on a city bus, buried a girl at age fifteen with deep scars on her wrists and an undetected form in her belly, planted want in sixty hearts in a town of one hundred, burned to death in a rumshop a young man who in his short life had cartwheeled seven times over the taste of Irish moss, raped sixteen virgins in a neighborhood known for fierce allegiances, enticed down the narrow throat of a bewhiskered man the bitter taste of a certain drug (and thereafter his own death), rallied even the soaring black john crows to fight over those slim dungheap pickings, and frightened away the ones who, from behind the gilded window bars of their inherited hopes, at the end of those long curving driveways of their aspirations, fled in terror to the warm, palm-filled city of exiles on the northern continent, where not even those palms, though more decorous, were indigenous, and where the only dolphins to be found were those which performed in glass tanks for tourists. It was a terrible time, Uncle McKenzie told us; despite the fact that the man they called the prime minister was a noble spirit and stout-hearted, of a long line of men who had arrived in the world at birth with white hair and blue eyes which, while revealing little of their origins in Africa, yet even at that tender age had gleamed with a fierce national pride and love of the people. During the sixth week of the dolphins' visitation, his blue eyes gazing out calmly enough yet sternly at millions of television viewers one evening, he announced that enough was enough, the dolphins were obviously a sign to everyone that it was time for wide-reaching reforms, *all* of our people have to be fed, we will *not* wind up like our neighboring nations to the north and east, we'll all have to tighten our belts and share the little we've got, I don't want to hear any complaints from those of you with mango leaves stuffed in your ears, if you don't like it we've got five flights a day to that northerly city of exiles, that noxious sinkhole of traitorous Swiss-bank quislings and dictators' descendants, make your choice. Not even twelve hours were allowed to pass until dawn of the following day, when, in frenzied riotousness, those who stuffed mango leaves in their ears, along with those who someday hoped to, launched a national campaign of outrage against the dolphins and the poor who had befriended them. That, Uncle McKenzie told us, was how he first met Icilda. She was out there on the causeway on the evening of the first anti-reform protests, a young girl kneeling by the side of the road in a yellow dress, a pink bandanna on her head, scorning the clamorous reactionaries who endeavored to convince her of the wrongful actions of the prime minister, as she nuzzled against her face a dolphin dying yet struggling to give birth on that narrow shore. It was the same creature that, the week before, had with that irrepressible smile shared with her forty-plus tones of the secret dolphinic language, confirmed in those same secret tones that she and the nation's wisest should never *ever* put even the smallest amount of their trust in bakra men, confided the as yet unrevealed truth that one distant day in the future the Rastas would finally be regarded nationally with the proper reverence they deserved, and, with that disarming prescience known to southern sea mammals, assured her that the moon's reflection on night waters was of course, as always, a matchless ally in the pursuits of youthful romantic love. Enraptured by that vision of a young woman in a yellow dress kneeling with the head of that sickly dolphin in her lap by the side of the road thick with riot-noise and human greed and anger, Uncle McKenzie made his way through the protestors to she who would shortly become, and remain long after her death decades later, the woman of all his dreams. He begged for her hand which up until then had known no other man's touch, and, oh, how he'd had to convince her, he told us, and console her too in her grief after the dolphin's passing and the appearance of those five stillborn young; yet he managed to assure her that, yes, he too was pro-reform, progressive, anti-imperialist, and no, he didn't stuff his ears with mango leaves, he had no dreams of a large house at the end of a winding driveway while people suffered in silent hunger on land and dolphins died on shore, he too despised the transnationals and the inhuman global straddlers, and no, Icilda, I've never loved anyone up until now, my love, my heart, the spirits of the blue mountains were saving me and all my youth for someone like you, Icilda, Icy. To hold. To hold this way. Come. They were married one year later with the white-headed prime minister's blessings and the voice of the singer behind them. Four years later, guided by the spirits of those dolphins that appeared in their dreams in gratitude and remembered solidarity, they journeyed north to a city of steel, bridges, tunnels, black water, concrete-colored skies, and unsmiling people who raced through their days in order to die sooner, all of which, however unsettling, would grant the two some promise, an agreeable sort of happiness, and years of passage in each other's arms; during their waking hours far only in literal distance from that green island that never left them. "Home," Uncle McKenzie would say then before the grave watchful eyes of O.K. Griffith and Mr. Winston, "that still my home, you see. And I going home someday to die." Standing very still then, seeing nothing, we thought; seeing again Icilda on that distant shore, the dying sea spirit in her lap; as all of us, moved by that tale of events and places we hadn't yet known and still hoped for, sank back into our selves, holding within those singular visions which still took the immediate shape of flesh in an old man's eyes. Mr. Winston would touch him on the arm then, lightly, drawing him and all of us back to the present and Sound Hill as the light began to fail with the merest murmur about our shoulders. They would depart in silence. Even then it was apparent to us how united in soul and reach they had become, stepping out from within those twilight afterthoughts to descend further, arise ever higher and higher and *higher* into the time-fields, the caresses, the — *!!here we are, my love!!* — of ghosts.

One. Become one at last. So the words and news came down to us, over us, quickly and silently taking shape, a whispered intelligence out of that most unending of currents that first slowly and now more quickly was rushing us all on to those final events. The first of which came with a shock: that, all at once, and for some time after, we couldn't tell either of them apart from the other. It was as if, overnight, as we slept, they had traded each completely for the other. It was Mr. Winston, not Uncle McKenzie, whom we watched winter-wrapping Icilda's nine backyard fig trees, muttering all the while about the duppies them that did live pon the hill just so and the damnblasted obeah woman who did live in May Pen, thief from the people them in Mandeville, vex up a whole heap of boogayaggahs in Half Way Tree and then when you hear from the shout did die in Spanish Town with nothing but a blasted rass-goat f' come sniff up her footbottom. It was Uncle McKenzie, speaking with all the life-knowledge so sonorously contained in Mr. Winston's voice — or so we thought, their voices and faces also having somehow become each other's — who laughed out of Miss Ardelia's side porch step about how he hadn't never in his life trusted no peckerwood and how these folks up north didn't know diddly squat of what they was missin compared to what we had back home — then all at once, in self-conscious laughter, became confused between NAACP, PNP, and JLP. And then it was quite clear to us from the way that laughter eased up between them that they had discovered between themselves the still unnamed actuality of love; which, while perhaps not yet manifestly real to them except in the current-realm of dreams, had, further back in time than any of us could guess, been predetermined by that same constant pair of unseen guiding hands — both through their shared dreams of each other and by way of those spirit-linkages of the past. So that we knew the presence of their wives nightly hovered above them in munificent protection as the two of them, furtively at first, and with a hesitation formed by decades of adherence to the most championed and unquestioned conventions, began to reach out through those dreams to hold first the divined presence of the other, then the actual other; holding each other's dream-spectres and then flesh as once they had held their wives; becoming in those still hours wife and husband and lover to each other. The current of that love swiftly filled out every lonely space of the two old men's reawakened hearts, filling them with that presence they had before sensed only on the edge of a further darkness, beyond the edge of the sea, and had never questioned. The current allowed them nothing of fear or shame. For by the time their lips brushed in dreams, then across those luminous and shifting night-fields where their shared tongues and skins and even the blood beneath were the same, we knew that they had walked enough with each other along the shores of death and grief so that at last, without any great effort, they were able to read each other's desires in every shade except green, had acquired the difficult skill of summoning one another out of harrowing dreams to the calming kisses and entry of the other, and ultimately possessed no fear whatsoever of wading through each other's night rivers in search of all the untold secrets lying at rest there. It really was as if, aloft in the pursuits of those new vision-gifts, they were finally free — not of care, but of the weighted vain nuisance of hope; for by that time they knew with certainty, rather than hoped with fear, that someday they would be united in complete silence and light with their wives and each other; in that certitude knowing that they could love each other without the abstractions of hope because the gift was already theirs: there remained nothing more to hope for except the gift's expansion into their unity in death.

So watching them, dreaming them, we too learned. Learned that the hunger for those whom we love, knowingly or not, doesn't die. Doesn't die even when the spirit stoking the needing fails, or when the watching eye glimpses the ghost-warning of its own impending death. We knew that a hunger so keen as Uncle McKenzie's and Mr. Winston's could not at their time of life either die or be destroyed. In our part of that hunger and yearning, as we slept and dreamt of them and moved ourselves back and forth across the sheets pressing with our own unappeased desires so urgent and wet against the flesh, we watched them straining along the steep banks of those rivers, burying their faces without rest in all that grew there; their mouths open, then filled, heavy with each other's pulsing flesh; their wrinkled hands moist from rivers shared, as, amidst odors and essences of what only the most private inward eye reveals, they thought still of resting the head they rested on the other in the bosoms of those other two watching ghosts who met one ancient eye with still another, descending — the lover of one, the comrade of another, and friends as they had always been and would be always. There.

— So it was and would be we remembered, as our days whitened further into deep winter and the sweep of that new silence all around brought forth the events which began with the memory of the smell of curried goat in a dead woman's kitchen and would finally unite the four of them forever.

That was how it began, we remembered   Yes, right there, slowly, inevitably, the windcurrents of that time and the season carrying the predictions of the long endless winterdark to come and then the attractions of love and recollection beginning in a dead woman's curried goat across the wide and far blue sea, accompanied by the echoings of years from that place of blue mountains and trees where so many years ago a young girl in a yellow dress had knelt by the side of a road with the face of a dying sea creature in her lap: the smells of embraces and memory lifted without end over every horizon of our dreams: then the dreams of the sleeping revolving earth as the singer crooned on about the poor whose bellies could never be full especially with their hearts fed upon by those who lounged at the end of long driveways and stuffed mango leaves in their ears: they at first paying no heed, do you remember, to the miraculous arrival of dolphins upon those shores and later to the memory-scents contained in the smell of curried goat from a dead woman's kitchen carried through that spirit-force to the sleeping nostrils of Uncle McKenzie who slept in Mr.

Winston's enfolding arms, until he our Uncle awakened on that morning which would signal the beginning and end to all things, the first of which was a walk through the unfolding winter dream that led him down those icy pathways and winterquiet streets and through the frostcolored late morning out of Sound Hill and up through Baychester and the Valley and then still up and over westward to White Plains Road where the music shops and the food shops and the stores with red black and green in their windows and drawings of the Nanny and the Bogle and the UNIA man all about and with green black and gold in between lined that avenue so noisy with traffic and the grumblings of the elevated subway: and now mark that, yes, even in that coldness young men were out feeling their bones and early morning rage with each other in the streets mark too how then he Uncle McKenzie with a light step walked past them to that grocery store owned by his countryman who would sell him those two pounds of goatmeat he planned to prepare at home for them alone, the two of them, Mr. Winston and himself livingdreaming their story, yes, they dreamt, their story for all time and ever after, yet a tale of entwined remembrances, the past:

— To walk out of there, Uncle McKenzie, white of hair, tall of stance, so lately light of step and always given to that deep music of ageless mountains beating within the blood: walking, yes, still smiling within the welcome hoarfrost of that private dream, except that that day Icilda was not walking with him, she could not come in those looming moments to steer him from danger as had always been her province and willful destiny both before and after her own death, for that day the dolphins of the past were calling her back to them across the channels of memory, beckoning, urging, so that thus called, you understand, so summoned back to that suffering and to that one in particular with its dead young, she could not refuse: and forthwith journeyed back across the seas and mountains and scorpion-filled deserts to that place and hour of the protestors and again to her own youth in a yellow dress and a pink bandanna, holding once again in her lap on the narrow causeway that desolate bottlenose as she soothed the feverish sorrow plaguing the air and so could not be there, there which

would be here in this time and place when that man she had always loved now walking in a winter dream of another waiting man held always close in their love and shared waiting for death, he the aged morning walker of that day suddenly awakened out of the cycle of snowflakes kissing his face on White Plains Road to see with horror with shock:

They're killing him, Icilda

— he thought: awakening then yes to see the young men who were his countrymen two of them or no three no FOUR raining blows down upon the boy outside the music shop blaring a song of the singer, raining blows upon the boy's head, a boy no more than fifteen years old holding up his useless hands, screaming, and now how true it came to be that yes, revelation, a hungry mob is an angry mob: Icilda, he thought as they reddened the snow with their fury and rage and called him Battyman and You goddamned fucking battyman and Kill him the bloodclaat battyman because

—: oh but they must have heard something about him, you see, or perhaps they thought he was looking at them in a certain way, whatever way he was looking at them, if he was looking at all, which to them would have been that way, the way men do not, musn't look at men, that way, they'll kill you for it   or maybe who can tell, at one time in the past he might have been clad in shorts, tight shorts showing too much, too little, the wrong shirt, the walk too fast, arms too slow, eyes too wide, lips or mouth or nose or who can tell?— but in any event it was notright notright so now kill the little rass pussyhole battybwoy they said

killing him Icilda

:— he thought amidst the screams, shouts: and in that one instant he our Uncle McKenzie as we watched in our dreams and screamed for him to leave them alone, not to go near them, we screamed to him but he not hearing:— he went forward with cries/shouts/trembling rage of

Leave him alone

Why you beating him

Leave him alone

— his greatest mistake we knew as we watched and shouted and tried to reach him through the dream, pull him back: but couldn't awaken

from it ourselves as we watched dawn on Uncle McKenzie the horror that his longtime comfort with the world of ghosts who loved him had scarce prepared him for the world of the living who did not, nor for the rageworld of the young who loved the old less than they loved themselves (which they did not), having been taught one thing only which was destruction, an outcome for which they too were destined; his greatest mistake, knowing nothing of this rage until

then the noise began   filling up the whitening air   whoops shrieks frenzy   finding another source for that fear   the driving forward of it   seeing only this latest enemy   seeing in that hysteria not really him hearing only the voice forbidding   feeling the ancient shame of their bones whitening in the sun   one pushing along the other   for O violence we have done/shall do again   they thought in that screaming as their bones whitened in the sun   the howl deep within their skins   For yet might we live they thought   yes through the blood they thought   live   precious   and the sacrifice   blood and the bones   the skin   the knife for sacrifice   there

then raining blows down upon him upon the thin whiteness of his head beneath the whitening sky

so there began the red   beneath the blows and the sacrifice   darkening the skin

darkening the snow and the field of the dream suddenly so dark: seeing   now there in the red Uncle McKenzie on his knees   the goat meat fallen beneath him   the red over his eyes   the knife glittering in the red   we couldn't reach you Uncle couldn't hold you through the dream   could only see you there

falling

falling

the red over your eyes now over all our eyes too for we too were responsible: had been dreaming of safety far too long, believing ourselves safe for a time not only from death but from the self-stalking, the fear: which was to be feared not so much in the night rivers of our dreams but here: right here   always here   in our days   our violent waking days

So that it was
had always been
Red.
Then darkness.
Leaving him there.

The police were able to identify him because he always carried his Social Security card. From Sound Hill, they ascertained from his address; had living kin who did not reside in either the city or the state. Who would have to be contacted. Which O.K. Griffith did. And the victim: would have to be taken to a city hospital, the police said, since no one was able to say anything about the condition of his insurance or even if he had any. That city hospital, not far from the Pelham Bay train station, where Mr. Winston and the rest of us found him: not in a room but on a dirty stained stretcher in the emergency room because there were no rooms, you see, so many people were dying, they said, this one and that one: Don't you people know, we've got a fucking huge disease out there that's killing everyone, and then so many of these sluts coming in with their faces bashed in, goddamn dope addicts and crackheads and all these young punks too with their guts or the few brains they have left shot out, we're living in violent times, it's a violent city, we're inundated, you'll have to be patient, we'll get an intern to tend to him as soon as we can, what do you expect, a miracle? — rushing through the cold white glare of so much human misery, holding their breath as we held ours so as not to inhale those odors, piss, shit, antiseptics, blood: so as not to believe, please, that Uncle McKenzie so suddenly was going to die that way in that place he had avoided for so long while men forty and fifty years younger than he turned up there without fail and nameless in the redred on nights of the full moon, bullets deep in their brains, knives plunged up to the handle in their throats: no, not there, we said, not on that low flat white hard stained mean metal stretcher

jammed between every other and every other going on and on
down the hallway and all holding a dying hand reaching out, a
shot-up stomach, a bleeding head and Lord Lord Jesus we thought
what kind of world was this what kind and what was happening
what had been happening to us always? The entire world screaming, except for him, just laying there, eyes closed; not speaking, not
even dreaming for once; merely waiting as Mr. Winston clutched
his hands, then bent over him calling *Now you Mac;* putting his
own face next to that face. Begging between those dry pleadings,
kisses, unheard assurances, please Mac. Now Mac. Come on now,
Mac, now can you raise up, Mac, please, or can you hear Mac. It's
Win, Mac. Mac. Then we looked not at Mr. Winston but into the
eyes of those passing who had looked into his eyes looking into
the closed face of his friend and lover and saw in their eyes beginning the low dark storms of that incredulous and loathing disgust.
The bitterness of knowing yet knowing nothing, understanding
nothing beyond the storm. Then feeling our own rage. Waiting
with Mr. Winston. Seeing nothing more. Waiting.

*(Wondering later was it all part of some other dream or real. Knowing
that it was real.* Seeing him open his eyes. One time only. Filled
with that same redness that never left him. Looking out right
then almost steady at the one touching him. Both looking.
Deep. Longslow. The fearpain in the redness for a moment leaving him. Then closing his eyes again. Saying something.
Quietquiet. Low, from deep down in the red and the night river
rising. Saying, Icilda. Icilda, girl, I finish. Finish in this country,
Massa God. I finish . . . . Winston. Jesus — :

— Don't bother go on with that — the other, touching him.
Uncle McKenzie's voice coming out of him. Standing over him
next to him still touching. Not caring not mattering either who
looked or how. But then all at once couldn't find what he was

looking for behind those closed eyes. Not anymore. Not anywhere. But wait. Maybe. Maybe . . . — but no. Couldn't find it. It
was gone. All gone. What had been there. Inside those eyes.
Between the hands. Deep in the chest. The light.)

Six hours later Uncle McKenzie stopped breathing. There, amidst
the noise, in the clutter of all that stench and suffering, he just
stopped. There was no time for any of us to say or do. It happened
so very fast, was suddenly so quiet. And then, as one of us who had
maintained watch throughout the entire time there would later
report, it was in that precise moment that a very old woman who
yet somehow bore the incandescently transfigured face of a young
girl, with dirt on her knees as if she had recently been kneeling by
the side of a road, and with a pattern of wetness on the lap of her
yellow dress as if an apparition from the sea had only just lain its
head there in a struggle between birth and death, walked unseen
by all the nurses into that emergency room and over to that particular stretcher, lowered her wet, gleaming face over the face of
the man who lay there and said something to him in that moment
which caused him immediately to sit up, lower the stretcher's pro-
tective side rods, step to his feet with the renewed vigor and erect
stance of a man fifty years younger, beckon with his face newly
transfigured to Mr. Winston (watching in disbelief as the woman
also beckoned to him), grasp his hand firmly, warmly, and walk the
three of them hand in hand down the dirty passageway under the
dim fluorescent lights past the stink and noise and cries, unseen by
the nurses and out the door to where, sheathed in light beneath a
new white straw hat, waited another woman, who with that same
odd yet joyous and almost otherworldly youthful lightness in her
step, joined them — taking hold of Mr. Winston's free hand as he
continued to hold Uncle McKenzie who held also the hand of the
woman in the yellow dress as she smiled back at him and, so walking, led them all on. Farther on. And on. Walking.

The nurse was examining the body of the man on the stretcher. Then said, quietly, The patient has expired. I'm so sorry. So very very sorry. Please accept — said something else we couldn't hear. And made the sign of the cross.

Mr. Winston was found dead in his house in Sound Hill at three o'clock that afternoon. His eyes were open, gazing out intently at something which in that wider, more silent distance might have figured as a distinct and even familiar form taking shape. The gaze remained intact beneath our ministering hands. It was then that we noticed that his left hand was clenched tight shut, as if holding something both withheld and held. The balled, curled-up fist staunchly resisted our attempts to open it. It was as if, quite by a last willful effort of the heart and thereupon inevitable, what remained held so tightly within had in lasting partnership with the holder sworn that it would not ever, and could never, be removed — as if the silence out of which the grasp had been formed exceeded both within and without, on every side and for all time, the imagined silence of death.

The funerals for Uncle McKenzie and Mr. Winston were held two days later at our church up in the Valley. After the services they were laid next to their wives and each other.

Yes. We were there.

THE FINAL INNING

AND WHETHER OR NOT DUANE HAD REALLY MADE A beautiful or even fly corpse with all of his fingernails and fierce teeth intact beneath the lid of that closed coffin, and why the fuck his mother had just *had* to wear that shitcolored crushed-velvet or whatever it was tacky suit (to match her just-as-tacky crushed-velvet also shitcolored hat with that old cheap-looking St. Patrick's–green fake daffodil on it), and if it was true that Uncle Brandon McCoy had made a goddamned fool out of himself again by crying like a big old droopingass baby in front of all those people instead of acting like a grown (old broken-down) man should even in the midst of all that grief for the fallen brother, and what it was exactly somebody had said to the minister (Reverend Dr. Smalls, old pompous fire-and-brimstone drunkass) about going on and eating up all the (greasy-nasty, Cee-Cee had said) greens so that there wasn't none left for nobody, not for *nobody,* honey — when it was all over and they were all over it and just dying to get home and take off heels and pantyhose and loosen up bra-straps and whatnot, those things, they all agreed, weren't even really the issues: by then they just wanted to leave it all behind (especially what had happened in the church) and get back to where they were now, which was back in Tamara's house in that most northeastern (and inaccessible, the people who lived there cursed and praised) Bronx neighborhood, Sound Hill; in her living room, with the heat on because it had gotten even colder, hadn't it, she said, and the television on too because it always was and like always now was showing some dumbass sitcom about two high yellow girls as usual who couldn't even keep their trashy-looking hair straight, do you believe the shit they were putting on TV these days, Jacquie said, but it couldn't get no worse than that other show about that black family that was all doctors and whatnot, Cee-Cee said, cause I ain't never seen nobody like that acting like all we got is fly furniture and no problems, did you? Nicky said; and all of them, even Jacquie's husband Gregory sitting off real quiet in the corner with two-year-old Gregory Jr. asleep on his knee and the *Sports Illustrated* open on the side table in front of him, said they hadn't, and laughed. Laughter out of and into sound and pulse as sharp or strained as anything else they might be feeling or making out and maybe even that one-half of one percent better.

The sad occasion had been over, more or less, for a few hours — ever since they'd all laid Duane away in the hard late-autumn earth of St. Raymond's out by Whitestone, beneath the watchful distrusting eyes of the fastidious-when-it-came-to-Negroes groundskeeping Italians (most of whom felt they themselves had pushed *this far* and even farther into the merciful hands of the Virgin in order to escape those colored hands stretched out today in grief and unbelieving fury to the hardedged sky — would the colored people even want heaven, too, now that they'd taken over everything else?). The main after-burial get-together was still going on at Miss Geneva Mack's — in the Valley, near the church used by some Sound Hill people, where the service had taken place — but after a few too many minutes of gossip that didn't interest anybody, kids who *weren't* cute, if only you knew, Ma'am, and just about enough senior citizen smalltalk of Mylanta and bloodclots and how it would come to us all someday and Lord, what a tragedy it was that such a fine young man had met the Savior so early but he sure had gone on up to Him with a beautiful-looking coffin, praise Jesus! — the five of them plus Gregory Jr. had piled easily enough again into Gregory Sr.'s car the same way they had on the way to the church. A little respite was in order now that they had done with the St. Raymond's part of it that everybody hated but for decency's sake couldn't miss, since all present had wanted to appear duly respectful, you know, the way you should for someone like Duane whom almost everyone had loved in spite of *that* (yes, *that,* but still, you had to have some feeling for the dead, didn't you?). Last regards had been paid at the cemetery to Duane's mother and stepfather (still in a severe state of shock after what had happened); Cee-Cee and Nicky and Tamara had finally been pulled away from chatting with the reverend, who had proved inconsolable despite his drunkenness: It wasn't none of it his fault, what had happened in church, he shouldn't even worry about it, they'd said, although everyone knew that if the old alcoholic nigger had put the whiskey *behind* his shelf instead of all out front *on* it for a change none of the disgraceful shit today would have happened. Now, back in Sound Hill, they were all tired and cold and disgusted and just flat out, that was all. Tamara had put on the lima beans, Cee-Cee was helping with the rice and Jacquie was trying to season the meat in that kitchen that was looking more nasty to her today than ever before because (yes, Tamara was her friend, but, well, speak the truth before God, girl, she thought) she had seen not one but two roaches about which she would be sure to tell Gregory later. But then petty shit like that didn't matter so much now after such a sad occasion, with everybody talking and the TV blaring and the 40s of Olde English out on the living-room table and Tamara looking for her house shoes and her husband Kevin still not back with their kids Jaycee and Laneese from Mrs. Shirley's: watching football with Mrs. Shirley's Harry after the funeral, now wasn't that some shit? she said; all the others except Gregory sucked their teeth and shook their heads. The house was still too damn cold, right down there on the Sound, after all, but the principal shit was Duane and *those others* too, still on everybody's mind after what had happened.

"Cause, girl," Tamara was saying to any one of them except Gregory, popping a halfcooked lima bean into her mouth and spitting out the skin, which she never ate, into the sink, "Lemme tell you. I ain't never think I'd live to see no shit like that. You know — "

"Word. You!" Cee-Cee said, pushing Jacquie out of the way to stand in a corner over the rice. The best corner, in fact, for affecting officiousness while nudging surreptitiously out from her behind the underwear that insisted on catching up in it beneath the folds of that stiff mourning dress she hardly ever wore.

"A damn shame. That's all that was," she said and lifted the lid off the rice pot to stir the water.

"What was?" Jacquie said, swaying to nobody's rhythm. "Why you holding your face over the pot, Cee-Cee? You think we want your make-up all in the rice?"

"Bitch, don't try it. You the one" — she replaced the lid on the pot and managed easily enough to rub her backside against the stove-door handle and there, she was free again — "you the one put on so much damn make-up couldn't nobody see that pimple on your chin you so de*ter*mined to try and hide — "

"Who you calling a bitch? Me and your grandmother."

"Your funky ass. Don't be talking about my grandmother. She could — "

"Now what y'all fussing about? Tamara, this food is not even ready." Nicky strolled into the kitchen on long legs not quite hidden beneath the most elegant-looking black wool pantsuit all of them had ever seen and would have done more than kill to have. She had already had some of the Olde English, finally had found her cigarettes, and now with the contentment of the smooth dark cat that always lolled somewhere in the marshy fields of her eyes slowly began to pull in sweet soft drags of a Newport.

"I forgot his name already," Jacquie said. "After he got up there and dissed everybody I wouldn't even want to — "

"Dissed? That's what you gone call it? *Dissed?*" Cee-Cee stretched out three fingers toward Nicky's cigarette in a gimme-one gesture. "That shit wasn't even about no dissing. That was just goddamn disrespecting blasphemy, that's all. I wish it had a been me sitting up there with Duane's mother. I woulda knocked the shit outa him first and put a foot in his ass second."

"*Okay.*"

"Y'all come on and sit in the living room," Tamara said, wiping her hands on the curtains over the kitchen window. "One thing I can't stand is sitting up in the kitchen talking about dead people while food be on the stove." And I can't stand Nicky with her nasty self putting no damn cigarette ashes in my sink neither, she thought but didn't say either as she pulled one more lima bean out of the pot and this time pulled the skin off her tongue before she flicked it off into the sink.

"Y'all still going on about what happened in the church?" Gregory said, looking up from the *Sports Illustrated* and over the head of his sleeping son just long enough to give Jacquie an appreciative glance before he returned to a photograph in the magazine that had caught his eye. The look was returned with another, deeper one, which could have passed between them comfortably enough then as only one edge of that almost unbearable love she possessed not only for the man whose gaze mirrored the silent ponderings and longings of her own (and whose lashes, like the arcing hummingbirds they yearned to become in dreams, nightly fluttered over the comforts her body offered that the dreams did not) but also for their child spread in smallish sleep across her husband's broad thighs. The child did not yet bear Gregory's unmistakably solitary look, which to her eyes had always spoken either of too many winding rivers already walked by the soul or the hands' constant reaching for what the ten fingers could not provide. Any or all of it might have worried or pleased her at the same time; speculations aside, they missed the look she gave him just then. Like so many other women who knew them, distinct but distrusted, only occasionally acknowledged other versions of themselves, they rarely looked far enough into those interiors that were both theirs and hers, the here-and-always silty brew and the joy, the source and sometime shadows of which none of them (through choice or necessity or the simple desire for safety, however they imagined it) had ever plumbed, had ever wanted to plumb. Their attention for the moment was anyway, as almost always, scattered: between the TV (they turned it off, they wanted music, it would go better with the Olde English) and Cee-Cee's Don't be mean girl, I gave you five cigarettes last week to Nicky's I know you did cause I gave you *six* the week before so now I guess you could go out and get you a pack, but then finally handing one over (Cee-Cee didn't never buy no cigarettes but still that was one of her main home girls), and Tamara putting on some Aretha and doing a jerky, rhythmless "white girl" dance to the first song that made them all laugh again, none of them had time to notice the new little things like that distant ticking sound in Gregory's voice when he spoke, or how hard up tighttight his right hand was gripping his little boy's small soft baby-shoulder.

"Lemme take him, Greg," Jacquie said. "I need to put his ass in the bed."

"You could put him right upstairs, girl," Tamara said. "Ooh, I love this song!"

"He all right. I got him," Gregory said, shifting thighs.

"Anyway, like I was saying," Cee-Cee said, exhaling a cloud of smoke and rolling her head back to rest it on the back of the couch where the three of them sat across from Gregory — Tamara was dancing — "I ain't never seen no shit like that neither. All in the church! And you know Duane's mother was through."

"Not just his mother," Jacquie said. "You ain't see Mr. Jackson?"

"I did," Tamara said.

"We *all* did, honey," Cee-Cee said. (The cigarette was sweet, the smoke was floating over her tongue, and *Breathe it in,* she thought, just like:) "That old man got up and started *screaming,* honey. 'You will not say these things about my son! You will leave this church now! Get out of God's house!' *Hon*ey . . . ?" She raised her head and looked out at them with both arms stretched out along the sofa back — the easy, lazy stance they all associated with her.

"I thought I was gone fall out myself," she said.

"We all was," Tamara said, shaking on to the chorus. "How could you not? I mean, now, that was wrong — "

"Damn right."

" — it was, you know? I mean now how you gone sit up in church at somebody's goddamn funeral and bring out all kindsa shit — "

"That probably ain't even true," Jacquie said.

"Well, I don't know about all that. But I'm saying how you gone get up there and do that shit when ain't nobody even want your white-looking ass up there in the first place?"

"He wasn't white," Gregory said. "The dude that got up and spoke? He wasn't no white. But I wish y'all would *stop* — "

"Lookded white to me," Cee-Cee said, chugging.

"Aw, girl, he did not. You gone sit there black as me and tell me you can't tell a — a half-breed when you see one? Come *on,*" Tamara said. She came and sat down on the floor next to Jacquie and looked up briefly at Nicky, who the entire time had remained silent and still, on her second glass.

"Hmmph. Half-breed. Somebody's business." Cee-Cee pronounced the words with particular contempt, as if describing someone who habitually shit on the only good side of his mother's bed. "See . . . that's why. Breeding, honey. Wouldn't no real black man do some shit like that."

"I don't know," Jacquie said. "A whole bunch of them stood up when he asked everybody to stand."

"Yeah," Tamara said. "The faggots did."

"Well, they was all faggots."

"Like I said," Cee-Cee came in again, "wouldn't no *real* black . . . "

"On *that* side of the church," Tamara said. "In the back, thank God. All sitting in a group. You see that shit?"

"You know we did," Cee-Cee said, putting out the cigarette.

"Faggots and bulldaggers. Ain't that some shit? With their hair all shaved off and zigzagged and earrings and nose rings — "

"Nasty. Probably all boggered up."

"That's how that shit spreads," Cee-Cee said.

"Girl . . . "

" — and *carrying* on — "

"Why y'all gotta keep talking about it?" Gregory said, shifting again and fastening his grip on his son and again staring down and out at that something anything not there but there.

"Why not? A goddamn freak show," Cee-Cee said, leaning forward. She snatched another cigarette out of Nicky's pack on the table, lit it that fast and exhaled two river-colored smoke streams from angry nostrils.

"Why the fuck not?" she asked again, turning to Gregory and then away and over to Tamara stretching her legs out on the rug. Now it was her turn for the Olde English. Aretha was crooning out that very oldie "Who's Zoomin Who?" and Tamara's lips were there with her and her hips too, lacking the grace but filled with the intent.

"It wasn't all that, Cee-Cee. You got a real problem when it comes to . . . " It was the first time Nicky had spoken since they had left the kitchen. The marshes in her eyes had filled with the afternoon light of that other place known only to her: the heavy sunset color of drowned fields, a small space of enclosed time hours, even light-years, beyond the chilly Sound Hill late afternoon.

"It wasn't even all that," she said.

"What you mean?" Cee-Cee said.

"I *mean,* you got a problem."

"What kinda problem?"

All eyes in the room drove toward the marshes and stopped there.

"I mean . . . like, you . . . — you don't like them."

"Them who?"

"You . . . well . . . umh . . . homos." (But oh no, now, she thought, she could be stronger than that with the Olde English. Braver and maybe even —)

"*Gay* people," she said.

"Well — " Cee-Cee was facing the marshes directly. They were deeper than they had ever appeared before. They had in fact, without warning or comfort, given way to untracked country which, even for those who thought (or had dared to think) they had always known the easiest way in — that simple road, the things you said or didn't, the half-smiles and the sliding glances, right? — confounded even the most scrupulous eye on the way back out into the farther brown that signaled both the marshes' end and the deeper waters' beginning.

"Well, no, I guess I don't — " (but it was all getting in her way, all around. Was that why her own voice suddenly sounded so — ? And what was there just beyond those marsh-reeds pulling her out into — ? The quick chill before that unknown whatever, nothing else and nothing noble, either, hurled her back onto firmer ground) " — like no fucking faggots, girlfriend. Not up in no damn *church*. Not all up in somebody's goddamn funeral. Not calling nobody out when . . . — you acting like there's something to like. You gone sit up here in this house in Sound Hill with Duane dead and buried over in St. Raymond's and his mother and Mr. Jackson over in Co-Op — "

"I know where we at."

"Ooh, yeah, Cee-Cee, Nicky *knows* where she at," Jacquie said and poked Nicky in the ribs, cause why we gotta go into all this now? she thought, feeling suddenly the surge of an unwelcome river rising up around their feet. The other woman smiled and slapped away her hand but they all knew that meant nothing. "Y'all know Miss Nicky ain't got just one but *two* men up on Gun Hill Road . . ."

"You stinking ho," Nicky said, almost laughing. "Liar!"

" — one name Billy and the other this Puerto Rican dude who ain't got shit in his pants to satisfy nobody — you know them Ricans just swear they all that" — they were all laughing easily enough now and the two were half-wrestling where they sat until Nicky let out a scream of half-real enough-now as Jacquie pulled at the weave that had cost eighty-five dollars at Jonay's up on White Plains Road and which, even in play, she wasn't about to have anybody mess up after the rain that afternoon had almost reclaimed it for free.

"Liar. Liar." (Straightening up and straightening out the hair, and Jacquie smiling in a relief wide enough for all: the river had returned to its proper place, wouldn't rise up and.) "You one ho and a half, honey. You gone go and bring in all you *think* you know about my business — "

"You said it wasn't true. Don't want nobody to talk about your business, baby? Don't have none, then."

"Like you."

"May-be," Cee-Cee came in again. "But I'ma tell y'all one thing. When I die ain't *nobody*" — she leaned forward suddenly, the lioness in her jaw — "ain't nobody gonna drag my shit all out in the street in no church. You know what I mean?"

"Not like how they did Duane, you mean," Nicky said. "Poor old Duane," she said, more quietly.

"Word! And you know" — Cee-Cee lowered her voice to the confidential tone — "I got to say, when he got up there and started to speak I got scared. I'm telling y'all, I thought I was gonna pee on my dress."

"Wouldn't be the first time," Jacquie said.

"Shut up."

"What you was scared of? That one of em was gone jump up and bite you?" Nicky snorted.

"On the titties, probably," Jacquie said and laughed over in Gregory's direction. He returned a weak smile. "So put on some Luther 'ready, Tamara. I don't want to hear no more 'retha's old fat ass."

"I was just gone do that."

"I knew they wasn't gone *bite* me," Cee-Cee was going on. "But I'm saying — I'm saying — "

"You thought Duane's mother was gone get up there and smack the shit outa him," Jacquie helped.

"Exactly. You said it!"

"Well, she didn't."

"Nope. Just sat there screaming and crying."

"So did everybody else," Tamara said.

"Why y'all gotta keep going on and on about this damn funeral?" Gregory put in again. "I just can't stand — "

"Aw, shut up. Your own Aunt Hattie almost had a damn heart attack."

"That's cause she ain't used to people talking about — talking about — "

"Faggots," Tamara helped this time. Luther's croons did not quite cover Nicky's and Gregory's flinches.

"Faggots." He heard the word —

(— yes, and felt it as it flew against his cheek as he sat there almost but not quite motionless, holding his son: holding him *faggots* and caressing him the word searing his flesh and thinking)

(: — again? thinking but didn't want to now oh no but yes of those places: parks, alleyways, redlit (bloodlit) bars: fuckrooms/darkrooms and those piss-streets he knew had known and: but no. Hadn't been him there. Had never been him among the ghosts and the searchers and the lonelyones, walking: looking, stroking and sliding, taking in; going in *now give it to me tight tighttight*: — never him back there but somebody else   one of the ghosts: :a spirit: :a dream or someotherbody fucking else there *lonely* and so he? the someotherbody sucking a pair of thighs or a bootstrap with lace so that he? — had wanted *remember aw shit now* to go down to that part the belly or the *aw yes* and travel it, Jesus: hold it or him the whole thing body and go to the feeling, Jesus: kissing and stroking and holding and take it and *aw fuck Jesus yes* and * * *: — *faggots* but naw don't be calling them that now naw but okay *sucker* and *punk* call them that; wandering again on those streets with the the the the: *Faggots.* He. Who had been unhappy and. Had wanted to wander, kiss manflesh. Find. Jacquie *but can't tell Jacquie.* — Wandering again and *he'd been so scared!* because yup one time he had kinda sorta without words told Duane about all of it, everything, parks, bathrooms, movies and the: — Duane who had understoood kind of, Duane like a brother down homie who wouldn't never say nothing to nobody, DuaneDuane dead now and — so now? he being Gregory who could? or couldn't go on with this kinda shit much more Jacquie   could? or couldn't lie much longer Jacquie   or keep on pretending to want to be with her *like that* when no he didn't really want to and honest to God one time thinking about Duane and *notsafe* and at the funeral shit-scared cause maybe one of them would have *known* or thought maybe could tell? he Gregory was a little *that way*, was close to them. Close to them, living as he did up there in Co-Op City nearby Sound Hill and Baychester and Gun Hill with a family but who still no goddamnit fuck it all would not couldn't ever stick up for their faggot asses nor get into it when the homies was beating up on them. Would not (couldn't) claim his hidden name among them and the shared desire, anger, simply to be allowed to live and be: not near his family, he thought; not with them, he thought. Holding his little baby boy. Jacquie nearby. Not with them. Never.)

"You see what I mean?" Jacquie was saying. "You could talk to the nigger til you dead in the face and he just go right on acting like he don't hear nobody." Her tone was the betty's outer crust firm to the touch but almost all of them knew where the goodfilling sweetsweet lay beneath it.

"He just sad, that's all," Cee-Cee said.

"No, he ain't sad, he sorry. Greg, answer Tamara. Did you know Duane was funny?"

"What?"

"Did you know Duane was a faggot, Greg?" Tamara asked him herself. "Cause — I swear to God, y'all, I ain't know til now. To*day*. You hear me?"

"Might not be true," Jacquie said.

"Oh, girl, it's true," Cee-Cee said. "And Tamara, you knew. No, don't open up your face to say nothing, girl! How you gone sit up there and say you ain't know when you living right here and Duane and his mother and Mr. Jackson used to come over here almost every week for Friday dinner — "

"*Used* to."

"Used to, could've, was gonna — but they did, right? — and you *used to* go with em up to Holy Rosary Church on Sunday and then y'all would come back here and hang out and whatnot

— don't tell me, girl, I know! — and him sitting up in here at your table switching his ass round the house helping you *dec*orate and shit and watching him swing them earrings and carrying on talking about going down to D.C. for some march and shit and all a that and you gone sit up here and tell me you ain't know? Come *on,* now. You woulda been blind if you didn't."

"Word," Jacquie said. "She got a point, T. Plus — "

" — Or stupid." Cee-Cee was not through. "I know you ain't stupid and you ain't blind neither so how the fuck you gone sit up here and say you ain't know?"

"Well . . . dag, Cee-Cee. He ain't never *told* me."

"That was one fine-ass nigger, too, girl," Jacquie said, glancing over at Gregory, but that was all right — he was staring out the window. Another light rain had begun to fall. "And had somebody on him," she added in a lower voice.

"I know. He ain't never *tell* nobody. But — "

"That's a lie, Cee-Cee. He told me," Nicky broke in.

"Told *you?* When?"

(Yes, he thought, the God's honest truth, he had told Nicky, but why? did you have to tell her or anybody up here Duane? why? couldn't you keep it downtown with all them downtown faggots (— :don't call them that: —) that came up to the funeral? why?)

(— But had *had* to, Duane had said: They were all his family and friends, weren't they? Had always loved him (they said), would always care for him (they said), wouldn't they? Hadn't become like whities who dissed their own at the drop of a hat, had they? Ooh but they didn't want nobody to know you had it, Duane. When they heard you had it said Yup serves his ass right cause you *know* he got it from hanging out with them nasty old white boys Village faggots downtown too much and: that's why you was *funny* they said. Even now they won't stop talking about it and Nicky was saying —)

"Yes, he did. Said he thought his mother mighta said something. Yes, he did. Coupla months ago. Oh yes he did."

"You lying!" Tamara said.

"Girl, you ever see me up in here lying?"

"His *moth*er? Ain't that some shit? I ain't even know she knew!"

"Hell yeah she knew." Nicky turned toward her cigarettes, lit one and sat back, closing her eyes for a moment. The Olde English had begun to feel reckless in her veins, as it had in everybody's.

"She just didn't want to say nothing, that's all," she said.

"Um-hmm. But see — I'm sorry — I can't blame her," Tamara said.

"I can."

"What you mean?" Cee-Cee said. Luther was still singing.

Nicky's eyes opened again and turned — flickered, ever so slightly — toward Gregory. The marshes were black as the night now descending, revealing only the shape of small scurrying things before the moon's glide.

"Because" — (her voice soft as the marsh-darkness he didn't turn his head to see, shimmying out toward him as if seeking a partner for that step-and-feint they might both have recognized on some other night — the most elusive, most interlocking dance of all) " — because, y'all . . . — they was gone bury him with — with a *lie*. Can you imagine?"

"Imagine what, girl?" Tamara said.

"She bugging," Cee-Cee said — but she was sitting very still.

"Naw, I ain't bugging. I know just what I'm saying. It's like — he lived his whole life — . . . see, y'all don't know, y'all didn't know Duane the way I knew him."

For the first time Gregory turned toward the marshes and felt their sweep of memory and night-knowledge shawl down over him through the silence. Luther sang no more.

" — the way he used to talk about how hard it was being so — outside the family and everything — "

"What you mean?" The new anxiety in Cee-Cee's voice could have built easily enough to agony someplace else: the simple shame of crucial words unspoken, the fearlatch left undone. He heard with them and knew — or thought he knew.

"What you saying, Nicky?" Cee-Cee went on and was leaning forward, almost on her feet. "He wasn't outside the family. All them people — his mother and Mr. Jackson and his Aunt Gracie and Sheila — that girl that got pregnant with Marcus — "

"She did? Get outa here."

" — they all loved him," Cee-Cee would not stop. "How you gone say he was outside the family when you saw the way everybody was crying and carrying on when they brought him in? Does that sound like somebody outside the family to you? Does it, Tamara?"

Tamara remained silent, a headshake saying neither yes nor no.

"Does it, Greg?"

(— holding his son verytight on his lap, tighttight like back in the church, and sitting, staring, at that too-shiny coffin; he, sitting there senseless, staring but not believing (no!) that what had been Duane was *in there* ninety pounds lighter than what Duane had used to be: that ain't even you in there, he had thought, O my God: not even no you with all them purple marks on your face (:the coffin had been closed:) and your hands with them purple marks on them and up on your chest too O my God Duane even on your eyes and in your mouth and you skinny like a damn rail with your hair all funny too (chemotherapy, radiation, drugs: had made what had been hair into — *that?*) O my God Duane: remembering and holding still on his lap tighttight his son   not even you   *wasn't even no you* he had thought

— Jacquie's shoulder pressed tight into him but she wouldn't cry, he'd thought, she wasn't no crying type; knowing he would much later. Yes, God. With his face pressed into that warm hot full space between her breasts, sobbing like a damn baby: that wasn't no Duane, he had half-wept silently at the cemetery into her softwarm body, Duane didn't die he didn't, just like Duane's mother screaming MY BABY MY BABY in the church and carrying on with all them others screaming *No, Jesus* to Jesus who didn't never listen. All of them sitting up and frozen, hands flying up to heaven when it had happened. The faggot)

" — got up outa his place, honey," Tamara was saying.

(— *his place* in the back where all of them had been asked (or no, told) to sit and who invited them anyway? Jacquie had asked him later but he couldn't answer that: wondering if the *I don't know* in his eyes behind the grief and the pain and so much else she didn't have no idea about had been good enough for her. But then it was like the faggot who had been crying with the rest of them had looked dead straight at him Gregory sitting there holding his son on his lap next to that strong-looking serious woman Jacquie his wife; had been as if the faggot had recognized something or maybe Duane had told him something about the men, Duane, about the blackmen and the brownmen and the whitemen who had done him, Gregory, shared fuckheat and wanting-someone-for-whatever-heat in all them dark places (:holding his son tight, tighttight Don't hold me so tight, Daddy, Greggie Jr. had cried out over the cries of the women with the sound of that light autumn rain falling over the church:) — had the faggot walking up there to the pulpit seen that in his eyes? the wanting and the searching and the? seen it? and gone on to push aside the minister and in his black leather jacket and jeans and boots wearing goddamn Lord Jesus not one earring but four and looking out at him and everybody past the minister who began to shout Sit down boy this is a funeral where you think you at as he the faggot began to say)

" 'You're killing us! With this silence! You won't stop, you keep on killing us!' " Tamara said, almost laughing, imitating —

(— just like that he thought, seeing it yet again, still holding his son tighttight: the one they had called a halfbreed, light-skinned, who even talked white like them trying-to-be-white downtown niggers on the West Side and the East Side and in the Village, that one: starting to shout from the pulpit with his back turned to the choir and all eyes looking at him in had it been disbelief? disgust? hate? or the rage of *We oughta kill that fucking faggot right now. Kill his motherfucking faggot ass. Outside the church or in it. Right here. Anywhere.* Or had those downturned mouths and pressed lips finally been feeling with the outrage and hatredscorn that more unavoidable discharge of loss: the need to spew out with the screams and shouts what the hands and heart couldn't contain, the eyes not witness and live: that their very same adored Duane Taylor Clayton Ross was laying up there with his hands you couldn't see folded over his chest all hidden beneath the wood and flowers and his mother and stepfather screaming over him and screaming even more when the faggot began to shout and you could see them everybody going from one to the other)

the faggot remember (:don't call him that:)	*the others: everybody*
and my name *(then louder)* my name is JAMES MITCHELL SCROGGINS and no you won't make me SHUT UP cause I'm PROUD to be here today as a GAY friend of DUANE'S and a *(shouting over the rage)* HUMAN BEING GODDAMNIT just like DUANE WAS TOO and now why won't you SAY IT	They, thinking: everybody yes with hands up in the air over hats and balding heads; hands fluttering to the top of the church and O my God Lord Sweet Jesus what is happening God who is this boy standing up there where's the minister well why don't you stop him what kinda going on is that and (faggot shit: growls: sissy

he died of AIDS of AIDS (*Lord God the screaming remember how their eyes looked everybody shouting* SIT DOWN WHERE YOU THINK YOU AT SIT DOWN) say it AIDS we all KNOW IT because I know some of you know I HAVE THIS DISEASE TOO and I took care of him so I know many of you KNOW ME and what you're doing today is WRONG WRONG Duane wasn't ASHAMED of it either but all of you people YOU'RE KILLING US you won't STOP you keep right on KILLING US like you didn't even want us to come today to SAY GOODBYE to our friend our LOVER and then we came but you made us wait out in the COLD RAIN and then SIT WAY IN THE BACK BACK OF THE CHURCH how can you KEEP ON DOING THIS when is it going to STOP now how can you bury him and say you LOVE HIM and not say one word about how HE LOVED

shit: abomination: growls) O Jesus Jesus Jesus! No my son ain't no homosexual no my cousin ain't no faggot no my nephew didn't have no damn AIDS the devil's disease don't you say that in this church and O you you filthy: — and the screaming and the children Mommy who's that man and look: O God Almighty the women the ladies crying and the men their nostrils flaring and saying muttering growling We should kick his motherfucking mulatto-looking ass and getting ready to do it too: but then you could see some people thinking from what you could see in their eyes the way their heads nodded soft and slow and the ladies' dark eyes so dark revealing that way showing so much so little under those tacky hats their eyes saying only in part You speak the truth up there boy but O God O Jesus but still you speak it all the same because it's all true all of it: under three hats three ladies in particular nodding Yeah

OTHER MEN   he loved all of us and WE LOVED HIM yes he had AIDS   it KILLED HIM   we us here now we should SAY IT   SAY IT   you're trying to IN him I'm bringing him OUT again for God's sake please I'm ask-ing you for once won't you just SAY IT   SAY IT

The faggot continuing   Jesus

— I want all of you now who were proud of Duane as a proud out open GAY MAN to stand up WITH ME STAND for a moment of silence STAND

we sure do know how he died but ain't nobody saying nothing cept "a long illness" and that boy is right rightright: could even be my grandson my godson or: but something and no it can't keep going on because He the One knows don't He: knows the truth about all of it and if we sitting right here with the dead boy's mama and can't even speak the truth now so damn late in the day when are we ever gone speak it and now just think think about it what in the hell kinda going on is that?

He had said

Stand

(the last inning   the inning was over)

"Yes, he did, honey," Tamara was saying — and every face there was attendant, looking or unwilling to look into that slow yet sudden shock of memory. "Asked us all to stand *up*. In the church. 'Which one a y'all *proud* a him? Stand up!' "

(— and everybody back there in pain, he thought. Crying. Eyes closed. Hurt by the truth. The *truth* truth. Couldn't take it. Not about nobody like you Duane. They all could take the truth about everything else but: about knocked-up teenagers, crack-head sons, numbers-running uncles, raped nieces, drive-by shootings, mixed-race marriages, retarded cousins, rat-filled projects, shitbigoted Koreans, pigfaced skinheads, African famines, Chinese massacres, psycho Jamaicans, right-wing terrorists, sellout nigger judges, even white-trash serial killers — but not about nobody they cared about supposed to be black and strong like you was Duane but with that faggot shit: what to them was whitefolks shit, another sick nasty fuckedup white thing like that nasty old AIDS, just like nasty whitefolks, not for no black man we know and Jesus have mercy Jesus don't want to talk about it never. Not to kiss another man, rock to slow dreams between his hips. Lay across his dusky thighs, smell his dusk, his musky parts in the hands; a palm to those musk-dusky parts moistened by the mouth. Not to love nor touch nor hold nor look him in the face and *see*. Never. Not one of our own. Not in the church. Too many rivers to cross. And specially not one a *them* telling your business about how he *loved* you and how you had *it* and how Jesus Savior he *had it* too. Couldn't take it. *I* couldn't take it, Duane. Can't.)

"I can't neither, Tamara," Jacquie was saying — a hint of that something of outrage or shame clouding into the storm in all their eyes that was now descending not as a cool easing rain but as that same old and loathsome bitter ash, weed: what would linger there long after the storm's eye and the parched brown field always beneath it, always so untended, had gone. It was there, from within those separate and gathered storms and the ash, that they sensed what she, out of that silence, suddenly knew — that he whom she loved, still holding their son on his broad lap, was (but for how long? and why?) in flight heavy with purpose and sadness away from her — from all of them.

(— because the faggot had wanted to show out, that was all, he thought: say No, *This* was Du-ane who died a *that thing*. That thing he Gregory knew he didn't have. *Did not have it* —)

" — so then, y'all," Nicky's voice, still soft, "see, Jimmy went back — "

"*Jimmy!* Jimmy!" Cee-Cee and Tamara shouted at the same time. "You — you know him?"

"Jimmy. James Mitchell Scroggins. Who got up. Yeah, Jimmy. I know him" — so softly, like music! — and looking straight at him. Penetrating, parting him. His hands on his son. Tighttight.

"How'd *you* know him?" Jacquie asked, moving her feet back. The river was rising again.

The other woman didn't answer. Her eyelids were drooping down. She settled herself back on the sofa. Stretched out her legs again as if the living room had once more become that which it could no longer be — comfortable, that was all, with nothing more than the smell of cooking rice and lima beans drifting in to them from the kitchen.

"I don't think y'all really want to know," she said from the twilight. "Do y'all?"

"Don't play, girl. Say what you got to say."

So alongside or even above their pursuit of something reckless, aloft, she spoke. "He used to be over there all the time," she said, very softly.

"Who? Not — "

"Jimmy. James."

"Over in — "

"Duane's apartment, Jacquie. Right on over there in Co-Op. The same one."

(Hearing the tiredness in her voice, he thought. Thinking as she was of that time of catheters and blood and —)

"He used to go over there, you mean?" It was Cee-Cee again, beginning to grasp the vaguest sense of it except for what was passing in silence between Nicky and the man seated there holding so tighttight his child-son on his lap: understanding maybe even the heavy steps behind the silence cast over what did not fit, what could not ever be imagined to fit, there.

"I guess" — Nicky, sitting up with that startling abruptness they would all remember later; Nicky all at once fierce; the marshes afire, the dry storm ignited, swirled into their midst — "I guess if y'all had gone over there more often y'all woulda seen him. Y'all woulda seen him holding Duane up in his arms like he was a little baby or I don't know what. Kissing up on him even with them purple spots all on his face. Telling him he loved him, he loved him so much and all kindsa shit. Wiping the shit outa his ass — "

(Holding his son. But Jesus don't let her go off on them. Jacquie getting ready to get up and *sit down Jacquie* and Tamara looking like she want to curse somebody out now please Nicky don't say no more girl)

"Nicky." Tamara's voice, not-calm-but-calm, crackling the incipient warning ice. "Don't be talking that kinda shit in here, girl. You see we all just come from a funeral and I don't *think* — "

" — and him holding him" — implacable, in the deep river dark now beyond the marshes — " — holding him, Tamara — where you going, Jacquie?"

"You see we got food on the stove, don't you? Kevin and them'll be back soon from — "

"Sit your behind down." More than the hint of a snarl.

"Girl . . . see, now, I know you must be bugging. This ain't even your damn — "

"*Sit down.*" Leaning forward very far; the eyes very bright; the storm-fire running wild. "Y'all don't want to hear it. We sitting up in here talking about faggots this and faggots that. Talking shit. Tamara, don't you open up your face to say nothing to me."

"I ain't say shit to you. But I'ma tell you now — "

(Holding him. Verytight. Tighttight.)

"You ain't gone tell me nothing. Y'all can't say shit to me cause — word, the whole time Duane was sick I ain't never seen not *one* a y'all up in his house. Not to stop by and visit. Not even to call. So now y'all can sit up in here talking about faggot so-and-so but when the shit was down y'all couldn't even *visit* the mother-fucker. I ain't never seen not *one* a y'all. Not one!"

"Hold on, girl!"

"I don't know who she think she talking to like she crazy. She — "

"You, Cee-Cee." Nicky got up to stand over her. The other woman's angry face didn't turn away from the possible smack it anticipated — if smack were to come, it would be easier to take than that acid-wash of the truth, the little jump-up truths or the greater wordless one, from which it had already turned long ago like the rest of them.

"I'm talking to you. And you, Tamara. And you, Jacquie."

"Don't put me in it."

"*In* it? You already in it. You don't even know how much you in it." Not looking at him. "You just as bad as everybody else, running your mouth *after* he's dead talking bout his *life*style and carrying on, but word, Jacquie, I ain't never seen your black ass neither when he had to have that old nasty catheter up in his chest. Y'all can talk a whole lotta shit, but what the fuck y'all really know about faggots? You ever kiss one?"

"Nicky!" But too late. Much too late. She had jumped way past what they would have once called their own innocence. It was only then that they saw that, like all those others who inhabited their eyes, she had in fact never been innocent, had never had any use for it, as, differently, they had never been either but did. They couldn't pull her back now, or even — especially — themselves.

"I'm telling y'all now" — swaying over Cee-Cee — " — y'all don't know nothing cause y'all didn't wanna know. I was going up there every day. Oh yes I was. Every damn day and I saw what y'all so busy calling faggots." Not looking at him. "Taking

care a him. Jimmy. Cause didn't nobody else do it. Not even —
not even his *mother*."

"Nicky — "

"Not even that bitch. You know she came by there two
days one time and ain't never come back. And Mr. Jackson ain't
never come. Guess maybe they couldn't take looking at all them
faggots."

"Nicky . . . "

"Reverend Smalls didn't neither. Miss Cee-Cee, where was
you at that whole time?"

(Her power. Fascinating him. Terrifying him. He couldn't
speak. Could only stare the way he had stared in church. But now
even his face was gone. He had left only a pair of hands to hold
on to things, a clenched asshole to relieve the icy lead in his bow-
els, a pair of legs with which he could run. Runrun away from
her voice saying)

" — so don't say shit, Jacquie, cause I *heard* Duane say —
Tamara, don't you walk outa here!"

"I ain't going no place, girl. But you are."

"You damn right. When I get ready. You listen. I heard him
say, on his *death*bed, 'Nicky girl, don't let Mama and them tell no
lies. They gone try to change it and say I died a something else. I
know she gone try cover it up,' he said. And she did. Everybody
did, tried to, til the one y'all keep calling the faggot, who got a
name, by the way, in case y'all forgot, his name is Jimmy, James M.
Scroggins — "

Tamara had already retrieved Nicky's coat from the hall
closet and then that fast (not hardly fast enough, they would say
later) was in front of her with it and then — since even that didn't
work — thrust it full force into those furious arms and jerked her
own head back toward the front door.

"You got five seconds to get outa here," she said.

"Or what? You gone throw me out? Bitch, ain't nobody

scared a you. Just cause *your* man fucks every ho up and down the Valley — "

"Get out! Get the fuck out!" — and there would have been a fight then for real if Cee-Cee hadn't sprung up and separated them and with Jacquie's help (who hadn't wanted to go near the crazy bitch, she would say later, but she hadn't been able to stand one more minute of all that goddamned cursing in front of her baby boy and her husband) got her to the front door and out into the dark cold Sound Hill evening with that constant breeze off the Sound more chilly tonight that carried her words down to Noah Harris' and O.K. Griffith's and the Walkers and the Goodmans and God knows even as far away as Pelham Parkway and Baychester: just get that lowclass uglymouthed bitch the fuck outa my house, Tamara was screaming, with Gregory Jr. awakened by all the commotion crying Mommy and then Daddy and Jacquie screaming back Shut up at the baby because Nicky had almost punched her in the mouth on the way out, shouting as she went that didn't none of them know what a *real* faggot was or a real man neither since it was what they'd called the faggots who'd kept Duane alive as long as they had, and y'all buncha bitches was as bad as the worst kinda crackers, and now quiet as y'all wanted to keep it (except there, for so many curious faces had begun to peek out from behind curtains and from over awnings along Sound Hill Avenue) everybody in Sound Hill *and* Baychester *and* the Valley knew Tamara's Kevin had picked up that nasty VD last summer from that old broken-toothed crackhead Jamaican ho up on White Plains Road, and wasn't it true that Cee-Cee's brother Jervis had gotten another one a them Puerto Rican bitches pregnant, cause everybody knew that yellow nigger didn't never date no black girl, and all a that wasn't even the real shit to what she *could* say but she knew at least one person there had loved Duane and anyway she had promised the dead she wouldn't never tell nobody's secret that shouldn't be told — looking back at Gregory once more with a last fire which scorched him to crucible ash on the spot, a moment of fiery intelligence from which he would never, for the rest of his nights and days in and out of that company and others, recover. It was only after they closed the door on all that outrage and pain (and then became aware of their own, gliding up the smooth back of their necks, gathering spit at the swallow-point in their throats, bristling on to the ever-so-delicate eyebrow's curve) that they realized that what could serve as distraction-relief and the greatest tragedy of all had actually occurred: the lima beans had burnt black, what had been the rice had scorched, and not two but three enormous roaches had gotten into the meat and ruined it, ruined it, ruined it, Tamara began to cry, her sisters standing all around with their faces hidden within those sudden useless cages of their hands — a flock of fragile birds clustered for safety beneath that lingering storm and every other yet to come, descending.

— Up, upup the stairs. Feeling all the light and shadow in the universe flying about him; holding onto his baby boy who had fallen asleep again on his shoulder at the end of all *that;* nobody wanting to mention Duane's name; nobody wanting to follow up on what had been said; nobody wanting to — ; then he had slipped away with his child and begun to climb the stairs, *time to put my baby boy to bed for real* he'd thought and would do now *cause I can do that much and maybe even a whole lot more,* he'd thought, *I got that kinda courage, enough for everybody* — now at the top of the stairs, almost believing his own nervechatter as he thought again of how that night — fuck yes, that night — he would nuzzle into that space always there between her breasts: always there warm, rich, deep, for him, he thought; where he could without fail find just enough of himself and know that she would always offer that shared part of the inner life to him without complaint or anger, without inquiry, without demanding too hard what she still thought he, even as far as the sheathed truth stripped naked and lean, could give: once somebody gave up their soul to you, he thought, you could always go back to that part of them where it was safe. That was true, he thought, opening the guest bedroom door, feeling his child pressing into him; that space would always be there for that smaller version of himself, he thought, prayed, and it was, at least tonight, wasn't it? — smiling that not happy but weary smile as he listened to Jacquie and the others downstairs fussing; thanking something deep within himself for still being able to feel within and without that no-questions part of her, as he felt within once more the rise of the stranger, the he-without-face or name, placeless, loose, as the grief began to settle over him again: for Duane; grief for whom he had loved, he thought, remembering, grief. . . . For all of them.

Duane who was with him now. Scolding him. Hovering. Admonishing him as he lay the sleeping child down on the star-patterned quilt made by Tamara's Aunt Gannell. His right hand beginning to stroke his baby's sleeping cheek as, lowering his face to that other, his left hand folded the broad blue quilt-thickness over the child, who smiled just then as if even from so far away in that dream-forest of tall dandelions through which he was now walking with two tiger-mamas, he felt the long passionate pro-tective kiss his father's mouth and eyes and entire body bestowed upon him. *With him now:* that presence, you, Duane? — that (he couldn't be imagining it, he thought) put a consoling arm about him. *But don't worry,* he mouthed out soundlessly to the darkness, *I ain't gone bring home nothing to make her sick, Duane.* Those deeper eyes watching him in the dark; admonishing, sorrowful. *Aw shit, Duane, you know I just let em suck on me a little, no more. Well no the truth like you know sometimes a whole lot more.* Lowering his eyes before the ghost or whatever it was watching, waiting; then bend-ing over his son whom he knew then more than ever he would defend from everything. Everything, Duane. Even you. You the dead and. . . . But now too much to remember, he thought, too many names, faces, things to take in, forget, release . . . so go on now. Leave. Go on, now, get out!. . . And then the thing, whatever it was or once had been, sorrowful, longing, mute and invisible as every other fallen body in that infinite outer and inner world, vanished into the darkness, and with that vanishing he knew it would appear no more.

Jacquie's footsteps on the stairs. Thinking (knowing? more than ever? praying) he didn't need Duane nor nobody to tell him what was right nor how to take care of his own family. How to protect them and himself and everybody. Didn't need no ghost to tell him nor no faggot screaming up in no church neither. I'm the one, he thought, the main one up on it, he thought; sensing Jacquie slip through the door behind him as she came up and squeezed a hand deep into the exhausted sunken field of his left shoulder. Before she sat down next to him on the bed for what he knew would be the beginning of a long something-or-other between them, a meeting of lips and lipstick, he pressed the covering in more tightly around Gregory Jr. and thought with some surprise *He's mine   I made him   I ain't never gone let nobody not nobody hurt him.* (She'd begun to massage his neck, he'd begun to give himself over to her, and aw yes, girl, all right, now. Yes.) Not nobody. Not no vicious gossip nor what nobody says. I'ma keep y'all safe from that, he thought. As sure as he knew his name and who he was. (He had always known his name, he thought, who he was.) Keep them very safe from ghosts and secrets and redrooms filled with: — *it wasn't safe,* some other ghost had once hissed into his innermost parts: *notsafe notsafe. Wasn't safe that time,* another had said, *who wants to be safe?* — keep them secure from all that and much more, he thought, lowering the grief-veil in his eyes as he gave what remained of him, the closures and the fells, into her openings. I got it all under control right here, he thought, stroking she who was with him now alive, Jesus, amen, yes; the other hand caressing his child; knowing now for all time in that darkness that this silence and shadow were *it,* where they had always lived, would continue to live: where he would keep them with every power possible, *safesafe.* Now there and falling back into the dark above the world where the dead and the ghosts slept and rose, walked, searching: his hands there now clasping them the living and the flesh and the protected hot blood to his chest tight tighttight, for that time and ever after shielded from that outer world of lies, safe from other people's eyes, he thought. Safe from the truth.

A REAL PLACE

How many are swinging

H ERE
where it is very quiet
a real place

Now it is very quiet   now he is no longer crying   now we
are listening again   listening and listening   for yes he is talking   talking again about what happened   down there in that
place   so very far to the south and green   green with mountains with rivers   where the people look like him   like us
where the farmers fall off their fields onto the mountains
where the cattle still are lowing in the fires   and the people are
burning   and the trees are red like the sea   endless red like
the sea   those rivers endless to the sea   filled with the people
burnt in the trees   filled with their hands   down there   so
far away   so close   the memory   he is telling us   what

happened to the people   inside   outside   everywhere   a
real place

Because yes he says I remember   remembering now but even
now not wanting to remember   there were so many different
noises   the sound of cattle in the fields   the sound of children
in the schoolyards   that came before they were in the trees
hanging black and red in the trees   and the televised executions
and the bayonets   tearing inside   things you cannot remember   things you must must not remember   the stench of flesh
burning on the hillside   the ashes of hands in the earth and the
smoke   and the screams   always the screams   and the sea

It is a whisper

I would like to remember the sound of hummingbirds
that sound   I would like
that noise
again
a whirr
and the color

there is nothing like it in nature

Now he is no longer crying   but yes he says once I was crying
it was just that one time in the room   the room where they
brought you to answer questions   always questions   that room
always the shouting   that room   that smelled of rats and excrement   where the people were screaming   crying   choking
a real place

A red river on the floor there

where the spiders were sleeping
red   sleeping

The room   always so dark   always so hot and the shouting
in between the kicks and the burns   always the shouting   we
were swinging upside down there   the blindfolds over our eyes
the excrement smeared on our mouths   the red river that
smelled like skin   skin so soft before the burns   old people's
skin   ours   the room   where they were going inside us
inside us with their guns and their hands   always shouting
inside us with the pushing part that tears   when you tear you
become part of the red river   down   down down   you are
tearing   down   down down   you are screaming   but it's
all right   all right they say all right   even when you're drowning they bring you up again   they bring you around for more
you learn   even when you're drowning   swinging   you must
swallow them   taste them   like excrement   taste them in
the red

You tear forever then

And she   the little girl   she was screaming   in the next room
she was screaming   saying stop   stop please   she was screaming
they were going inside her with a cactus   then themselves

What you can't remember
what you have to remember
it is

Because memory he says   that is the all of it and the end   the
all of all life and feeling   where you live   where you die
suspended   not like when you're swinging   that kind of
suspension   swinging upside down   your hands tied behind

you   your face in the piss bucket   it is not like that   the
memory takes you away from it   even as they prepare to go
inside you   to open you up to the tearing parts   the memory
it takes you away   back to the time before their hands   before
their guns and the tearing parts

That's what I most want to remember he says   that time before
them   was there ever a time before them   when we lived simply beneath the sun   the sun on our backs and we   alive and
feeding the goats and cattle and we   tending the earth in the
highest hills   thinking there could be nothing more to any of it
than the sea and the sky   another place

The sound of hummingbirds
that whirr

That was before they came   they had been there before and had
never left   that was the truth   they had never left   always
one of them behind an election   always one of them planning
an assassination   yet another siege   but that had never touched
the people in the hills   the people who held their goats and slept
on leaves   the people who knew the worth of pigs   will never
touch us we thought   we're not important enough   we   too much
of the earth   we thought   another coup   another execu-
tion   and we'll still be here we thought   like the sea and the
sky   ageless   still here

The sea has a blank face   not sometimes but always   its face
is blank   telling you nothing you can truly remember   the
rivers flowing into it are red   now it is crying and choking on
excrement   choking on the bodies that have no faces   they
are dark   swollen   have no faces   all of them are crying
without their faces   the sea drives salt into their wounds   the
last place where the redness shows

If you walk into it it will tell you   it's all right to die   it will
tell you   it told us when we were swinging   our hands tied
behind us   we were swinging   the electric shocks and still we
were swinging   the shit in our mouths and we were swinging
even the barbed wire beatings on our backs   we were swinging
I didn't swing only once   when they cut me down and did that
to me   nice and tight they said and   laughing and filling my
throat and   one by one they laughed and   too much to
remember   when they open you up and   by that time you're
already dead   in the sea   in the red   choking   you have
no face   no throat   no hands

None of them who beat you are faces   only voices   always
shouting   you hear their voices so full of questions with the
shouting   so full of   spit   always shouting   asking who
you know and the shouting   who did this   and the shouting
who went there   who signed this   who's working with this
one   with that one   who is conspiring   who betraying
even if you tell them lies still they go inside you   there are no
stories that are enough   you can't tell them you know only of
goats   can't tell them that when you're swinging   nothing is
ever enough

Now the goats are burning on the hills
I see them

burning

the goats and the shacks

Now there can be no memory there

it was a real place

with faces   people
now it can be   nothing
ashes
no place

But yes he says   he who is I says   you don't have to touch me
I'm all right   you don't have to   touch   please do not touch
no nor smile either   no smiles   not ever

Now he is no longer crying   now I am no longer   I can talk
about her he says   I say   my mother   dead   now dead
I am   she   I can talk about her   I   I can   talk

I am talking

I can remember her   I can

She was the one there

The one I said was the little girl screaming   yes it was her   I'm
fine you don't have to touch me   please   don't   I'm sorry
I was pretending   please forgive me   I was pretending   there
were so many little girls there screaming   so many of them
swinging upside down   screaming when I heard that voice
yes   that voice   I started to pretend

not her not her I said

Not her   not her   not in that room I said   no   they aren't
going inside her   they aren't putting a cactus into her   they
aren't putting the tearing parts into her   I was upside down
swinging   the rope was hurting my arms   swinging   I
was pretending   but the sea said yes   yesyes   it was her

That was another time they cut me down   not the others   just
me   cut me down   we're going inside her now they said
move it you son of a bitch they said   nice and tight like a   why
don't you watch us open your mother   open her way up in the
twat   that might loosen your tongue a little bit they said   they
were smiling   but I   couldn't speak I   had no face

It was all the sea
it was the river   it was
a real place

And she was screaming   hanging upside down she was screaming   when the first one cut her down and went in her from
behind she was screaming   you'll have to break her jaw they
said and still she was screaming   beat her with the barbed wire
billy club they said and still she was   screaming   the men
laughing and the women veryopen   her   the men with voices
beating her and opening   still they didn't win   even with the
screaming   the red river came pouring out of her   out of her
mouth out of her nostrils   she was in the river with a red face
they had only the voices left   she was opened up   gone

That was my mother

Why am I laughing   that's what the dead do isn't it they laugh
the dead go dancing on the sea and forget things   it's all right
now you don't have to touch me   I'm dead now you don't have
to   touch   still I remember her river   I wish I could go on
pretending forever   I wish I could   say it was another little
girl they were tearing   I wish I knew the currents of that sea
it feels so good against the skin   against the faceless face   when
all you have left are the bones   and the sky

Now it is very quiet   now again he is remembering   he who
is I is remembering   I have to take back my face from the river
now I am no longer crying   now we no longer are   now
instead we are walking   millions of us or more   walking
across the sea   across time and   out of that dream   out of
that room   above the fields   above the burning and the trees
wetting our faces in the river   the red water is all you have to
drink   all you have to   take   the salt feels good in your
wounds   it closes you up where they went inside   where they
opened   yes   I remember   a real place   down there   where
I came from   where I came from I say   that place of rivers
and fields and mountains   where still the cattle are lowing in
the valleys   where still the machine guns are tearing the skin
another coup   another country   another man killing people
in the national palace   only why is it always our people   why
is it always   we

Now it is very quiet he says   I say   quiet   I want it to be
for once   one time   very quiet   listening to the silence   the
memory   I might still have another chance   I might not be
dead yet   maybe there is still time to die   then the time to
live   I think that's right   it must be   must be   right   yes
I'm all right   all right I say don't mind me   I'm trying hard
not to remember   still   trying hard to remember   what
didn't happen   what always happens   down there   a real
place   because look   do you see   now I see them again   all
of them   I see them   me   we   burning in the hills   in
the trees   and the soldiers   coming down again with the guns
and now   now I say   the memory is not dead   we are not
dead I say   in the memory she is not   the girls and the men
but listen   you have to listen   you will hear it   yes   hear
it   the soldiers   the guns   the fire   opening again   inside
and now can you tell me   can anyone tell us   all of us   where

is the truest memory   where is the death and the sea   is it
right here   inside   where they've already gone inside   where
the spirit sings and dies   O the spirit   singing   dying   the
life and the creation   or is it still there   down there   outside   inside   in that place so far away   so close   where
there are rivers and mountains   outside   inside   where
there is red   outside   inside   down there   so far away
close   where they are tearing   where now again it is very quiet
now and always   here   all around   listen   it is quiet   in
the sea   in the river   in the red   the memory   the silence
outside   inside   where the spirit swings   where it dies
where we all are swinging   all around   swinging   yes listen
now   we are here   all of us   swinging   a dark room   a
red river   inside our lives   inside   in   always   a real place

THE PIT

THE KILLING OF CHILDREN IN OUR TOWN HAS BECOME quite common now, ordinary as the bread we yet bake each day. We've lived here since, it seems, time immemorial, but little since that time, in our memory, has changed. Our town, like those neighboring, has running water now, and even electricity, but still a dryness and darkness prevail. The killings, like the dryness, are as regular as the daily beatings of our grandmothers in the streets, and the slaughters of those who, between summer locusts and hurricanes, attempt to save them; as our daughters, before they disappear from our sight forever, are raped (in the cane fields, in the mountains) after being pulled from our arms, from our shacks, in those hours when the roads are dark again, and no one except those very few, in their boots, may walk. We don't speak of these things now as much as we once did, having learned that speech, like the persistence of memory, here serves little purpose; or rather, here in particular, on hillsides no longer strategically important to the north (the last of the marines are already gone), serves a purpose many of us would rather avoid.

Thus our memories, like what we'd rend in different circumstances, have gradually congealed on our tongues. Better that way for us all, finally, some think, for already precious few of us from the early days remain here; in that way, especially during the darkened hours when faces and other parts disappear, we're not so different from the many others along here and beyond, except for what we now know, have known for so long, to be the presence of the pit.

To reach the pit, you must walk three hours' way out of our town, on a dusty road, rock-strewn, that borders and, at varied points, rises sharply above the sea. That in itself isn't unusual in a place such as this where the sea, surrounding us and our lives as it always has, forms an integral part of our history. Those who fled, or were forced, to the shores on those distant nights, we thought, were surely ultimately better off than those who wound up at the pit; for the sea, caressing and forgetful as it has always been, leaves behind no trace to which the spirit might return on some troubled night, to wander. Wander. If you've heard those sounds coming from the pit on nights of the clear moon, wafting on the perpetual star-apple breeze, you'll know what we mean.

Why, then, were they there on that day, those two, and how, exactly, did they wind up there? None of us even now can really say, having learned never to raise questions like that, although — as always — our imaginations can tell us plenty. Don't believe that, like the family down the road and those three others up on the hill, they were marched there blindfolded, bound, and gagged, a rifle's mouth to their back, for — this we did know — they had hidden long and well. In their case, forget what you've heard about all the murdered journalists uncovered in pathetic rural hideaways (like our town), and the news clips regarding throat-slitted clerics, tortured nuns, revoked amnesties, and the disemboweled, tree-scorched human rights workers who, even unto the bone and ash piles they became, wept over earth sacred and profaned. As was generally agreed by those who claimed to know, they weren't that important. They weren't part of any urban insurrections or upland revolts; weren't, like many of the canecutters in the last general strike, hunted down, caught by the scruff of the neck, and rifle-butted by people we'd in some cases known, who, even as mercenaries, still resembled us; nor, as later happened to some of those farther down the shore, were they burnt out of a shack after the others, sleeping within, had succumbed to the smoke and flames. No. In their instance, it was simply a case of that adamant curiosity which so often drives the young to the uneasy edge; for they were only boys, after all, young ones, who — like many of us — couldn't at that time fully believe the warning stories they'd been told, nor the accrued evidence of the embers that had smoldered along that road for years. In their case, of course, they happened upon the pit during a period when the ones with guns and bayonets and boots — district chiefs, civilians, and others — had departed from our vicinity for a while, to enforce elsewhere our latest ruler's latest edicts; which happenstance, and its unexpected turn, in part accounts for that day's unforeseen events, and this recounting's strange outcome.

The elder child — yes, you could see, definitely the elder: his eyes, if not his height, stunted by poverty and raggedy diet, told you so — was, everyone thought, roughly twelve years old or so at the time of these events. Like others in his condition — on his own, without any home to claim him or guiding hand to care for and feed him — he had been living on garbage for more than a year, and had from all appearances so far managed to do well in avoiding the rotten meats and fish that, with so many muffled explosions of spores followed by maggots' fiendish internal workings, had killed countless other hungry children. There was never as much garbage in our town, of course, and of such rich variety, as daily rotted in the capital; and, gruelingly distant though that journey was for a lonesome child, proceeding on foot in infinite patience over a road littered with marauding militias only too eager to slice apart yet another filthy urchin, he did make it there when the desire and need took him, and each time returned without dramatic incident, fairly unscathed. Amidst days of fierce competition for those filthy leavings and so many nights of running with the other children from the police who raped first and mutilated afterwards (the marines had tried to stop that — officers of state could have sex with people without *raping* them, they said), we knew that he sold himself, of course. It amazes some of us still to this day, recalling images of that tawdry capital most could scarce afford to see, that anyone in the world with proper eyes and a sense of what could and couldn't be would pay any amount of money for such a filthy, tattered specimen — for a child, clearly, made crafty not by choice but necessity, whose eyes, like those of so many others, revealed tales in colors no one ever wished to see. But then his sorrow-tale about wanting the money to send home to his mother, in whose existence he still needed so passionately to believe (she had been burned alive in a northern town's public square one year and a half earlier, at the end of two badly thwarted populist uprisings, about which, by way of that same global press, you'll doubtless already have heard), likely as not inflamed their hearts as well. For — as anyone knows — it's easy enough to permit a child to do anything for you, almost anything at all, if deep down you're convinced that you're in fact doing that face beneath you only a kindness.

The other — the younger, of indeterminate age, in part because of his mangled, scarred face — was, then and always, our true responsibility, so to speak; but at that time, and even before, recalling now, one about which it seemed we could do little. A few of our older women, who in that time before running water daily carried leaden buckets on their heads from the river with their surviving babies on their backs and "saw" things in the wiser light of age and brutal experience, remarked that the boy, like the dwarfed trees in the grieving glens by the river, was clearly crossed: malformed in the head, they meant, or maybe somehow retarded. Such a state wouldn't have been unusual, given the gravity of our own. But certainly not crossed in the heart, they added, as if that might somehow help. Another, who has since spoken to us from the somber isolation of the pit, said No, the child wasn't retarded, but inward. Inward in that he'd gone inward, having seen all that he'd seen, to the interior country of shadows and muted light, where all, even for one his age, was silence; that most immutable place of all, where the light was softest and most resistant to the pulls of outward reality and vision that plagued us all, from which he would never again venture into the outer world. Wouldn't speak, not to any of us, leastways not in a voice easily understood. Walked always with his eyes cast low upon the ground, as if seeking to decipher there the pathetic steady trundlings of worker ants. Walked with one hand just about the underside, beneath the jaw, of his slightly deformed-looking head. Had been that way ever since his mother and sister years before, on a blazing afternoon months before the many curfews to come, had been knocked to their knees down by the river by those with boots and guns, and, with shots that had ricocheted off the farther hills, rousing drowsing butterflies out of midday torpor and immediately launching the dwarfed glen trees into a fit of uncontrollable weeping, been blown into scattered fragments along with six other hapless women and left there to stare wide-eyed up at the sky that, with nary a glance before those streams, had continued on its way without a murmur out to the sea and the farthest corners of the world, shimmering down as always the heavy heat-haze which in that scorching hour had always driven us to the cooler succor of our interiors, but that day didn't. Although the boy — picture him: small, tattered, scar-faced, malnourished, slight of frame and knock-kneed — had run forward in that moment on his useless legs, at that time a toddler's, toward his mother and sister, screaming out things no adult could or would understand, he hadn't been shot in the instant because the soldiers in the very next minute had turned to pump their remaining bullets into the body of another woman running up from downriver to save him. That, of course, was when the first miracle of several to come occurred: when, as several of us witnessed only seconds after those fatal explosions, the bodies of all the women lying there were swept up by the hands of a somnolent river breeze never before felt in these parts, and borne aloft into the highest of the leaning trees that for centuries had without even the slightest complaining sigh shaded them in their labors; swept up into the leaves and the green, leaving behind only the blood that, bearing hot witness in the red tongue of somatic secrets, had quickly hissed and drained into the waiting earth. Those who saw the transformation insisted afterward that it was in the arms of those trees that the child thenceforth slept, still there and outwardly silent as his most inward memories, until the later time when everything changed. For, try as we did to pull him into our homes, especially on nights when jeeps roared through our dreams in search of blood and memory, he never once responded to our calls during that time, and it was from that day forward until the hour of the mercurial prophet that he did not utter amongst us or anyone else one single word.

Given those events, it was only natural that the two of them came together — the elder boy and the younger. Being boys, they clearly still possessed in their deepest hearts the yearning for the things kittens, like lions or grown men cast in the graven images of their more daring, consecrated heroes, must do. But then, as was obvious from the start, they each were the only place, aside from their separate innermost countries, they had to go. Most of the other children they'd known in the area had either been killed or had long been in fearful hiding; their families, far and wide, had under our ruler's long-arm reach been mostly decimated in widespread raids; and, while they two hadn't quite grown up together, they gravitated toward each other with the grave caution and stealthy assurance of the last true brothers they knew and felt themselves to be. When, on a cloudy afternoon after the most recent occupation, the elder one came flying into our public square with a small sackful of money he boasted he'd snatched from a well-known, wealthy whoremonger with fantastically long hands and a mouthful of gold teeth pried from the stiffened jaws of thirteen executed past presidents, he immediately ran, shoeless and filthy as ever, to share the sack's delights with the oldest, poorest woman of our town, who during the eighth siege of an infamous year had lost seven sons in seven minutes to the bristling fire of six machine guns, and, like the glen trees, hadn't stopped weeping since, causing us to fear that, like the agonized matriarch of that ancient tale, she might without any undue effort or longing end up a parched stone forever wet with tears. She didn't, finally, and to our surprise and relief even stepped out of those gray shoals to thank the urchin for his kindness, but, that fast, he was already off to the younger, for whom he'd brought back from some elusive capital recess ("where all the trees are onyx, and speak in hollow tongues," he would tell the mute, as all-knowing friend and benefactor) a bag of glittering green- and yellow-backed turtles that, with shocking pink-painted eyelids, an amphibian's fey intelligence, and the savage wit and love of harmless skulduggery possessed by all living reptiles so transformed into garish curios, were in reality the disguised holy familiars of beneficent patron saints, as he'd been told by an ancient wizard given to soaring midnight flights above the sea with winged horses that nightly neighed forth on those ghostly flights the many parabolic epigrams sent in love and nostalgic longing to the living by the dead. Related as the spirit-steeds were in spectral blood and fortitude to the clever abiding turtles, the wizard had told the child, they would forever protect from destruction those who, by chance or destiny, above the sea or from within a vortex of miraculous light, came into their presence. Whether any of that was true or not, none of us at that time knew; but the mute, in all his four and a half feet of gravity, twisted features, and continued silence, delighted in the gift and, poker-faced as always, quickly ascended with them and his friend into the safer arms of the watching trees.

Who was it, then, who told us how they got there? To the pit? An old woman, gabbling, probably; a whirlwind flock of noisome crows; the weary disenchantment of a vine sinking its teeth into an impassive wall. It's difficult now to remember. The very next day, on a morning redolent still of the night's previous longings and the sea's churning dissatisfactions, they set out: "Come on down out of that tree, you — you shrimp!" the older boy cried, ruffling the younger's head as, sleepy-eyed, with a veil of tender leaves in his hair that had kept tree insects in search of riotous color from crawling through his dreams, he tumbled downward out of those watchful guarding branches.

"I've got something to show you," his big brother said, "something you can't ever tell anyone about." The younger child, speechless as usual, merely gazed upon him with those eyes still very much a feral kitten's, wary of intrusion and fiercely vigilant of their secrets; it was clear then to his protector, however, as it was to those who watched from assorted morning tasks, that everything in his aspect's marked silence said, Yes.

How they arrived there without any trouble on the way remains a mystery to this day. True, that morning none of the usual regimental bands were in the area; but uniformed laggards had been known on occasion to doze away entire mornings and the afternoon's hottest hours in the road-bordering fields, as jeeps loaded down with militiamen on their way to further massacres were often heard racing over the dusty cliffs above the sea. The sight of two small rag-tattered boys walking along that lonely road, and their skulls' lovely shapes beneath the youth-soft flesh, would of course have been too much for the soldiers, revolvers held tightly against their genitals, to resist. Yet make it they did, in the hour when the sun was at its highest; feeling that heavy fire burning into their backs as the rest of us prepared to retire until its fury had ceased. It was there and then, as a great dark bird crossed in front of the sun with its wings outlining the arc from the horizon to the sky's upper blue where still crept a few trembling clouds, that the elder took the younger's hand in his own and, holding it aloft, pointed down to the spreading sight that met their eyes far below the scrub-brushed promontory where they stood.

"Look there, shrimp," he whispered. The air's stilled quality was enough to encourage — demand — fearful whispered reverence. "There. Down that way. See? That's ... that's *it*. That's the pit."

The younger child — from thence onward known as Shrimp, until, in the time of the oracle, we learned his true name — looked out, squinting, at the sight below. He might have been squinting merely from the sun's force, sharply reflected off the sea beyond the view, or at what glimmered in the pulsating tableau before them. As his guardian-brother had said, it was the pit; unremarkable at first glance, appearing to be only a broad earthen field set in a deep valley, roughly ninety feet or so below them; a valley at some time or another clearly excavated, inch by inch, by the straining labor of human hands. It resembled nothing more, in a way, than the peculiarly rectangularized crater of a long-extinct volcano, or a quirky, somehow disturbing human attempt to reorder the burnt-out scar of some past meteor's dying outrage; ringed all about by the sober cliffs that, on the far side facing them, led steadily down to the sea's accusing refrains. It was the second, deeper look they gave it, however, unable to move their eyes once they saw it, that caused their gazes to widen, as they focused on what no one had ever been meant to see.

For the very earth itself was moving — dark brown and rich from millennia of rainfall and haphazard neglect, untilled and —

just then — apparently bare. Moving, not with the tremulous force of the earthquakes to which this discarded end of the world had long ago grown accustomed, but rather with the very heavings of the sea itself: a tidal wave's reckless roll and sweep toward a sleeping shore. The shiftings appeared to move in utter silence, yet they soon saw that, aside from the distant wave-refrains and the wind's saw along their necks, other sounds also were rising — muffled, softly discordant, as of the keening of felled birds — from an indistinct area just above the earth. It was as they listened and continued listening, necks craned forward and hearts and bodies still, that they saw the next strange thing: that, for as far as they looked in whatever direction, the pit appeared to extend without end — without limit. When they looked toward the sea, the shifting earth traveled the length of their gaze, over the far cliffs and down to the shore; when they looked to the south, toward that farther region of misted forests where, it was said, the winged horses were known to breed and school their skittish foals in the ghostly art of nocturnal flight, the steady carpet of moving brown ran before their eyes to the forests' edge. They turned to regard the mountains behind them, and there too the unceasing image spread before them over and beyond the mountains. The sole direction in which the pit seemed not to travel was back toward the town, from which in those moments they glimpsed only a single line, oddly serrated and of the most glittering silver, suspended just above the moving ground as if dangled there by an invisible hand, wavering faintly in the breeze and rising higher over the dark hills behind them before its descent, with the sound of a sigh, into the bucking earth below.

No — of course they shouldn't have kept going. Shouldn't have attempted the uncertain and surely insane journey down there. Yet, compelled as they were by that young adventurer's curiosity, in wonder drawn to the disquieting earth and strange silver line, they proceeded down with moderate difficulty; the elder all the while holding tightly the smaller hand of that word-less other whom he hadn't yet discovered, like many a bossy big brother, he actually loved. They couldn't know then, as they walked nearer to shadows that had in fact always loomed over their lives, that they were under the watchful guidance of the tree that nightly wrapped the smaller boy in its arms. In a few min-utes, that wouldn't matter either.

Down, farther down, until, at the bottom, the human-scratched-out valley's surrounding walls towered over them. It was all at once dark as early evening, despite the sun's still-feverish burning far above, but when the elder squeezed his mute charge's hand and whispered, "You scared, Shrimp?" the only response was a returned squeeze and a calmly increased veiling of those feral eyes; and then, given what happened to them afterward, and the fiery prophet's words made flesh, none of the living would ever know what they'd thought of that sojourn into the pit.

"Stop. Shrimp, *look*" — as, in that same vale where all around they suddenly heard what sounded like cries of pain, they saw yet another strange thing: a shrunken old woman, standing only one hundred yards or so distant. Naked. They could neither avert their eyes nor believe them. An old woman they recognized. Her breasts open and torn. A large hole between them. A rivulet there, dribbling. Dribbling without end. Her hands, reaching. Up, up. The mouth — open, screaming? — but without sound. Without sound not only of what had been taken, but also of things sullied, destroyed. Without sound about her sons. One . . . two . . . three, four, five . . . six . . . her seven sons shot and killed. Mowed down before her eyes. And the gasoline. Poured, slowly, over their nerve-twitching bodies. A stench of sizzling flesh. Burnt hair. Cooked hands. A riverwash of screams. The tongues cut out. But yes. A sizzling of gasoline. A smarting. Melting. A riverwash of screams. Flesh further blackened before her eyes. It does not smell clean. Such is the fate of the suspected. So says a

voice. Speaking of radicals. Leftists. Spies. Declared enemies of
state. What the marines do not believe. That such things still
occur here and elsewhere. That is why they intervened, they say.
Now they are gone, say they, and all is fine. Councils of state no
longer need denounce. Flags of victory have since unfurled.
Presidents have smiled and said, Okay. Ratifications issued, adju-
tants recalled. Trade sanctions enforced, exiles returned. For it is
known and was. Known that melted hands cannot cut the cane;
that scorched limbs cannot fold the hems; that burnt knees cannot, no, not bend to clean the surveillance posts, and that the seas
will evermore be flooded with the northward-bound panicked of
their kind. But all of them forgetting. Forgetting that the sea does
not cool, but erases. Erases the skiffs and the leaking rafts; sweeps
downward the blackened hands and the charred remains. The sea
does not cool; it forgets. And still, in the sea of memory, she is
screaming. Without sound, for she is dead. About how the soldiers had come for her only that morning. Yes, she was from that
town. From our town and all of them. What do you want, she'd
said. Where are we going, she'd asked. But it didn't matter, they'd
laughed. It never mattered, they laughed, haven't-you-learned-
yet-you-stupid-old-bitch? they say. Laughing. Their hands all over
her, feeling her up that quickly: just put your superannuated ass in
there. With the others. In the van. Young and old. A slamming of
rifle butts, a kicking with boots. A glen of sighing trees. That
town, our town. A silent public square, and the many who locked
themselves away each night from the sound of boots and jeeps on
a dirt road, until the arrival of those four who took her and the
others away, but before they arrived at the pit they had all four put
both themselves and their guns up her cunt, her cunt, she says,
screaming: their words, unfolding their tongues, laughing   Yes,
you old bitch, they say, laughing   Nobody's whore and an
enemy of the nation, have you ever been fucked with an Enfield,
with an M-16, you miserable old cunt? — laughing: and take her

to the pit, screaming, Look up and kiss the sky good-bye, bitch, laughing, now you'll join those bastard sons you love so much, aiming, firing   one   two   three   four   five   into her chest, now firing   down into her tattered cunt, now laughing   as she falls backwards, falling, back such a very long way down into the pit, falling   to lie there on her back with the wounded parts exposed and continuing only to look up at them O so very far far above as the nerves still all they are twitching and the four of them still are standing and laughing aiming as they prepare to dispatch the others, waiting, but now where are her sons, she is screaming (without sound), she's dead, isn't she (without sound), they've taken everything away, haven't they, so now where are they, you bastards, she says, where . . . one, two, three, four, five, six . . . where? Without sound

The two watchers stood fixed, unable to move before that insane dance of screams, but, even as they couldn't be certain as to the beating of their own hearts, other shadows, moving things, took shape: a woman without hands, holding up only two shining nubs, ran toward them, sobbing, mistaking them in that panic for her two grandchildren; a young man, a machete's rusted remains in his chest and his eyes gone, ran about also naked, screaming for the sound of his father's voice; a small girl begged her mother or someone to make the soldier stop, Mama, hurting again, Mama . . . tight, first time and last; a few other children again wept before choking once more in the curling smoke of remembered flames; an elder choked still on the metal cylinder that, with a burst of hot steel, had only that morning blown his face apart . . . and the towns. Calling. Breath, noise, silence. For yet the ropes rub now raw the wrists, the bayonets lance yes again still yes the thighs, the gasoline drizzles smooth and O how smooth upon the skin. Flints are raised. And all about them, the earth is moving, and it is in that precise second that the younger child, who up until then has remained still and not opened his mouth, parts his lips to raise his voice, with that blistering chorus, in a scream. A scream unending, he screams and screams, and it is not until his friend holds him close, sensing yet another newly arrived danger, that his sobs end with a single word, gasped out: "Nadiya," and then, "Nadiya, there — " as he points off toward a farther corner of the pit where a figure appears to wander amidst all those others. "Nadiya, Nadiya," he shouts, and might call out again but for the other's hand clapped fast over his mouth.

In that instant both saw what the older child had heard on its way: a van, on the road high above the pit, that with a harsh squeal of brakes presently came to a stop.

"All right . . . — bastards — " A voice inside the van, to the accompaniment of several quiet-to-loud clicks. "Fuckers. Out. On the road. Fast!" Barked to another voice that, in an undertone of fear and disgust, commences in a steady stream: "All right, come on, now, you heard the man . . . what's wrong, honey? Haven't had enough dicks up your ass? Didn't we fuck you good enough? Oh, this one wants to give a last blow-job before he goes! — Now, cunt. Uh huh. Move it. Uh huh. You want us to rip that little bastard out of your belly right now? Okay . . . . Don't worry, we'll be giving you a *personalized* abortion. Uh huh. Don't worry about the bleeding. You'll all be bleeding enough for a fucking cunt pool in a minute. Move! If you — "

All noise quieted in the pit.

"That's all of them," the first voice says. Belonging to a man who might be anyone from the region, but for his military fatigues. The other man — armed with a rifle in addition to the holstered guns both men carry — wearing only a white T-shirt, black pants, and sunglasses.

"Is it?" the second says. Beginning to count: one, two, three . . . five, six, seven . . . eleven, twelve, thirteen . . . fifteen.

"Right-O," he says. "Ready?"

"Ready."

A sudden, broad sigh-to-cry, as of weeping; scattered noises attempted through the muffles of gags forced into and tied about mouths; silenced almost immediately by a single shot's report, fired just above their heads.

"Bastards!" the first man shouts. "So you'll try to scream now? Why didn't you scream before, when you were planting bombs and blowing up bridges? Killing innocent people and women with children — " Stopping for a moment to pass a brief smile in the direction of the woman to whom remarks about a personalized abortion had been addressed — small, almost completely unremarkable, he sees, but for the seven-month full balloon of that belly — then licks his lips with a slow, soft flick, as if savoring still some unspoken and even profane remembrance. From behind blank eyes that close tightly in the next moment, she does not return his gaze. "Plotting terrorist acts. Attempts to assassinate the president. *Our president*" — his voice dipped to *sotto voce,* holding something like the actuality of horrified awe, or another two-visaged, elliptical thing like it — for anything, surely, might be believed on this road, in time; on certain roads all things, in time, must be — that quickly raises again, now with a curious rising but controlled hysteria, to the anterior interrogator's tone: "Our *President,* who art in fucking *heaven* — "

"Hallowed be his name," says the other, snickering.

"Hallowed be his holy fucking name!" roars the first, shaking his head back and forth — the hands not yet touching his gun, though, near his crotch, clearly are itching — "so why didn't you bastards scream then? Huh? Cocksuckers? Why?"

"*Fuck* you." The words of one of the fifteen, faintly audible through the gag. A teenager, not more than sixteen or thereabouts: tall, thin-chested, dark. A boy both boys are certain they have seen before.

"Fuck *me?*" The first man already turned toward him. Eyebrows raised, and smiling that smile. Walking closer; signaling the second to follow. The first man's hands small, soft; like the earth, now mildly trembling. Even he does not know that, like many others', though fond of midnight steel and other heartwrenching things, in secret they are actually birds' wings, but cannot fly. At one time, on the edge of another pit, facing this boy or someone else whom, in that other place or still another, he might have loved and suffered to the point of the hatred that is both deepest loss and faith, he would have thought of how the very sky seemed to discourage it — flight, acts of love or valor, or faith. How the work, this work, like a certain type of falling, made for strange relations with dreams and with light. How, at times, like now, the waking skin appears to wrap too tightly about that which seethes beneath it. How the hands, compelled to silence others, can never contain what won't be kept within. Why, perhaps, edging toward his gun, they are trembling. Because yes, he thinks, it's true. They really are birds' wings, beating. Responding to whatever it is down there, inside or outside; higher, lower. And who would have thought it would be so hard, he thinks. So very hard to keep them still when it's your time to die.

"Is that what you said?" he says. "You want to fuck me? But — let me see now — " Still smiling. Stroking his chin with a gesture as unlikely as the cornsilk in his tone. "I don't think that's right. I don't think so." The other man now waiting beside him. "I don't think you'll fuck me," he continues, very softly, "because I've already fucked *you*. Twice. Three times. Isn't that right?" he says over one shoulder to the other.

"That's right," the other says, laughing.

The remaining fourteen prisoners completely still. Staring straight ahead or with eyes closed. Their hands, like their bodies, motionless in the secured bonds.

"Up the ass. Remember? Huh?" Reaching into his holster.

"Remember how you, you —

"Wanted it?" A small laugh. Furious birds' wings.

"Huh? How you screamed for it? You little whoreshit?" He spits a full wad into the youth's face, then slowly, with a slight forward rocking motion of his hips accompanied by that same licking of his lips and a gentle squeezing together and releasing of the full, firm buttocks muscles cupped close in his tight military fatigues, draws out a .357 and, with those same trembling hands, trembling, clenching, describes slow, almost tender caressing circles over the boy's naked chest; taking care to linger over the soft, plum-colored nipples, ripe as a parted mouth; then pulls the beautiful piece that is his falling and his flesh up to the slender neck; pushing, again gently, against the smooth throat there, as if seeking entry into that where the gliding surge still throbs; where the full-bodied passion of all yearning — life itself — is with a single thrust discharged.

"So I don't think," signaling with his eyebrows to the other man, who moves in yet closer, "that you'll ever be fucking me. Not now. Right?" He moved aside with a quick step as his comrade took aim and, with one swift jab, slammed his rifle butt into the boy's groin, then aimed the rifle under the smooth jaw and fired. A few of the others screamed through their gags, but, aside from the dull thumps the body made as it fell backward and down into the pit and the chiding calls of a few birds startled by the blast into sudden flight, no other sound issued. The pregnant woman wept, but softly.

"Ye-es," the first man said, gazing calmly down into the ravine where the body came to rest, "I think I'll definitely be fucking you. Remind me to fuck your slut of a mother too when we get back. She . . . could use some filling." He turned to the second man, made an impatient gesture and spat once more. "All right, already. I've had it with this group. Let's go."

Thirteen single shots were fired, each preceding the falling sound, into the pit, of the body it was fired into. The pregnant woman was the last to be shot, but even though a special six rounds were fired directly into her belly and then another six into her chest, neck, and shoulders, she still didn't fall as immediately as the others did, and the two men would not be able to help but marvel afterward at what a gorgeous specimen the cunt probably had been before she'd gotten knocked up by some shitbag subversive, and the new guns were really something, weren't they, tcha! because just look at her, a pile of shit now, that was all, just shit, fucking whore . . . a waste of tits and ass.

With some distaste — blood on his boots was an inconvenience, an occasional part of the job but a pain not to be borne by his wife and three creeping children, whom he adored — the first man kicked the woman's soggy remains over into the pit.

"One group down. Six to go." The other man laughed. They got into the van together and, with an abrupt roar that again startled the returned birds, were gone.

The other two, crouching all the while at the bottom of the pit, didn't know that during the executions they had not, in fact, been in danger; that that place and all around were environs of another side — another of many — and, as such, wouldn't ever — couldn't, quite — reveal them, on their side, trapped there. They continued to tremble, however, holding each other, certain that at any moment the swift click of revolvers, aimed to snuff out their small heat, would snap at their backs. It was only after the earth, spouting more of that what-it-was-and-wild they recognized, again began to rock, and the voices (joined by the newest apparition of one bullet-riddled unborn child) began again to call before that fantastic quadrille without end, that they felt the strength that enabled them to scale those walls excavated by human hands, clamber over the rocks above, and run, run, run for their lives and their very sanity all the way back, quick, quick, children, they ran. Back to what they'd left behind. Back to our town.

Later, the elder would recall that, on reaching the top of the pit, his younger brother had looked back only once before they began to run, and whimpered in a very small voice that single word he had uttered before. Nadiya.

And so that very afternoon, only hours after their safe return, what came to be known as the But how? and crazy miracle occurred: the smaller boy, for the first time ever since we'd known him, began to speak. It was toward evening, in the hour when we began making preparations to steel ourselves into our homes, when, after some time of silent sequestration in their tree, the two walked out into the town square: one — to everyone's surprise, the elder — feebly stepping, his suddenly sunken face now marked by tracks of glistening tears, as he repeatedly jerked his head around to look for that gun at his back; the other high-stepping, almost strutting like the most naive toddler or swaggering soldier; a grim, fixed determination hardening the scarred, previously soft smallness of his face. Although a few rushed out from assorted tasks to snatch them into hidden safety for the night, all motion instantly ceased when the younger boy — his voice fully stentorian and nowhere near the expected mewl of one his size — planted his feet firmly on the square's central point and said, "Dead. All," pointing toward the road that led to the pit, "in that ground that moves. It shakes. Remember? How many? Mass graves and hidden. Thick. Remember? How many? And you," pointing out at everyone, that expression on his face, "you all knew. You *know*. So why the fuck didn't you say? Why won't you say even now, among yourselves? Now? Here?"

Nobody spoke. The leaves of that great tree of life, caught between ourselves and the other side and badly scorched by sky-fire, had come to rest in our midst. Then someone, in a voice filled with the embers of the greater fire that was on its way, spoke: "This child must be mad." An old, male voice.

"Devil-taken," said another.

"The devil." The swift lights of his gaze flew straight out

from those eyes more feral than ever. Yellow and brownredgold. Don't look into them, they say, for what you see there just might — (Yes). Look into them, they say, for what you don't see there might — (And yes). Clearly the eyes no longer merely of a child (had perhaps never been) but of one who had seen too much, heard, known, and not turned away. Hadn't been able to.

"Fuck the devil." Not quite said but breathed. How can such words, the very air through and about them, be soft enough to curl bark off myrtle, slide smooth snakeskin over the hotmusk of advancing shoes? Now all movement stops where, so gathered and disbelieving, they stand, though ants, loading spoils and bitter found things, yet crawl unto dark holes, moist tender places. When he says, "The devil is *this*," and points downward and all around, then back up toward the road, his eyes are closed. Closed when he says, "Who comes at night. Does. The things redsplit in trees. Who? Lips should remain part of the skin. Arms should stay with hands. Knuckles shouldn't be left in the grass. Why are the broken nails bent all the way around? Babies should be warm in the womb, not open in the head where the rocks are hard. The devil? you said? Who ropes your mothers' throats in the afternoons? That one? And scratches their secrets til the skin peels? Oh, that one? Who tears their hanging parts at night? Oh, yes, that one? Called devil? Who?" His eyes are still closed though the words are clear — not said but this time spat. Closed as bark curls off myrtle and grapevines, as distant drums beat in chests and hands.

"It's there." His voice soft water. Moving closer. "Your devil. Not screaming and crying with the others but there. Here. Every night and day. Where your mouths and hands have shadows like your eyes. Here and ready. Where you fall. The arms flap like crows' wings when you fall. Did you know? Like this." Both his arms flew out into a grotesque flapping motion and might have carried him off to the source of those visions until, with a single, choked sound, he fell sputtering to the ground and lay still. Eyes closed.

Nobody moved. Although we all should long have been inside our homes, we stayed fixed there — caught up in the currents of that wind rising up off the sea, sweeping down from the road, carrying with it those blue voices of the past, muffled cries from throttled throats, the groans of vanquished hopes and solitary visions vanished beneath blindfolds and the furies of mass rapes and midnight raids. Filling the night. That was when our own sounds began, as we backed away from the sighs of those memories and the child-figure lying there with that expression on his scarred face: backed into our own inner spaces and the safer dark and solitude of no-sound uttered in recognition of the weird chorus we in fact were, had been, and (before the coming deeper silence and re-acquaintance with speaking shadows) were yet to be.

Most of us resolutely avoided him thereafter, convinced that his untoward time at the pit, and maybe even some unspeakable, previously undisclosed evil from his past, had transformed him into a witch, a freak, another example of nature (or someone's conjure) gone awry, before whose cutting glance we crossed ourselves and silently invoked the names of the abiding ones whenever he crossed our paths. He certainly was no longer a child. The journey up the road had snatched away his former quietude, apparently for all time, and replaced it with the spit-and-fire that blistered cane, caused even the sun to blanch, and stopped snails dead in their slime. No one, not even our sagest, thought it stupid that we should be so held in thrall by a mere child, for on those afternoons when (now without his protector, who of late had taken up a miserable, profoundly reduced existence in the beneficent trees) he returned from sojourns to the pit to hold forth in our square with the most shocking pronouncements, it was clear to everyone that he was obviously possessed by some lingering breath not of genial otherworldly succor but of maleficent and vengeful grace. He was no longer the Shrimp: "My name is Theo," he said one day, "that's T-h-e-o, and what the fuck are you going to do, assholes, when they come again? Hide? I guess I'll see you at the pit, then," he would say, invariably laughing that maniacal laugh. But such rips were only the beginning. Gradually it dawned on more than a few of us that what he was in fact doing was challenging, even forcing us when possible, to do what we'd never before done and still couldn't bear to: plainly, to face down a history which, to our knowledge, had never before been either documented for the world's tribunals nor widely told, and which, from all appearances in our world and others, out of the silence in which we lived and from between the shadows that nightly limned our dreams' comforting haze, might never be — in short, the history of ourselves; of knowledge and collaboration entwined with ignorance, shame, and the continuing erasure into non-ness of those who, so banished for all time to exile and the expunging of memory, had officially ceased to exist. "Because who knows their names?" he would shout. "Do you? Or you? Remember?" — pointing at several people scurrying past.

"Someone should knock the little fucker down from there," one of us — a man known as J. — said one day; referring to where Theo stood on the edge of our president's statue in the square. "Knock him on his ass and show him what time it is," he said, and it appeared that, in the company of several others who had also had it up to there with the child's carrying on, he was going to do just that, but the group was stopped short as Theo, seeing them approach, began in that voice of smooth water-snakeskin:

"Oh. Uh huh. You. And you," pointing to another, "and all of you," indicating some on the outside, quickly surrounded by a larger crowd. "Why not? Kill me, yes? You've already killed the others, haven't you?"

"Shut up!" One of the men, advancing closer.

"What is the matter with this child?" a woman asked, pushing forward.

"Demons, tcha."

"Obvious."

"Fire ants eat up his mind."

"Or night birds . . . "

"Moon nettles in the blood."

"Foreign sickness."

"Demons." The water-voice. The changeling's smile. "Sickness?" The laugh. "But now seeing things you shouldn't see everywhere but and here so yes not seeing what's there and so. But how? You-blind-people-can't-see and that's a fact. Why don't you ask them?" he said, pointing to some of the advancing men. "They know."

"Know what?" asked another woman.

"About the demons. Money in the hand. Soft, you know. For better land in the fertile valleys if they — "

"Shut up, you little bastard," one of the men at the end of the child's pointed finger said, almost upon him. "Now we're going to — "

"What do you mean — money and the valleys?" the woman demanded, pushing farther forward. Two of her three children had been shot not far from those valleys.

"Them. *Them,*" the boy shouted. "How many do they think they turned in? Denouncements. What do you think? Living among you as your neighbors, your brothers and lovers, sharing your tears and cursing the ones with guns in the daylight, laughing into the darkness at night? How many? Ask them!"

"You dirty bastard — " One of the men, reaching for him, but then the breeze began again, a heavy dirge carrying that old complaint of the sea, laden with the bitterness of cruel regrets and the spiraling anthems of betrayals, shadow-rhymes of broken fingers and stretched necks: sweeping down, echoing Theo's words, citing in the voices of the dispatched those present who had handed over their own, innocent all. Naming and named.

Transfixed, everyone listened, but only for a moment, for the crowd had quickly transposed into a curling wave from that sea, and would immediately have engulfed the traitors into its snarling crest had not Theo in that very minute held up his hand for quiet.

"Leave them," he said, "and let them run, if they like. They were only the first. God knows they won't be the last. Which one of *you*," he said, tapping the side of his head, "in here loves the pit more than yourselves? Who'll be next? There are too many already!"

"We should kill them," someone called, to a rising chorus of Murderers! Killers! that swelled even as the breeze again began to blow, but all motion upon the cowering assassins once more ceased, with the breeze, at the sound of the boy's voice.

"Leave them," he said. "They can only run. But what good is running when death is racing on every side to meet you? How far can you go when it already knows your smell? Your *stench*," he added, glaring out at someone else in the crowd who quickly retreated before that stare.

"You were in Samarra yesterday and the day before and the day before that," he said, focusing again directly on the enemies, "and you'll be there again tomorrow, forever. Go," he said, waving them on, in a voice both scornful and tender, "and may your own dreams of death and destruction keep you from that road on which you're already walking. There are all kinds of pits," he added, looking back at us. "So resist, or don't resist. Go on, now," he finished, to them. "Good-bye."

They weren't seen again in our town from that day forward. It was only much later, after everything else was over, that we learned that they all had been caught and arrested two days later in the next town by soldiers who bore their exact faces and who had lived their very same lives, and who in the need to murder those lost, crying images of themselves shot them as traitors, quartered them, and stuck their ruined heads on poles before a crowd of thousands. What was happening everywhere, by our intelligence; what had never ceased happening.

And so before the end, though caught up as we were in those recent confusions that had always been with us, it loomed clear that Theo, frightening as his forbidding aspect had become, had obviously been transformed among us into the voice of a fiery prophet. A fearless seer who, in the tones of that oracle that guided his restless visions, would speak until death or deliverance — his or our own — of our most pressing sorrows, joys, and tensions — and fears, of course. Though he eschewed that role as such — "I'm not a fucking prophet, assholes, you'll just have to know when to resist and when not to," he said, shocking the more abstemious with that salty language rivaled only by that of the silver-necklaced hermaphroditic parrots pampered by officers' whores in the capital — when he spoke, from thence onward, we listened. More betrayals were revealed and corroborated as truth by that increasingly frequent breeze off the sea that each day grew louder, angrier, more impatient. In most cases, the malefactors were released, as, to our horror, all of them were sooner or later executed by their marauding murderous brethren.

With time and the outward whirlings of our lives, however, one hour's spiraling into another, one revelation and consequence into another and still another and (clearly without the benefit of a spirit's loft or grace) backed by those pointed guns and the subsequent feeling of falling into the nothingness that wasn't death but the void that since time incipient had all around been everyone's and unavoidable, it came to pass that, with each revelation's renewed fury, many of us began to feel within the perimeters of that most inward country in which each of us lived, alone (and, without the solace of touch or true understanding of who we truly were or had always longed to be with the spirit and affection of someone we loved, sometimes died), that none of us could trust the other. For, in that aloneness, increasingly distanced from ourselves and those around us, if in desperate times we hadn't yet betrayed a neighbor or friend — even, or especially, the precious, pitiful comfort of one's own — which of us, in more taxing moments, might not betray tomorrow? It was that fear that added to our general distress: that, for whatever it had been worth — the small and friendly wage of daily communal exchange, fellow-feeling, and the given trust that our faces amongst each other's had indeed been faces, not masks, united in common force — if we'd never had anything to call our own aside from our history, dreams, our children as our future and hope, and the land so often snatched from our hands, we could say at least with pride that we had always known ourselves; that our hearts could stand with our hands and say *we* — that *we* were *we,* who had endured and were; more than what many others could say who weren't themselves but rather conscribed by that whatever-or-which that without fail led them forward by the sniffing nose into desolation, spiritlessness, sorrow. But with the increased challenge of lowered veils among us, the jeeps' roaring into our lives and so much clever interweaving of more veils, it soon became clear that we really weren't — couldn't be — completely ourselves at all. Rather, we had succumbed to the common plight of the many who, despising what they hadn't learned to value most in themselves, sought to erase it: in the traitors' case, the *it* being quite literally the unified self of our selves. So ravaged among us the treachery-illness, caused by that familiar weakness and unequal memory. So highly communicable among fellow travelers, it left in its wake only the brooding fever of an increasing isolation, which, two steps before the feared fall, fed again into the illness. And again. And again. So that although Theo's proclamations captured our attention and buttressed our relief at being rid, in a way, of so many traitors and cowards, we began to feel the effects of a crushing depression borne on the weight of his truths, so much heavy wood tossed upon the fragile stems of our still-moving hopes and fears: the ultimate inevitable truth that eventually none of us, though we had known, loved, lived with and occasionally loathed one another ever since we could remember, could be trusted, and that, as it turned out, so often the true enemy to triumph and ascension — to that secret and most shining goal of our greatest selves — lay hidden within us. Thus a sense of alienation from ourselves — we'd long ago been alienated from the world — began to have its way; our conversations grew more hushed, circumspect, and never occurred without the guarded lowering of eyes: the suspicion of doubleness and potential betrayal in that face facing our own. "Many kinds of pits," Theo had said; it was true, even with the strange comfort of those distant winged horses' pinions coursing through our most intimate reveries. So that, even as we fell prey to one type of fall and, so falling, fell still further; even as we heard within those caverns the shouts and calls of who and what still lived there, we knew, after Theo's words, that if it weren't now fully within our power to resist one thing and then still another, one day it truly would be impossible not to. Yet our unhappiness continued: "I'll be glad when he's gone," one woman murmured one evening, and many, though they would never say it, shared that feeling in their deepest of hearts.

Theo didn't go, any more than the daily breeze that, full of his words and those dunning voices, steadily swept each night into our homes — accompanied always by that nagging refrain about resisting or no. While the boy who'd once protected him was in flesh and breath slowly fading into the fiber of the watchful trees, sprouting sallow leaves in his hair and even in the moist recesses of his armpits, Theo continued daily to make his solitary trips to the pit, returning each day with actual words and messages from the dead: So-and-so says she never left you, she's with you even now, sweetness, by your side, can't you feel? intoned one; be careful on the roads at daybreak, warned another, the forerunners won't be able to intervene for you when they come for you with gasoline and matches this time, they'll soon come for you now, take care; spiders are growing ever faster in your brain, only a reflection of the true malicious nature of your soul, stay clear! — so cautioned the uncles, grands, great-grands and children of others; along with the many tales of yearning and solitude, the dead enjoining the living to learn from the living things around us, learn from the silence within, from what we'd always been taught to fear. . . . Learn. And grew in number, whenever they arrived causing fresh outbreaks of weeping, distress, and — perhaps the first clear sign of what was on its way — the bile of vengeful anger. Although many begged Theo to carry back messages of reassurance and continued devotion to the pit for them, he steadfastly refused. "The dead are dead, so. Always will be," turning out that noxious scowl, "and have every damn right to be so lonely and miserable when not even a pig's crotch-hole is being done for them on earth. Would you rather join them, and spend the rest of your time in a pit? A falling pit? When you have all this" — pointing around — "and time. Time to resist . . . — Resist *that*," he finished, pointing once more up toward the road, "and learn not to resist what you need to know. What you know. All right? Uh huh." And he would depart, a solitary gremlin obviously weighted down by his own parables — a prophet, especially a truthful one, always feels the boding weight — but implacably ruled by them in a destiny over which he clearly had no control. Had he not also suffered raw losses to the pit? Which of us could comfort that part within him? Which knew how to? For all his cold drama — the truth, spoken forth, always ripped a more fearsome swath than he did — we knew that the events of that distant morning beneath the watching trees by the river had never completely left him, and that, had he not possessed the force of the oracle bestowed upon him by the agent that saw fit to so stir us, his lifeblood's small quick would long ago have been snuffed out as easily as a paltry candle's flame. Those earlier executions had hurled him without compassion or care into a depthless, secretly feared pit of his own. Thus we knew he mourned for the grieving and for himself — for all of us — even as he scowled; part of that scowl, we knew, reaching from his own inability to soothe their grief and his own, creased within what we all shared.

It would all end with a huge crash, though much sooner than everyone expected. Three days later, on a bright sunless morning which augured heavy clouds for that afternoon and evening, Theo called everyone out into the square. Even then we could see how dramatically his aspect had changed. He was no longer the imperious gnome, short-tempered and bristling with scathing looks, but rather frankly urging, more vulnerable than usual and even slightly scattered, with a nervous air that caused some to roll their eyes with a Now what? feeling; between increasing tensions and the general unease caused by his speeches, all were closer to the edge, just shy of the jump. The change arrested everyone.

"Listen to me!" he began to shout. No breeze arose. "You wouldn't listen before. I know none of you understand how the pit lulls. You know, it drugs. Works spells on you just by being there. Now who's going to wind up there tomorrow? Who the first to fall when they come? Fall backward, into —

"Silence," he went on, but almost whispering. "Silence without end, so. What more can they want? Are you going to give them more than that? Now are you going to learn that the dead are the dead, tcha, and that you all —

" — have hearts, don't you? Are you going to listen to them or — "

"I've just about had it with this child," a woman in the crowd said.

"Me, too," someone else said. "Get down off there!"

All at once everyone was pressing forward, hands outstretched for that small, wild figure: not to kill him (of course not!

everyone would say later — that wasn't our way. Not *our* way) but, having had enough of his pint-sized doomsaying, yearning to spank the hell out of him, slam his bare backside. Make him by force into a child again. A few hands did reach him. Proceeded to pull him this way and that; smacked him about the head with all the rage and frustration not turned elsewhere; but then, beneath the disciplining blows, he became the seer once more; eyes reverted to the lights behind which blazed the oracle. Only one of those glances at his attackers enables him to shake himself free as, blown back by that fire, they fall before him. Already he is walking backward through the crowd, out of the square, disheveled head held high; planting his steps firmly on the road to the sea and the pit as he speaks with the old water and now again the breeze in his voice: "All right then. You all know me. Know me well. And I know you. Know you and I, I — " A pause during which he regards no one until: " — *love* you. All right? All of you. More than you. . . . Right now, so. And you — I — " But does not finish; begins instead, shocking everyone, to cry. Crying the way they cried when bullets parted the flesh and ripped where the mouth had just learned to hold the nipple, the way they cried when bones crunched beneath the metal and she did not come home, they did not know her name, they laughed when you even mentioned her, that-fucking-whore-who-is-no-one, they said, can't you understand that, you little black-mongrel son of a bitch. Before them, so exposed, he is again aware of the ridiculous size and shape of the gnome, how pathetic his words sound to them, how ugly to them and everyone appears his dirty brown shitfuck face. "I *hope* you'll know what to do when the time comes," he finishes, already receded. "It's — " Then completely gone; awkward child-steps up the hill. It was then, at the edge, that we saw that long, thin silver line, serrated as a swordfish's snout and now deep scarlet, light up the entire sky from east to west, ending in that area toward which he'd gone. In the moment, no one divined what that fire-light portended; nor guessed, as the breeze resuscitated at his back with its eerie chorus, that that would be the last time any of us would ever see him; nor knew for certain, until it all was over, that it would be a long-building fire's smoke and ash, in part, that would ensure that all that happened afterward never happened again in quite that way, in just that sort of way, in our town.

None of us ever knew who started it. The first shot, and all that followed. So we would all say later. Say in the light of fire billowed down to earth that maybe it really had been our thickened shame at how we'd treated Theo, or hadn't treated him, that had caused it; or the sourness, so long locked within our chests in the face of guns, that did it. Or the memory of bodies living and vanished pressing against the face, or the rifle butts' slamming into what they called the cunt, or the bayoneted infant's cry, or, or . . . who knows? We only remember now that when the first soldier arrived that night, followed by a phalanx of twelve and several more jeeps, for the first time ever we refused to open our doors. All of us. We might have been thinking of Theo then, recalling his words and feeling the pit's presence out there and within, where memory serves strange and sullen purpose. For that night not one of us flinched; stood fast by children, husbands, wives, infants; remembered the ones who'd been ripped faceless and live from laps, from wombs, with nothing but laughter to stroke the loss. So remembering, bidding the young ones to be quiet and listening to those voices returned in the breeze, we found ourselves an entire *we* once again, this time versed in the brutal language of the enemy: Yeah, come on, you sons of bitches, we muttered, then began to shout, come on now and fuck with us, we're ready for you this time, bastards, you won't come in here tonight and rape our children and our wives, no castrating our elders and lynching tonight, fucking prickhearted cowards, come on, cocksuckers, make the first move now, we're ready for you this time, we're ready. Now. And now. In the brief silence that followed, we knew that all of us — praying, watching, trembling, hissing to them outside to go and kiss our fucking asses — were clutching in that place, right there, Theo and his former protector. Waiting. Knowing that everything he'd said about resisting or not resisting was there. Clear.

It didn't seem that any of us could have had guns equal to the first sudden blast that, with a blinding flash, caused first one young soldier and then another to fall within seconds of each other, huge black holes splattered in their chests, screaming as they went down in the stench of their own filth. As far as we knew, nobody had grenades either, and so couldn't explain how five militiamen suddenly found themselves madly dancing, until they burned to death, in a circle of fire and light that seemed to come from nowhere — out of the night or the sky, from an unseen hand among us. We did learn, quickly, that the entire town was ablaze. The dry hills in the distance were burning, as were the sky and the sea. Screaming soldiers, sporting pinions of fire, scattered in all directions as, terrified, some people ran out from the safety of their homes, children and elders beside them and animals howling at their heels, and were immediately shot down by the hysterical militia. Two bloody things, scorched beyond recognition and unable to stop twitching, lay smoldering by the roadside, as shacks enveloped in flame roared and toppled, in several cases trapping the occupants within. We couldn't know then that the entire nation was afire that night, blazing down to the reefs and beyond in what would shortly be known as one of the most ferocious uprisings the region had ever seen. Little thought was given to such things just then, or to the guaranteed future reprisals, renewed sanctions, and official lies sure to come, for as we ran about in that hell grabbing whatever still-living hand reached out as flames licked at heels and headrags, we heard the first scream of those two; then the second. The first had come from the watching trees, holding still in their limbs the body of that child who, like many filthy urchins before him, had once rested his face on garbage heaps festering with swarming rats and the worms that loved dead whorechildren's parts, as he'd burrowed with them in the filth of those who had and the ones who didn't for those sorry pickings. The trees were being incinerated by the soldiers, and even as they swirled skyward in a detritus of ashes and embers, we heard the last cries of the boy taken inside them. Swirling upward. Then out over the sea. Gone.

The second couldn't have been what we thought it was — but it was, of course. Another militia came upon him as they were dumping bodies, minus wedding rings and teeth's fillings, into the pit: just another scruffy-looking child, who'd lately been cursed, or blessed, with the weird gift of seeing, and who in that language had spoken out loud about affairs quite ordinary in this part of the world and others. Just then, in hushed tones and with closed eyes, believed in that kneeling posture to be speaking with the dead, a half-dead victim, or even with an imaginary friend — someone named Nadiya, we were later told — he turned once only, as if attempting once more and always to speak in that more cryptic language descended from trees and rivers, saying *But now look, look,* so it was heard, saying *Yes, I know, mornings and life, these gifts, I know,* saying *but there's something cruel in this day that holds the warmth of sunlight but also in the eyes so many shadows,* so cycled down an echo and passing strange, *and now I see, no one here but me, no one here at all to love, and I I am searching for,* and so uttered it was that distant tongue memory voicewaver that few would understand, that few have ever heard, that was speaking and praying when the soldiers opened fire on him and, with stunning aim, blew open the back of his head clear through to his face. A spray of blood showered onto the first officer's boots, goddamnit, fucking piss-peasants, someone said, they spray all over creation, just like cats. Amidst the laughter and rush to reload almost no one

heard that last searching word, "Nadiya," float upward from the
dead boy's lips, but it didn't matter anyway by the time they
kicked the dirty little bastard, that was it, move the little shithouse
son of a bitch, they said, along with seventeen mutilated others,
into the dark yawning boredom of the pit.

That night, from out of nowhere or from that place where vision
and spirit abound, we saw streaking across the skies in galloping
pairs a fleet of forty neighing winged horses followed by sixteen
whinnying foals, prancing above and around the moon and
emblazing the night with their membranous wings, and it was that
stellar sign and no other that swiftly summoned from our throats
the names of all our hoary archangels and reckless saints, as we
lifted heads and hands to the coursers and saw with our own eyes
that circle of silver hoofprints form a gleaming ring around the
moon as they galloped on to those farther fields of the distant
beyond, as we discovered then and for all time in the trail of those
hoofs the most elusive secret and others, which, like all human
possibility itself or merely a beginning belief in it, were boundless,
eternal, and, as signed by that glimmering trail threaded about the
moon, would not disappear from our skies or memory for another
seventeen years of continued struggle, armed fire, and death. Part
of a story someone had told, long ago . . . a wizard, or ourselves.
Who all looked up then and watched. We. Together. And watched
some more. Continued watching, for a while.

We're told that little remains of our town now, although the
killing of children, and others, continues there. Though most of
us have long since left for what we believe to be safer places, the
voices of that time and place yet stay with us. Should you per-
chance sometime see two small tattered boys wandering, close to
death or even already gone, please make sure to tell us, for it will
very likely be that we know them. If they haven't wound up in

the pit after all, as so many others have, well . . . but there can be no telling. For even now the pit is calling us. Do you hear it? Calling. Forever close . . . far away, unending. Without sound. Calling so many of us. Voices, names. For even now —

And now:

WHOSE SONG?

YES, NOW THEY'RE WAITING TO RAPE HER, BUT HOW CAN they know? The girl with strum-vales, entire forests, behind her eyes. Who has already known the touch of moondewed kisses, nightwing sighs, on her teenage skin. Cassandra. Lightskinned, lean. Lovelier to them for the light. How can they know? The darkskinned ones aren't even hardly what they want. They have been taught, have learned well and well. Them black bitches, that's some skank shit, they sing. Give you VD on the woody, make your shit fall off. How can they know? Have been taught. Cassandra, fifteen, in the light. On her way to the forests. In the light. Hasn't known a man yet. Hasn't wanted to. How can they know? She prefers Tanya's lips, the skin-touch of silk. Tanya, girlfriend, sixteen and fine, dark glider, schoolmate-lover, large-nippled, -thighed. Tanya. Who makes her come and come again when the mamas are away, when houses settle back into silent time and wrens swoopflutter their wings down into the nightbird's song. Tanya and Cassandra. Kissing. Holding. Climbing and gliding. What the grown girls do, they think, belly-kissing but shy. Holding. She makes me feel my skin, burrowing in. Which one of them thinks that? Which one flies? Who can tell? Climbing and gliding. Coming. Wet. Coming. Laughing. Smelling. Girlsex, she-love, and the nightbird's song. Thrilling and trilling. Smooth bellies, giving face, brushing on and on. Cassandra. Tanya swooping down, brown girls, dusky flesh. How can they know? The boys have been watching them, have begun to know things about them watchers know or guess. The boys, touching themselves in nightly rage, watching them. Wanting more of Cassandra because she doesn't want them. Wanting to set the forests on fire, cockbrush those glens. How can they know? They are there and they are there and they are watching. Now.

Sing this tale, then, of a Sound Hill rape. Sing it, low and mournful, soft, beneath the kneeling trees on either side of the rusty bridge out by Eastchester Creek; where the sun hangs low over the sound and water meets the sky; where the departed walk along Shore Road and the joggers run; where morning rabbits leap away from the pounding jogger's step. Sing it far and wide, this sorrow song woven into the cresting nightbird's blue. Sing it, in that far-off place, far up away from it all, where the black people live and think they've at last found peace; where there are homes, small homes and large, with modest yards, fruit hedges, taxus, juniper trees; where the silver hoses, coiled, sag and lean; where the withered arms hanging out of second-story windows are the arms of that lingering ghost or aging lonely busybody everybody knows. In that northerly corner of the city where no elevated IRT train yet comes; where the infrequent buses to Orchard Beach and Pelham Bay sigh out spent lives and empty nights when they run; where the sound pulls watersmell through troubled dreams and midnight pains, the sleeping loneliness and silence of a distant place. Sound Hill, beneath your leaning trees and waterwash, who do you grieve for now? Sound Hill girl of the trees and the girlflesh, where are you now? Will those waters of the sound flow beside you now? Caress you with light-kisses and bless you now? The City Island currents and the birds rush by you now? O sing it. Sing it for that yellow girl, dark girl, brown girl homely or fine, everygirl displaced, neither free nor named. Sing it for that girl swinging her axe through the relentless days, suckling a child or selling her ass in the cheap hotels down by the highway truckers' stop for chump change. Sing it for this girl, swishing her skirt and T-shirt, an almost-free thing, instinctual, throwing her head back to the breeze. Her face lifted to the sky. Now, Jesus. Walk here, Lamb. In thy presence there shall be light and light. Grace. Cadence. A witness or a cry. Come, now. All together. And.

How could we know? Three boys in a car, we heard, but couldn't be neighbors of ours. Had to be from some other part of the world, we thought; the projects or the Valley. Not from here. In this place every face knows every eye, we thought, what's up here in the heart always is clear. But they were not kind nor good, neither kin nor known. If they were anything at all besides unseen, they were maimed. Three boys, three boys. In a car. Long legs, lean hands. In a car. Bitter mouths, tight asses, and the fear of fear. Boys or men and hard. In their car. Who did not like it. Did not like the way those forest eyes gazed out at those darker desert ones, at the eyes of that other who had known what it was to be dark and loathed. Yo, darkskinned bitch. So it had been said. Yo, skillet ass. Don't be cutting your eyes at me, bitch, I'll fuck your black ass up. It had been said. Ugly black bitch. You need some dick. Them eyes gone get you killed, rolling them at me like that. It had been said. Had to be, *had* to be from over by Edenwald, we thought. Rowdy, raunchy, no kind of class. Nasty homies on the prowl, not from this 'hood. How could we know? Three boys, fretful, frightened, angry. In a row. The burning rope had come to them long ago in willed and willful dreams, scored mean circles and scars into their once-gorgeous throats. The eyes that had once looked up in wonder from their mother's arms had been beaten, hammered into rings, dark pain-pools that belied their depth. Deeper. Where they lived, named and unnamed. How could they know? Know that those butterflies and orchids of the other world, that ice-green velvet of the other world, the precious stones that got up and wept before the unfeeling sky and the bears that slept away entire centuries with memories of that once-warm sweet milk on their lips, were not for them? So beaten, so denied, as they were and as they believed, their own hands had grown to claws over the years; savaged their own skin. Needles? Maybe, we thought. In the reviling at large, who could tell? Pipes, bottles? Vials? So we thought. Of course. Who could know, and who who knew would tell? Who who knew would sing through the veil the words of that song, about the someone-or-thing that had torn out their insides and left them there, far from the velvet and the butterflies and the orchid-time? The knower's voice, if voice it was, only whispered down bitter rains when they howled, and left us only the curve of their skulls beneath the scarred flesh on those nights, bony white, when the moon smiled.

And she, so she: alone that day. Fresh and wet still from Tanya's arms, pajama invitations and TV nights, after-dark giggles and touches, kisses, while belowstairs the mama slept through world news, terrorist bombings, cleansings ethnic and unclean. Alone that day, the day after, yellow girl, walking out by the golden grayswishing Sound, higher up along the Shore Road way and higher, higher up where no one ever walks alone, higher still by where the dead bodies every year turn up (four Puerto Rican girl-things cut up, garbage-bagged, found there last year: bloated hands, swollen knees, and the broken parts); O higher still, Cassandra, where the fat joggers run, higher still past the horse stables and the smell of hay, higher yet getting on to where the whitefolks live and the sundowns die. Higher. Seeking watersmell and sheen for those forests in her eyes; seeking that summer sun-down heat on her skin; seeking something away from 'hood catcalls and yo, bitch, let me in. Would you think she doesn't already know what peacefulness means, contains? She's already learned of the dangers of the too-high skirt, the things some of them say they'd like to put between her knees. The blouse that reveals, the pants that show too much hip. Ropes hers and theirs. Now seeking only a place where she can walk away, across the water if need be, away from the beer cans hurled from cars, the What's up, bitch yells and the burning circle-scars. Cassandra, Cassandra. Are you a bitch out here? The sun wexing goldsplash across her now says no. The water stretching out to Long Island summerheat on the other side says no, and the birds wheeling overhead, *okay, okay,* they cry, call down the skytone, concurring: the word is no. Peace and freedom, seasmell and free. A dark girl's scent riding on her thighs. Cassandra. Tanya. Sing it.

But they watching. The three. Singing. Listen: a bitch ain't nothing but a ho, sing those three. Have been taught. (But by whom?) Taught and taut. Taught low and harsh, that rhythm. Fierce melody. Melodylessness in mixture, lovelessness in joy. Drunk on flame, and who the fuck that bitch think she is anyway? they say — for they had seen her before, spoken to her and her kind; courted her favor, her attentions, in that car. Can't talk to nobody, bitch, you think you all a that? Can't speak to nobody, bitch, you think your pussy talks and shit? How could they know then? — of her forests, smoldering? Know and feel? — how in that growing silent heat those inner trees had uprooted, hurled stark branches at the outer sky? The firestorm and after-rain remained unseen. Only the lashes fluttered, and the inner earth grew hard. With those ropes choking so many of them in dreams, aware of the circles burnt into their skins, how could they know? How could they not know?

Robbie. Dee. Bernard. Three and three. Young and old. Too old for those jeans sliding down their asses. Too young for the rope and the circle's clutch. Too old to love so much their own wet dreams splashed out onto she they summoned out of that uncentered roiling world. She, summoned, to walk forth before their fire as the bitch or cunt. So they thought, would think and sing: still too young for the nursing of that keening need, the unconscious conscious wish to obliterate through vicious dreams who they were and are, have been, and are not. Blackmen-brothers, lovers, sons of strugglers. Sharecroppers, cocksuckers, black bucks and whores. Have been and are, might still be, and are not. A song. To do away with what they have and have not; what they can be, they think, are told by that outer chorus they can be — black boys, pretty boys, big dicks, tight asses, pretty boys, black scum, or funky homie trash — and cannot. Their hearts replaced by gnashing teeth, dirt; the underscraping grinch, an always-howl. Robbie Dee Bernard. Who have names and eyelids, fears, homie-homes. Watching now. Looking out for a replacement for those shredded skins. Cause that bitch think she all a that, they sing. Word, got that lightskin, good hair, think she fly. Got them titties that need some dick up in between. The flavor. Not like them darkskinned bitches, they sing. (But do the words have joy?) Got to cut this bitch down to size, the chorus goes. A tune. Phat pussy. Word, G! Said hey-ho! Said a-hey-ho! Word, my brother. My nigger. Sing it.

So driving. Looking. Watching. Seeing. Their words a blue song, the undercolor of the nightbird's wing. Is it a song you have heard before? Heard it sung sweet and clear to someone you hate before? Listen: —Oh shit, yo, there she go. Right up there. Straight on. Swinging her ass like a high-yellow ho. Said hey-ho! Turn up the volume on my man J Live J. Drive up, yo. Spook the bitch. Gonna get some serious pussy outa this shit.— Driving, slowing, slowing down. Feeling the circles, feeling their own necks. Burning skins, cockheads fullstretched and hard. Will she have a chance, dreaming of girlkisses, against that hard? In the sun. Here. And.

Pulling up. —So, Miss Lightskin, they sing, what you doing out here? Walking by yourself, you ain't scared? Ain't scared somebody gonna try to get some of your skin? Them titties looking kinda fly, girl. Come on, now. Get in.

Was it then that she felt the smoldering in those glens about to break? The sun gleaming down silver whiteheat on her back? *And O how she had only longed to walk the walk.* To continue on and on and on and through to those copses where, at the feet of that very old and most wise woman-tree of all, she might gaze into those stiller waters of minnow-fishes, minnow-girls, and there yes! quell quell quell quell quell the flames. As one of them then broke through her glens, to shout that she wasn't nothing anyway but a yellow bitch with a whole lotta attitude and a skanky cunt. As (oh yes, it was true, rivers and fire, snake daggers and black bitches, she had had enough) she flung back words on what exactly he should do with his mother's cunt, cause your mother, nigger, is the only motherfucking bitch out here. And then? Who could say or know? The 5-0 were nowhere in sight; all passing cars had passed; only the wheeling birds and that drifting sun above were witnesses to what they could not prevent. Cassandra, Cassandra. —Get in the car, bitch.— —Fuck no, I won't. Leave me alone. Leave me— trying to say Fuck off, y'all leave me the fuck alone, but whose hand was that, then, grabbing for her breast? Whose hand *is* that, on her ass, pressing now, right now, up into her flesh? —Stop it, y'all. Get the fuck off before— screaming and crying. Cursing, running. Sneakered feet on asphalt, pursuit, and the laughter loud. An easy catch. —We got you now, bitch.— Who can hear? The sun can only stare, and the sky is gone.

Driving, driving, driving on. Where can they take her? Where will they? They all want some, want to be fair. Fair is fair: three dicks, one cunt. That is their song. Driving on. Pelham Bay Park? they think. But naw, too many people, niggers and Ricans with a whole buncha kids and shit. (The sun going down. Driving on.) How about under the bridge, by Eastchester Creek? That's it, G! Holding her, holding, but can't somebody slap the bitch to make her shut up? Quit crying, bitch. Goddamn. A crying-ass bitch in a little funky-ass car. Now weeping more. Driving on. —Gonna call the police, she says, crying more; choking in that way they like, for then (oh, yes, they know) in that way from smooth head to hairy base will she choke on them. They laugh. —What fucking 5-0 you gonna call, bitch? You lucky we ain't take your yellow ass over to the projects. Fuck your shit in the elevator, throw your ass off the roof. These bitches, they laugh. Just shut up and sit back. Sit back, sit back.— Driving on.

Now the one they call Robbie is talking to her. —Open it, he says. Robbie, O Robbie. Eager and edgy, large-eyed and fine. Robbie, who has a name, unspoken hopes; private dreams. How can they know? Will he be dead within a year like so many others? A mirrored image in a mirror that shows them nothing? A wicked knife's slide from a brother's hand to his hidden chewed-up heart? Shattered glass, regret. Feeling now only the circle around his neck that keeps all in thrall. For now he must be a man for them. Must show the steel. Robbie don't be fronting, he prays they think, Robbie be hard. Will they like you better, Robbie, then, if you be hard? Will the big boys finally love you, take you in, Robbie, if you be hard? But it's deep sometimes, isn't it, Robbie, with all that hard? Deep and low. . . . He knows. Knows the clear tint of that pain. Alone and lonely . . . unknown, trying to be hard. Not like it was back then when *then when he said you was pretty.* Remember? All up in his arms . . . one of your boys, Darrell J. In his arms. Where nobody couldn't see. Didn't have to be hard. Rubbing up, rubbing. Kissing up on you. Licking. Talking shit about lovelove and all a that *But naw man* he said the first time (Darrell J., summertime, 10 P.M., off the court, hotwet, crew gone home, had an extra 40, sweaty chest neck face, big hands, shoulders, smile, was fine), *just chillin whyn't you come on hang out?* — so said Darrell J. with the hands and the yo yo yo yo going on and on with them eyes and *mouth tongue up in his skin* my man — : kissing up on Robbie the second time, pretty Robbie, the third time and the fourth and the *we did and he* kissing licking holding y'all two and O Robbie Robbie Robbie. A homie's song. Feeling then. Underneath him, pretty. In his arms. *Where nobody couldn't see   didn't have to be hard   kissing up on him shy shy and*   himinyou youinhim Robbie, Robbie. Where has the memory gone? Back then, straddling hips, homiekisses and the nightbird's song. But can't go back there, can you? To feel and feel. Gots to be hard. Can't ever touch him again, undress him, kiss his thing . . . feel it pressing against the teeth and the slow-hipped song. Black skin on skin and

— *but he was holding onto me and sliding, sliding way up inside sucking coming inside me in me in hot naw didn't need no jimmy aw shit now hold on holding him and I was I was Robbie Robbie Robbie Darrell J. together we was and I we I we came we hotwet on his belly my side sliding over him under him holding and we came we* but naw, man, can't even be *doing* that motherfucking punk shit out here. You crazy? You bugging? Niggers be getting smoked dusty for that shit. Y'all ain't never seen *me* do that. Gots to be hard. — So open it, bitch, he says. Lemme get my fingers on up in there. Awright, awright. Damn, man, he says, nobody don't got a jimmy? This bitch stinks, man, he says, know I'ma probably get some VD shit on my hands and shit. They laugh. — He a man, all right. Robbie! Ain't no faggot, yo. Not like we *heard.* They laugh. — Just put a sock on it, the one they call Dee says. Chillchill, yo. Everybody gonna get their chance.

And the sun. Going down, going down. Light ending now, fire and ice, blue time watersheen and the darkened plunge. Sink, golden sun. Rest your bronze head in the Sound and the sea beyond. The birds, going down, going down. Movement of trees, light swathed in leaves. Going down, going down. And.

Hard to see now, but that's okay, they say. This bitch got enough for everybody here under the bridge. No one's around now, only rusty cars and rats. Who cares if they shove that filthy rag into her mouth and tie it there? It's full of turpentine and shit, but the night doesn't care. The same night that once covered them in swamps from fiery light. Will someone come in white robes to save a lightskinned bitch this time?

Hot. Dark. On the backseat. Burning bright. Burning. On the backseat. Fire and rage. —Naw, man, Robbie, not so hard, man. You gone wear the shit out fore I get my chance.— Who said that? Which one in the dark? O but can't tell, for all are hidden now, and all are hard. The motherfucking *rig*orous shit, one of them says. Shut up, bitch. Was that you, Bernard? Did you miss your daddy when he went off with the one your mama called a dirty nigger whore, Bernard? Was that where you first learned everything there was to learn, and nothing? — there, Bernard? When he punched you in the face and left you behind, little boy Bernard? You cried. Without. A song unheard. A song like the shadowrain — wasn't it? The shadowrain that's always there so deep, deep down inside your eyes, Bernard. Cold rain inside. Tears and tears. Then fists and kicks on a black shitboy's head. Little punk-looking nigger dumped in a foster home, age ten, named Bernard. Fuckhead faggot ass, the boys there said. The ones who stuck it up in you. Again and again. The second and the third . . . —don't hurt me, don't!— screamed that one they called the faggot ass pussy bitch. You, Bernard. How could they know? Know that the little bitch punk scrunched up under the bed had seen the whole night and afterward and after alone? Bernard? *Hurts, mama. Daddy* — . Rain. Little faggot ass punk. Break his fucking face, yo. Kick his faggot ass down the stairs. Then he gone suck my dick. Suck it, bitch, fore we put this motherfucking hammer up your ass. The one you trusted most of all in that place, in all those places . . . everywhere? Bernard? The one who said he'd have your back no matter what. Little man, my man, he said. Smiling down. His teeth so white and wide. Smiling down. Smiling when he got you by the throat, sat on your chest and made you swallow it. Swallow it, bitch, he sang. Smiling down. Choking, choked. Deep inside the throat. Where has the memory gone? Something broken, then a hand. A reaching-out howl within the rain. A nightbird's rage. A punk, used up. Leave the nigger there, yo, they said. Til the next time. And the next. On the floor. Under the bed. Under. Bleeding under. You, Bernard.

The words to every song on earth are buried deep somewhere. Songs that must be sung, that must never be sung. That must be released from deep within the chest yet pulled back and held. Plaintive and low, they rail; buried forever beneath the passing flesh, alone and cold, they scream. The singer must clutch them to the heart, where they are sanctified, nurtured, healed. Songs which finally must be released yet recalled, in that place where no one except the singer ever comes, in one hand caressing the keys of life wounded, ravaged, in the other those of the precious skin and life revealed. The three of them and Cassandra know the words. Lying beneath them now and blind, she knows the words. Tasting turpentine and fire, she knows the words. —Hell no, yo, that bitch ain't dead.— A voice. —Fucked up, yo. The rag's in her mouth, how we gone get some mouth action now?— —Aw, man, fuck that shit.— Who says that? —My turn. My turn.— They know the words.

Now comes Dee. Can't even really see her, has to navigate. Wiggles his ass a little, farts softly to let off stress. —Damn, Dee, nasty motherfucker! they laugh. But he is busy, on to something. Sniffs and sniffs. At the bitch's asshole. At her cunt. —Cause yeah, yo, he says, y'all know what's up with this shit. They be saying this bitch done got into some bulldagger shit. Likes to suck pussy, bulldagger shit.— Word? —The phattest bitch around, yo, he says. Bulldagger shit.

Dee. DeeDee. Someone's boy. Has a place that's home. Eastchester, or Mount V. Has a heart that hates his skin and a mind half gone. Is ugly now, got cut up, but smoked the nigger who did it. Can't sleep at night, wanders seas; really wants to die. The lonely bottle might do it if the whiffs up don't. The empty hand might do it if the desire can't. What has been loved and not loved, what seeks still a place. The same hand, pushed by the once-winsome heart, that before painted angels, animals, miraculous creatures. Blank walls leaped into life, lightspeed and light. When (so it seemed) the whole world was light. But was discouraged, led into tunnels, and then of course was cut. The eyes went dim. Miraculous creatures. Where have the visions gone? Look, now, at that circle around his neck. Will he live? Two young ones and a dark girl waiting back there for him, frightened — will he live? Crushed angels drowned in St. Ides — will he live? When he sells the (yes, that) next week to the undercover 5-0 and is set up, will he live? When they shoot him in the back and laugh at the stain that comforts them, will he live?

But now he's happy, has found it! — the hole. The soft little hole, so tight, down there, as he reaches up to squeeze her breasts. Her eyes are closed but she knows the words. *That bitch ain't dead.* How can they know? When there is time there's time, and the time is now. Time to bang the bulldagger out of her, he sings. Listen to his song: —I'ma give you a baby, bitch.— (She knows the words). —Got that lightskin, think you all that, right, bitch? Word, I want me some lightskin on my dick, yo. When I get done this heifer ain't gone be *half* a ho. You know know? Gonna get mines, til you know who you dis and who you don't. Til you know we the ones in *control,* sing it! Got the flavor.— Dim-eyed, banging out his rage. Now, a man. Banging out his fear like the others, ain't even hardly no faggot ass. Def jam and slam, bang bang shebam. On and on as he shoots high, shoots far . . . laughter, but then a sense of falling, careening . . . sudden fear. It doesn't matter. The song goes on.

Night. Hell, no, broods the dim, that bitch ain't dead. Hasn't uttered half a sound since they began; hasn't opened her eyes to let the night look in again; hasn't breathed to the soft beating of the nightbird's wing. The turpentine rag in place. Cassandra, Cassandra. The rag, in place. Cassandra. Is she feeling something now? Cassandra. Will they do anything more to her now? Cassandra, will they leave you there? Focusing on flies, not meeting each other's eyes, will they leave you there? Running back from the burning forests behind their own eyes, the crackling and the shame? Will they leave you there? —Push that bitch out on the ground, the one they call Dee says. Over there, by them cars and shit.— Rusty cars, a dumping ground. So, Cassandra. Yes. They'll leave you there.

Were they afraid? Happy? Who can tell? Three dark boys, three men, driving away in a battered car. Three boy-men, unseen, flesh, minds, heart. Flame. In their car. O my God, three rapists, the pretty lady in her Volvo thinks, locking her doors at the traffic light. In their car. Blood on the backseat, cum stains, even hair. Who can tell? It's time to get open now. Time to numb the fear. —Get out the whiff, yo.— 40s and a blunt. —That bitch got what she deserved.— Those words, whiffs up, retreat, *she deserved it, deserved it* — and they are gone. Mirrored images in shattered glass, desire and longing, chill throbbing, and they are gone. The circles cleaving their necks. Flesh, blood and flame. A whiff and a 40. —We fucked that bitch good, G.— Night. Nightnight. Hush dark silence. Fade. They are gone.

Cassandra. What nightbirds are searching and diving for you now? What plundered forests are waiting for you now? The girl-trees are waiting for you, and so is she. Tanya. The girl-trees. Mama. How can they know? Their eyes are waiting, searching, and will soon be gray. The rats are waiting. They are gray. Cassandra, Cassandra. When the red lights come flashing on you, will they know? Fifteen, ripped open. Will they know? Lightskinned bitch

nigger ho, went that song. Will they know? Girl-trees in a burning forest . . . they will know. And the night. . . .

Where is she, they're wondering, why hasn't she come home?
They can't know what the rats and the car-carcasses know.
Cassandra? they are calling. Why don't you answer when
night-voices call you home?
Night. . . .

Listen now to the many night voices calling, calling soft,
Cassandra. Come. Carrying. Up. *Cassandra. Come. Out* and *up.*
What remains is what remains. *Out* and *up.* They will carry her.
A feeling of hands and light. Then the red lights will come. *Up*
and *up.* But will she see? Will she hear? Will she know?

The girl-trees are screaming. That is their song.

It will not appear on tomorrow's morning news.

But then — come now, ask yourself — whose song, finally, shall
this be? Of four dark girls, or four hundred, on their way to lasting fire in Sunday school? Of a broken-backed woman, legs bent?
Her tune? Of a pair of hands, stitching for — (but they'll never
grow). Of four brothers rapping, chugging? — a slapbeat in the
chorus? Doing time? Something they should know?

A song of grieving ships, bodies, torch-lit roads?

(— *But then now O yes remember, remember well that time, face, place or
thing: how those ten thousand million billion other ashes eyelids arms
uncountable dark ceaseless burnt and even faces once fluttered, fluttered forever, in someone's dream unending, dream of no escape, beneath a black-
blueblack sea: fluttered, flutter still and descend, now faces ashes eyelids dark
reflection and skin forever flame: descend, descend over laughing crowds.*)

A song of red earth roads. Women crying and men. Red hands, gray mouths, and the circle's clutch. A song, a song. Of sorrowing suns. Of destruction, self-destruction, when eyes lay low. A song —

But whose song is it? Is it yours? Or mine?

Hers?

Or theirs ... — ?

— But a song. A heedless, feckless tune. Here, where the night-time knows. And, well —

Yes, well —

— So, Cassandra. Now, Cassandra.

Sing it.

ACKNOWLEDGMENTS

Joyce Magdalene Glave; Thomas Edward Glave, Sr.; Phyllis Melbourne; Marcella Glave Abbott; Ethel Lindo; Assotto Saint; Maureen T. Reddy; Nehassaiu deGannes; Norman Riley; Kathleen McAuley; Robin Lewis; Angela Feaster; Charles Henry Rowell; Wilson Harris; Clarence Major; Gloria Naylor; Nadine Gordimer; Carole Maso; Wole Soyinka; David H. Lynn; Harry Belafonte; David Bergman; Mervyn Morris; Dorothy McLean; Salamishah Tillet; Daylanne English; Aishah Rahman; Marilyn Reizbaum; Terry Wolverton; Robert Drake; Brian Bouldrey; Sidney Brinkley; Luiz Valente; John Edgar Wideman; Daniel Wideman; Rohan Preston; Larry Dark; Louise Erdrich; Ginger Thornton; Arnold Weinstein; Bowdoin College; Brown University; Princeton University; Altos de Chavon; Fine Arts Center in Provincetown; Millay Colony for the Arts; Bronx Council on the Arts; New York Foundation for the Arts; University of Miami Caribbean Writers Institute; NEA/Travel Grants Fund for Artists; Djerassi Foundation; Fulbright Fellowships; Gay Men of African Descent; Elaine Katzenberger; Stacey Lewis; Nancy J. Peters; B.G. Firmani; Jacob Forman; Michael Rosen; Eric Fergerson; Baychester, North Bronx; Kingston, Jamaica; Nehemiah; Ishmael.

Thomas Glave was born in the Bronx and grew up there and in Kingston, Jamaica. A 1993 Honors graduate of Bowdoin College and a graduate of Brown University, he traveled as a Fulbright Scholar in 1998-99 to Jamaica, where he studied Jamaican historiography and Jamaican-Caribbean intellectual and literary traditions. While in Jamaica, Glave worked on issues of social justice, and helped found the Jamaica Forum of Lesbians, All-Sexuals, and Gays (J-FLAG).

Thomas Glave is currently an assistant professor of English at the State University of New York, Binghamton. While *Whose Song? And Other Stories* is his first book, he has been published and praised in many prestigious literary journals including *Callaloo, Black Renaissance/Renaissance Noire, The Massachusetts Review,* and *The Kenyon Review.* His work has received many awards, among them the prestigious O. Henry Prize — he is the second gay black writer, after James Baldwin, to claim that honor. His fiction has also appeared in numerous anthologies, including *Children of the Night: The Best Short Stories by Black Writers, Men on Men 6: Best New Gay Fiction, His 2: Brilliant New Fiction by Gay Writers, Soulfires: Young Black Men on Love and Violence, Best American Gay Fiction 3,* and *Prize Stories 1997: The O. Henry Awards.*